Prais...

S...

"Setting up a new mystery on the final page, Green keeps the action and laughs flowing in equal measure. Here's hoping for many more adventures of this terrific quartet. Recommended." —*SFRevu*

"The series really picks up to that same masterful level of storytelling [Green] is known for. And he delivers with this excellent work of classic, good old ghost-hunter fun that we've come to love from the genre." —*The Gatehouse*

"It continually amazes me how Green can pump out such original stories . . . Worth the read." —*Crooked Reviews*

"An extremely fast-paced book with some great gallows humor, introspection, and references to both the Nightside and Secret Histories series . . . I found it intriguing and highly enjoyable with some crazy action and twisted characters." —*The Bibliophilic Book Blog*

## GHOST OF A DREAM

"Green once again mixes and matches genres with gleeful abandon . . . Readers who enjoy a roller-coaster ride through a haunted house (well, theater, but I'm mixing metaphors here) will love this novel . . . A terrific continuation of the Ghost Finders' adventures, with loads of horrors, thrills, and shocks." —*SFRevu*

*continued . . .*

# GHOST OF A SMILE

"Packed with creepy thrills, *Ghost of a Smile* is a mighty strong follow-up in this brand-new series. Ghost hunting has never been quite this exciting. Recommended."

—*SFRevu*

"[With] plenty of action and chills, this book keeps pages turning even as a feeling of dread builds. The dialogue between the three characters is snappy and humorous, as is the chemistry between them." —*NewsandSentinel.com*

"*Ghost of a Smile* is a lovely blend of popcorn adventure and atmospheric thriller, and good for a few hours of distraction and entertainment. That's one of the reasons why Green's books always leap right to the top of my reading list." —*The Green Man Review*

"[Green] gleefully tweaks the natural fear of experimentation (and the inscrutable motivations of the men behind it), bringing some real-world paranoia into his fantasy-laden playground. It's a gamble that pays off nicely . . . With his Nightside series ending soon, the Ghost Finders books are quickly proving to be worthy replacements."

—*Sacramento Book Review*

# GHOST OF A CHANCE

"Thoroughly entertaining."

—Jim Butcher, #1 *New York Times* bestselling author of the Dresden Files

"If future novels in Green's new Ghost Finders series are as engaging as this one, they will hold up admirably against his previous work . . . Readers will appreciate the camaraderie and snappy dialogue." —*Publishers Weekly*

"Terrific." —*SFRevu*

"It's fast-paced, filled with nifty concepts and memorable characters, and quite enjoyable." —*The Green Man Review*

"I'm a huge fan of Simon R. Green's Nightside novels, and he continues to impress with *Ghost of a Chance*. He continues to put out great stories and gives readers deeply flawed characters that you still want to root for. This book is a great start to a new series that I will keep reading."
—*Bitten by Books*

## Praise for the Novels of the Nightside

"A fast, fun little roller coaster of a story." —Jim Butcher

"If you like your noir pitch-black, then return to the Nightside." —*University City Review*

"If you're looking for fast-paced, no-holds-barred dark urban fantasy, you need look no further: the Nightside is the place for you." —*SFRevu*

"Sam Spade meets Sirius Black . . . in the Case of the Cosmic MacGuffin . . . Crabby wit and inventively gruesome set pieces." —*Entertainment Weekly*

"A fast, intelligently written tale that is fun to read."
—*The Green Man Review*

"Plenty of action packed in from London to Glastonbury . . . should definitely please fantasy action fans." —*Booklist*

*Ghost Finders Novels*

GHOST OF A CHANCE
GHOST OF A SMILE
GHOST OF A DREAM
SPIRITS FROM BEYOND
VOICES FROM BEYOND

*Novels of the Nightside*

SOMETHING FROM THE
NIGHTSIDE
AGENTS OF LIGHT AND
DARKNESS
NIGHTINGALE'S LAMENT
HEX AND THE CITY
PATHS NOT TAKEN
SHARPER THAN A SERPENT'S
TOOTH

HELL TO PAY
THE UNNATURAL INQUIRER
JUST ANOTHER JUDGEMENT
DAY
THE GOOD, THE BAD, AND THE
UNCANNY
A HARD DAY'S KNIGHT
THE BRIDE WORE BLACK
LEATHER

*Secret Histories Novels*

THE MAN WITH THE
GOLDEN TORC
DAEMONS ARE FOREVER
THE SPY WHO HAUNTED ME
FROM HELL WITH LOVE

FOR HEAVEN'S EYES ONLY
LIVE AND LET DROOD
CASINO INFERNALE
PROPERTY OF A LADY FAIRE

*Deathstalker Novels*

DEATHSTALKER
DEATHSTALKER REBELLION
DEATHSTALKER WAR
DEATHSTALKER HONOR

DEATHSTALKER DESTINY
DEATHSTALKER LEGACY
DEATHSTALKER RETURN
DEATHSTALKER CODA

*Hawk and Fisher Novels*

SWORDS OF HAVEN
GUARDS OF HAVEN

*Also by Simon R. Green*

BLUE MOON RISING
BEYOND THE BLUE MOON
ONCE IN A BLUE MOON
DRINKING MIDNIGHT WINE

*Omnibus*

A WALK ON THE NIGHTSIDE

# VOICES FROM BEYOND

## SIMON R. GREEN

ACE BOOKS, NEW YORK

**THE BERKLEY PUBLISHING GROUP**
**Published by the Penguin Group**
**Penguin Group (USA) LLC**
**375 Hudson Street, New York, New York 10014**

USA • Canada • UK • Ireland • Australia • New Zealand • India • South Africa • China

penguin.com

A Penguin Random House Company

VOICES FROM BEYOND

An Ace Book / published by arrangement with the author

Ace Books are published by The Berkley Publishing Group.
ACE and the "A" design are trademarks of Penguin Group (USA) LLC.

For information, address: The Berkley Publishing Group,
a division of Penguin Group (USA) LLC,
375 Hudson Street, New York, New York 10014.

ISBN: 978-0-425-25994-8

PUBLISHING HISTORY
Ace mass-market edition / September 2014

PRINTED IN THE UNITED STATES OF AMERICA

10  9  8  7  6  5  4  3  2  1

Cover art by Don Sipley.
Cover design by Judith Lagerman.
Interior text design by Laura K. Corless.

Ghosts exist for a purpose. Unfinished business, delayed revenge, or to carry a message. Sometimes the dead can go to a lot of trouble to bring a desperate warning of some terrible thing that's coming.

Whatever the reason, don't blame the messenger for the message.

# ONE

## NOBODY HOME

From the outside, it looked like any other house. An everyday, semi-detached property, half-way down a side street, on a perfectly ordinary South London estate. On a perfectly ordinary evening in late autumn. Except, lights were blazing in every window. As though whoever was inside this particular house was afraid of the dark. Or something in the dark.

A Land Rover came screeching down the street at speed, sometimes on one side of the road and sometimes on the other, before finally slamming to a halt outside the house. The car rocked back and forth a few times, as though getting used to being suddenly at rest, then the engine shut down. No-one got out. The three people inside sat where they were, so they could take a good look at the house and its surroundings from a safe distance. The last of the light was going out of the evening, and the house stood half-silhouetted against a dark and lowering sky. The windows all blazed very brightly, but there was no sign of movement inside the house. The street-lamps burned orange and amber, illuminating an empty scene. It was all very quiet; nobody about. The house had the feeling of a brightly lit stage, with the action yet to begin. After a while, the Land Rover's driver turned around in her seat to address her two companions.

"It all looks normal enough to me," said Melody Chambers.

"I never trust normal," said JC Chance. "It usually means the universe is trying to hide something from me. And rarely in a good way."

"I've got a bad feeling about this place," said Happy Jack Palmer.

"You've always got a bad feeling," said Melody, crushingly.

"And I'm always right!"

"That's as may be," said JC. "I still want to know what in God's name made you choose a Land Rover as our team transport? Were they all out of tractors and combine harvesters?"

Melody heaved a deep, put-upon sigh. She was very good at it. She'd had a lot of practice. "I chose this marvellous example of reliable engineering because I got fed up with my scientific equipment always being left behind, or turning up too late to be of any use. How can I be the Ghost Finder girl science geek if I don't have any investigative equipment to work with? So I went down to the Carnacki Institute car pool and chose this. Because it's a real work-horse of a vehicle; and because it was the only thing they had big enough to hold all my marvellous machines."

JC nodded slowly. "Not exactly the most inconspicuous thing to turn up in, though, is it?" he murmured. "We are supposed to do our good deeds on the quiet, with no-one's ever knowing. On the grounds that if the general public ever finds out why the Ghost Finders exist, and what we have to do, there will be a mass panic and general pants-wetting of biblical proportions."

Melody sniffed loudly. "I get the job done. I put ghosts in their place and kick supernatural arse, in a strictly scientific way. And look good doing it. You can worry about public perception."

"Oh, I do," said JC. "Really. You have no idea."

Melody kicked open the driver's door and got out. She glared at the semi-detached house waiting for them, as though daring it to give her any problems. The lights in every window stared unflinchingly back; with not a trace of anyone's moving behind them. JC pushed open his door and got out of the back seat, slowly and carefully, then took his time stretching his long limbs. They made clear cracking and creaking sounds on the quiet of the empty street. When he was ready, he moved in beside Melody and studied the house dubiously.

JC was tall and lean and too handsome for his own good, or anyone else's. Thirty years old now, and loudly protesting he didn't give a damn, JC Chance had pale, striking features under a rock star's mane of long, wavy, black hair. He had a prominent nose, an easy smile, and wore dark sunglasses all the time for a very good reason. He also wore a rich, ice-cream white three-piece suit of quite devastating style and elegance, along with an old school tie he stole. JC was team leader because he was the only one brave and arrogant enough to always lead from the front, striding into danger with a careless smile and far more confidence than was safe for him or his companions.

Melody Chambers was advancing into her thirties, and fighting it every step of the way. Conventionally good-looking, in a threatening sort of way, she was short and gamine thin, forever burning with raw nervous energy. She wore her auburn hair scraped back in a severe bow, couldn't be bothered with even the most basic make-up, and scowled at the world through serious glasses with dull, functional frames. Her clothes had never even heard of style or fashion; and Melody had once shocked and scandalised an entire roomful of women by loudly declaring she didn't give a damn about shoes. Or any kind of accessory you couldn't use as a weapon.

"Odd . . ." JC said finally. "I know it's evening, but there ought to be someone out and about. Hurrying home late from work, or out jogging, or simply walking the dog . . . It's as though all the people here have sensed it's not safe to be outside at the moment."

"Good," said Melody. "I hate innocent bystanders. Always getting in the way, and underfoot, and dying horribly from collateral damage."

"Except for when you use them to hide behind," said JC.

"Except for then," Melody agreed. She shot the house one last warning glance then marched round to the back of the Land Rover to unload her precious equipment.

"Don't anyone feel obliged to help me with all the hard work and heavy lifting!" she said loudly.

"Don't worry," said JC. "We won't."

He banged ruthlessly on the door to the Land Rover's passenger seat until it finally swung open, and Happy Jack

Palmer half fell out. He got his feet under him with something of an effort and pushed the car door shut with an irritated scowl. He then leaned back against the door until he recovered his balance and his thoughts. He looked vaguely up and down the street, as though hoping it might provide him with some idea as to why he was there; and then he produced a small silver pill box from inside his jacket. He popped open the lid and stirred the multi-coloured contents with a finger before selecting two dark green pills decorated with muddy yellow lightning bolts. He knocked them back, dry-swallowing with the ease of long practice, then hiccoughed loudly a few times. He straightened up, pushing himself away from the car door, and made the pill box disappear about his person. His eyes were suddenly a lot brighter, and he smiled a smile with far too many teeth in it. JC looked at him expressionlessly.

"Are you still on the mother's little helpers? The mental medication? We haven't even started the investigation yet."

"It's the only way I can cope with Melody's driving," said Happy.

"I heard that!" said a loud voice from the rear of the Land Rover.

"You were meant to!" Happy said coldly. He slumped a little. "God, I'm tired, JC. I'm always tired. I need something to wake me up and get me moving. Is that the house? I don't like it. It looks like it's staring back at me."

He studied the house in a sullen, antagonistic way, as though daring it to come out fighting. JC left him to it and went to join Melody at the back of the Land Rover as she piled up boxes full of scientific equipment at the side of the road. She didn't even look at him but kept on working.

"He didn't sleep well last night," she said roughly. "He doesn't like to sleep. Says it makes him feel . . . vulnerable. That things might try and get inside his head while his defences are down. And with a telepath as sensitive as him, who's to say he's wrong?"

"Surely he can find a pill to help him sleep?" said JC.

"He can; but his system's already so compromised with industrial-strength chemicals, some of them only suspected by modern science, that it takes something pretty damned powerful to affect him. He's afraid to take that kind of pill too often in case he builds up a tolerance. Then he wouldn't have anything to turn to when he really needed it. He needs more and more pills, JC! Bigger, stronger doses, all the time. Just to function. I don't like where this is going; but I don't see what else I can do to help. Sex isn't enough to distract him any more, and love isn't enough to make him strong. Sometimes I think it's only the job that keeps him going."

"He hates the job," said JC.

"I know!"

They both looked down the street, to where Happy was bouncing slowly up and down on his toes, studying the waiting semi-detached like a boxer about to enter the ring for a fight he strongly suspects is fixed.

Happy Jack Palmer was the Ghost Finder team telepath and full-time gloomy bugger. As he often said, *If you could see the world as clearly as I do, you'd be clinically depressed, too.* Well into his thirties now, and openly fed up with it, Happy was short and stocky and prematurely balding. He might have been attractive if he ever stopped scowling and sulking long enough. He wore grubby jeans and a T-shirt bearing the message JUST BECAUSE I'M PARA-

NOID, IT DOESN'T MEAN I'M NOT OUT TO GET YOU, along with a battered black leather jacket whose most recent tears had been roughly stapled back together. He took so many pills he rattled when he coughed. Just enough, he said, to keep the world and all the awful things in it safely outside his head.

Melody finally finished loading the more important pieces of her machinery onto a trolley and dragged it down the street to join Happy in front of the house. JC strolled along behind her. He knew better than to offer any assistance because no-one touched Melody's toys except her. The three Ghost Finders stood together, looking the semi-detached over carefully.

"Are you picking up anything, Happy?" said JC, after a while.

"Something bad happened here," said Happy. "Quite recently."

"Obviously," Melody said crushingly. "Or we wouldn't be here, would we? What kind of bad?"

Happy thought about it. "Really bad."

"Good!" JC said cheerfully. "The only interesting kind. Let us all go rushing in there and poke it with sticks."

"After you," said Happy.

JC grinned easily and strode up the paved path to the front door. Happy slouched after him, while Melody trundled along in the rear with her trolley. The path cut straight through a neatly trimmed lawn, decorated with a scattered handful of morose-looking garden gnomes. Happy gave each of them a dark, suspicious glare as he passed. The three sets of footsteps sounded very loud on the quiet street, counterpointed with loud creakings from Melody's heavy-laden trolley. JC frowned slightly as he realised he couldn't hear anything else. The evening was almost totally silent, as though it were holding its breath and listening. The footsteps sounded so clearly on the quiet path that whoever was inside the house had to know they were there; but no-one appeared at any of the brightly lit windows to look out.

"Does anyone in the house know we're coming?" said Melody.

"Someone does," said JC. "A Professor Volke put in a panic call to the Institute, about an hour ago, from this address. Apparently he's someone's cousin. Knew enough about us, and what we do, to scream to us for help when whatever it was went horribly wrong."

"What did he say the problem was?" said Happy.

"I don't know," said JC. "This was all arranged in a rush. There's no file, no case notes. We got the call because we were the closest team, and could get here the fastest. The professor is supposed to supply us with all the grisly and entertaining details."

"No case file, no details, no warnings," said Happy. "Oh, this can only go well."

JC crashed to a halt before the front door. Happy stopped a comfortable distance behind him. Melody leaned on her trolley, breathing heavily. JC rang the bell, knocked briskly on the door, and kicked it a few times for good measure. He raised quite a din; but there was no response from inside. JC tried the door handle, but the door was locked.

"Now what do we do, oh wise and learned team leader?" said Happy.

"I suppose we could break a window . . ." said JC.

"Get out of the way," said Melody.

She pushed past Happy and JC and produced a slender spikey object from a hidden pocket. She eased it into the lock and wiggled it about; and the lock threw up its hands and surrendered. Melody pushed the front door open with a flourish. JC considered the thing in her hand thoughtfully.

"How long have you been able to open locks, Melody?"

She shrugged and smiled, and made the picklock disappear about her person. "Girl's entitled to a hobby . . ."

"I am changing all my locks, the moment I get back," said JC.

"Go right ahead," said Melody. "See what good it does you."

They went inside, closing the door carefully behind them.

The three Ghost Finders moved slowly and cautiously down the long, narrow hallway, looking about them, careful to touch nothing. All the lights were on, every bulb glowing brightly, but there was no-one present to greet them. A terrible, oppressive silence lay over everything, seeming to stifle even the smallest noise. Happy winced and rubbed at his forehead.

"Bad atmosphere," he complained.

"What kind of bad?" JC said patiently.

"Malignant," said Happy. "Toxic."

"As in actually, immediately life-threatening?" said JC.

"What do you think?" said Happy.

"Why do cheerful, friendly people never come back as ghosts?" said Melody, plaintively. "Why do we never meet happy smiley people from the vasty deeps, who are actually pleased to see us?"

"The answer is almost certainly implicit in the question," said JC. "People at peace and at rest don't need to come back. It's the ones who have a complaint to make who end up disturbing the living. Let's try the lounge."

He moved quickly down the hall, throwing open each door as he came to it and peering into the room beyond. Until he found the lounge and went inside. Happy skulked along behind him, while Melody struggled fiercely with her trolley as the wheels caught and spun on the rucked-up carpet. The lounge turned out to be a pleasantly spacious room, with comfortable chairs and a huge red leather settee, along with all the usual comforts and luxuries, including a really big wide-screen television. Set a little to one side was a long, narrow coffee table, with four young men and women sitting on the floor around it. They were all wearing assorted jeans and sweaters, and had that indefinable but unmistakable look of students. None of them looked up as the Ghost Finders entered the room. None of them made a sound, or moved a muscle. They sat in place, staring straight ahead of them, with blank faces and empty eyes.

JC started to address them, then stopped as he realised how very still they all were, and how completely empty their faces seemed. He moved slowly forward, one step at a time, until he could lean over and study their faces close-up. They didn't react, but they were all still breathing, very gently. JC relaxed a little. Where there's even a little life, there's hope. He gestured for Happy and Melody to stay back, and moved cautiously around the four seated figures, looking them over, with his hands clasped behind his back so he could be sure he wouldn't touch anything. He leaned in past the students to look at the coffee table. An old-fashioned wooden Ouija board had been set out on the tabletop in front of the four students. All the usual markings, in old-fashioned lettering, so a message could be spelled out. There was no sign of the usual upturned glass, but there were fragments of broken glass all across the table and on the carpeted floor around it.

"A Ouija board?" said Happy, coming forward very cautiously for a better look. "Oh, that's never good. Those things should be banned. They open doors, and never to anywhere good. Giving one of those things to a bunch of amateurs is like giving a hand-grenade to a group of toddlers. There are bound to be tears before bedtime."

JC snapped his fingers fiercely in front of each empty student face in turn, but there was no reaction. He straightened up and turned to look consideringly at a camera on a tripod, set up not far away, aimed at the coffee table. JC gestured to Melody, and she came forward to look the camera over.

"Expensive," she said briskly. "State-of-the-art, all the latest bells and whistles. The kind of camera that does most of the work for you. Some really nifty filters, and extra options . . . for when you need to be sure you won't miss *anything*. What was going on here? What were these four doing . . . that someone needed to record every detail of it for posterity?"

"Is the camera still working?" said JC. "Still recording?"

"No. Someone's put it on stand-by."

"And it isn't transmitting to anywhere else?"

"No. It's set to record."

They all looked up sharply as they heard quiet but definite sounds from someone's moving about, upstairs. The slow, furtive footsteps of someone hoping not to be noticed. JC's head moved slowly as he followed the footsteps from one side of the ceiling to the other. The sounds stopped, abruptly. JC hurried out of the lounge, with Happy and Melody right behind him.

·············

Back in the hallway, it was still and quiet again. JC led the way up the stairs. He made no sound at all as he ascended the carpeted steps; and neither did Happy and Melody. Learning to walk unseen and undetected was one of the first things you learned when working cases like this. Sneaking up on ghosts took special skill. They reached the landing at the top of the stairs, and JC gestured for the others to split up, so they could each take one of the three doors leading off the hall. The silence was so complete now, so heavy, it had an almost solid presence. Melody moved in close beside JC, so she could murmur in his ear.

"How many people are there supposed to be in this house?"

"Beats me," said JC, quietly. "No case file, remember? But we haven't found Professor Volke yet. Or his body . . ."

Happy pointed an only slightly unsteady finger at the door nearest him, and JC and Melody padded over to stand beside him.

"Someone's in there," said Happy.

"Can't you tell who it is?" said JC.

Happy sniffed. "The atmosphere in this house is really messed up. There's so much information present, the aether is saturated. It's like trying to see through thick fog."

JC looked at Melody. "He makes this shit up, doesn't he?"

"Probably," said Melody.

"All right," said JC. "Plan B it is. Brute force and ignorance; everything forward and trust in the Lord."

"After you," said Melody.

"Why would the professor be hiding from us?" said Happy.

"Let's ask him," said JC.

He stepped smartly forward and kicked the door in. It slammed back against the inner wall, making a hell of a racket. JC launched himself into the room, with Happy and Melody reasonably close behind him. The bedroom was empty except for the usual bed, fittings and furnishings, and one very large wall closet. Happy did the pointing thing again, and JC walked right up to the closed closet door. He coughed loudly, then knocked on the door, very politely.

"Hello, Professor Volke! We know you're in there; please come out and talk to us. Or I will be forced to rescue you from this closet, with extreme violence and no concern at all for your personal dignity."

There was a pause, and the door opened a crack. A wide eye peered out, studying JC with open trepidation. JC gave the eye his most charming smile.

"Please come out, Professor. There's a good chap. Nothing at all to worry about, now. The cavalry has arrived."

The door opened, and Professor Volke stepped slowly out. He stood half crouching before JC, twitching and trembling, as though expecting to be attacked at any moment. He looked quickly at Happy and Melody and must have seen something in the way they were looking at him because he straightened up and tried to pull what remained of his dignity about him. He looked to be in his late forties, fashionably dressed in a sloppy way. His greying hair was ragged and tousled, in contrast to his neatly trimmed goatee beard. His face was unhealthily pale, and his eyes were worryingly wide and unblinking. His hands shook. Something had thrown a hell of a scare into him. He looked like he was ready to dive right back into the wall closet at the slightest provocation—or even if anyone spoke harshly to him. JC kept the charming smile going.

"Hello, Professor Volke," he said carefully. "You're perfectly safe now. We're here! We are Ghost Finders, from the Carnacki Institute. You called us for help, remember? It's our job to Do Something about ghosts and ghoulies and long-leggity beasties, and make them play nice with others. Can you tell us what it is that's happened here?"

"You've got to get me out of here!" said the professor. He clearly wanted to shout, but his voice was so strained by stress and shock, he could only manage a rough whisper. "We have to leave. We can't stay here. It's too dangerous!"

"Sounds like a plan to me," said Happy.

"Hush now, Happy, grown-ups talking," said JC, not taking his gaze off the professor. "We can't leave just yet, Professor Volke. We need to determine exactly what's happened, and what the nature of the threat is, so we can do something extreme and final about it. Please come downstairs with us and fill us in on all the appalling details."

The professor tried to get back in the wall closet. JC grabbed him by one ear and hauled him out again. The professor made loud signs of distress but had no choice but to go along when JC led him firmly out of the bedroom and back down the stairs, not releasing his hold on the professor's ear for one moment. Happy and Melody brought up the rear. The professor protested loudly and bitterly all the way down the stairs and into the hall but shut up the moment he saw the door to the lounge standing open ahead of him. He seemed to shrink in on himself, and all the fight went out of him. JC let go of the man's ear and ushered him politely into the lounge. The professor took one look at the four young students sitting unnaturally still around the coffee table and made a high, whining noise. He got away from JC and made a dash for the door, but Happy and Melody were there to block it. The professor turned back reluctantly, looking everywhere round the room except at the four young people.

"Tell us what happened here, Professor," said JC, in his most encouraging manner. "You can start by telling us what kind of professor you are and what you and these four were doing here."

"I am Adrian Volke," the professor said haltingly. "Head of the Psychology Department at Thames University. They . . . are four of my students. Angie and Elspeth, Dominic and Martin. First-class minds, all of them."

"Very good, Professor Volke," said JC. "Now, what were you trying to do here? And why were you recording everything?"

"I set up suitable conditions for a séance, using a Ouija board," said the professor. His voice grew in confidence as he moved onto familiar ground. "It was a psychological experiment. I wanted to see what would happen, or could be made to happen, under the right conditions."

"But something went wrong, didn't it?" said JC.

The professor nodded miserably. "You have to help me! I never intended for any of this to happen. I didn't know what to do . . ." He seemed to realise how pathetic he sounded because his head came up abruptly, and he glared defiantly at JC. "You have to help me understand what happened here. Help me put this right again. A scandal of this nature could ruin my professional reputation!"

"Relax, Prof," said JC. "We are the big guns from the Carnacki Institute. Ghosts and ghoulies cringe at our approach. We'll sort this out for you and help restore your poor students."

If the professor noticed the dig at his apparent lack of concern for his students, he didn't seem to care. The distraught academic wrung his shaking hands together and shook his head miserably.

"I shouldn't have called the Institute. I don't believe in . . . that sort of thing. But after what happened in this room, right in front of me, I couldn't think what else to do."

"It's all right, Prof," said JC. "We understand. No atheists in haunted houses . . ."

"I don't believe in ghosts!" said the professor.

"Tough," said Melody. "They believe in you."

The professor looked at her uneasily. "There's no supernatural element to the use of a Ouija board. Everyone knows that, these days. Impulses in the unconscious mind move the fingers that move the glass, causing it to spell out hidden thoughts and desires. I was simply interested in setting up the right conditions for an experiment in suggestibility. If I could make my students believe enough in what they were doing, reinforce their natural desire to get results, would they make things happen? Or believe they had? I was looking to create a situation of controlled hysteria, to provoke a reaction. But . . . look at them!"

He still couldn't bring himself to look directly at the

four unmoving students. He gestured in their direction, then clasped his hands tightly together, to stop them shaking. He was trying hard to hang on to his professorial dignity and failing. He looked more like a child expecting to be punished for doing something he knew he shouldn't have. JC considered the man thoughtfully. The professor had clearly seen or experienced something very much outside his scientific comfort zone. The professor straightened up again under the pressure of JC's regard. He made himself look at his students.

"I suppose it could be . . . some kind of extreme shock? A fugue state? Some kind of psychic transmission, even, from them to me, drawing me into their hysteric state and making me see things . . ."

"Don't strain yourself, Professor," said Melody. "Your brand of science doesn't have the answers to cover something like this. It's not big enough."

The professor bristled immediately and glared at her. "My science covers the known world! What else is there?"

"Don't get me started," said Melody.

"Everything casts a shadow, Professor Volke," said JC. "And we operate in the shadows. Come along, Prof; it's time to tell the tale. What did you do here, exactly; and what did you see?"

But the professor turned away, stubbornly shaking his head. He wasn't ready to talk, to commit himself to accepting that what he had seen was really real. JC turned to Melody.

"Can you access what the camera recorded earlier? Maybe plug its output into that really big-ass television?"

"Piece of cake," said Melody.

She performed a quick and brutal fix with a series of

cables, and the television screen was suddenly full of
heavy buzzing static. The professor saw what was happening, and made another dash for the door, but Happy was
still there, blocking it. The professor raised a hand, as
though to push Happy out of the way. Happy gave him a
hard look; and the professor lowered his hand and turned
away. He looked reluctantly at what was happening on the
television screen, and everyone came forward to stand before the screen. To watch what had happened, earlier.

,,,,,,,,,,,,,,,,,,,,,,,,,,

On the screen, four graduate students sat happily around
the coffee table, drinking wine from plastic cups, chatting
easily together, and making caustic comments about the
Ouija board set out before them. Except . . . now and again,
one or other of the students would glance at the wooden
board, in a wary and suspicious way, as though it was another person in the room. One that couldn't be trusted to
behave. But still, they all seemed relaxed enough, laughing
and teasing each other and not taking any of it too seriously.

Angie was a heavily freckled redhead, going out of her
way to make it clear she was convinced nothing would
happen. "I mean, really; come on! The whole Ouija-board
thing has been thoroughly discredited by modern thinking! We're only here because Professor Volke bribed and
bullied us into turning up. Isn't that right, Professor?"

"Don't look at the camera, Angie," said the professor's
voice, from off screen. "Concentrate on the board, please.
We need to get this started."

"Exactly!" said Angie. "The sooner we get started, the
sooner we can call it a day and go to the pub!"

Elspeth was tall and slender and very blonde. "I would

like to believe," she said artlessly. "Really, I would! But I've been to graveyards, and old houses and haunted pubs, and never experienced anything. It would be terribly thrilling, though, wouldn't it? If something really did happen here?"

"You'd run a mile," said Angie. "You can't even cope with spiders in the bath."

"Probably," Elspeth conceded. "But! I would still like to see . . . something . . ."

Dominic was a large, rugby-playing type, who turned out to be surprisingly quiet and thoughtful. He was broad and wide, with skin so black it had blue highlights. "I am determined to keep an open mind," he said firmly. "We can't expect to get anything out of this if we go into it with our minds closed to new experiences. We have to hold ourselves open to . . . possibilities. Isn't that right, Professor?"

"This is your experiment," said the professor, off-camera. "I'm only here to record what happens."

"Yeah; right." That was the final student, Martin. Tall and lean and openly sardonic. "How can it be our experiment when you've arranged everything? None of us are here because we want to be. You pressured us into this. What did he promise the rest of you, guaranteed better grades? Oh, you don't have to say anything. I freely admit I'm here because my grades are in the toilet, and my only hope to stay on the course is with the professor's help and support. So if he wants us to play parlour games, while he films it, I can live with that. As long as I get to keep my clothes on . . . But you had better hold up your end of the bargain, Professor."

"I am sure we'll all get something useful out of this," said the professor's voice. "Please place the glass provided on the Ouija board, upside down, then each of you should place a forefinger on the glass."

With a certain amount of giggling, and embarrassed glances at each other, the four students did as they were told. A glass was ceremoniously turned upside down and placed in the centre of the board, inside the circle of letters, in easy reach of the Yes and No positions. One by one, they all placed a finger on the upturned glass, doing their best to keep their faces suitably solemn.

"All right," said Martin. "What do we do now?"

"I think we're supposed to ask it things, aren't we?" said Elspeth. "I saw this film once . . ."

"I am not saying, *Is there anybody there?*" said Dominic. "There are limits."

"Now relax, and let our unconscious minds take over," said Angie. "No doubt we'll find ourselves spelling out all kinds of revealing thoughts and wishes . . ."

"Why isn't the glass moving?" said Elspeth.

"Because you're not taking it seriously," said the professor's voice. "Stop talking. Concentrate your thoughts on the glass. Feel the atmosphere. Just . . . let things happen."

All four students settled themselves as comfortably as they could and stared fixedly at the upturned glass. And slowly, almost without realising it, their bodies relaxed. Their breathing became synchronised. They were all concentrating on the same thing, not even thinking about the professor and his camera any more. For a long moment, nothing happened. And then Angie snatched her finger back from the glass. The tension of the moment was immediately broken, and everyone let out their breath in a rush. They sat back from the board, taking their fingers off the glass, breathing heavily. Elspeth glared at Angie.

"What did you do that for? I really felt we were achieving . . . something!"

Angie looked apologetically off screen. "Sorry, Professor. I had this . . . feeling, that something bad was about to happen."

"Please take this seriously, everyone," said the professor's voice. "Fingers back on the glass, and concentrate."

Four arms stretched across the coffee table, and four fingers pressed down on the upturned glass. Martin was looking openly contemptuous now. Elspeth shuddered suddenly.

"Hey! Did everyone else feel that?"

"Feel what?" asked Dominic.

"Like . . . a sudden cold breeze," said Elspeth, looking around uncertainly.

"Rubbish," said Martin.

"I did feel it!" said Elspeth. "Look; I've got goose pimples!"

"I didn't feel anything," said Angie. "And I'm right next to you."

"What are you all feeling?" said the professor's voice. "I need you to articulate your feelings, for the record. What is going through your minds, right now?"

"I'm feeling completely ridiculous," said Martin. "And I'm starting to wonder if any grade is enough to justify this."

"It feels like . . . someone's watching us," said Elspeth. "And no, I don't mean the camera. It feels like there's someone else here, in the room with us . . ."

All four students looked round the room, not taking their fingertips off the glass. Elspeth looked spooked. Angie and Dominic looked impatient. Martin seemed increasingly angry.

"There's no-one here but us idiots," he said firmly. "I don't feel any dread presence, and I didn't feel any breeze. Can we please get on with this, and get it over and done with, before I die of terminal shame?"

"I guess we do have to start with the traditional question, after all," said Dominic. "Come on; I'll start the ball rolling. Is there anybody there . . . ?"

And all of them were shocked silent as the upturned glass immediately began racing round and round the wooden board, moving so fast the students had to struggle to keep their fingers on it. The glass was moving so quickly, they couldn't even make out what it was trying to spell. It shot back and forth, all over the board, then went round and round in circles, dragging the students' arms after it.

"Martin!" said Dominic, so angry he could hardly speak. "This is you, isn't it?"

"How could I be doing this?" Martin protested. His face was very pale. "Look at how fast the bloody thing's moving!"

"No-one is to take their fingers off the glass," the professor said urgently.

"I can't!" said Elspeth, her voice rising. "I'm trying to let go, and I can't! It's stuck!"

The glass jerked viciously this way and that across the wooden board, in swift, angry movements. Angie was crying quietly. Dominic was struggling to get his feet under him, so he could get up from the table, but the glass jerked his hand back and forth so rapidly he couldn't get his balance. Elspeth looked quickly around her, as though catching sight of something out of the corner of her eye. Martin looked shocked. All four students were open-mouthed and wide-eyed at what was happening right in front of them.

"Professor?" said Martin. "Are you getting this? I'm not doing this; I swear I'm not doing any of this!"

"What's the glass doing?" said Angie. "Why isn't it spelling anything? How are we supposed to . . . communicate, like this?"

"Something's here in the room with us!" Elspeth said loudly. "I can feel it, staring over my shoulder!"

"There's no-one here but us!" said Dominic. "Everyone, take your finger off the glass!"

The glass exploded—shattered, and blew apart. All four students cried out in shock and pain as they were hit by flying glass splinters. They recoiled from the board and the table, snatching their freed hands back. No-one was badly hurt, only a few scratches; but there were bits of broken glass all over the table and all over their clothes. The students brushed the glass fragments away with almost hysterical speed. They looked at each other, breathing hard. All the good humour and scepticism were gone, slapped right out of them. Something had definitely happened even if they weren't sure what.

Strange lights flared suddenly, all around them. Great blasts of vivid colour, come and gone in a moment. The air shimmered, like a heat haze. Ripples moved slowly across the carpet, spreading out from the coffee table like waves on the surface of a disturbed pond. The students cried out and huddled together. Loud, knocking noises sounded in the walls and the ceiling, moving round and round the room as though chasing each other. As though something were banging on the outside of the world, trying to get in. The wooden Ouija board suddenly rose from the table, shooting up through the air till it slammed flat against the ceiling overhead. It clung there, entirely unsupported. The coffee table jumped and shuddered, rocking back and forth on its spindly legs. Elspeth pulled away from the others, and looked wildly about her.

"There's someone else in this room! Someone else is here with us!"

Angie burst into tears. She turned to Dominic, who put a protective arm around her and glared defiantly about the room. Martin was on his feet, his hands clenched into fists, ready to lash out at anything. Elspeth looked fiercely off-camera, at the professor.

"We've got to get out of here! We can't stay here!"

"No-one is to leave!" said the professor's voice. He was trying hard to sound like someone still in control.

"Go to Hell!" snarled Martin. "This isn't what we signed up for!"

"If anyone leaves, they can forget about any help with their course work, or their grades," said the professor's voice. "This is important work we're doing . . ."

"Stuff your help!" said Dominic. "Get out from behind that camera and do something! This isn't your experiment any more!"

The coffee table stopped moving. The flaring lights disappeared, and the loud, knocking noises broke off. Everything was still and quiet in the lounge. The four students fell silent, looking around them with wide, shocked eyes. The Ouija board, pressed against the ceiling, dropped back down, hitting the coffee table with a dull, flat sound. Everyone jumped. And then, all four students slowly relaxed, bit by bit, as the room remained still and peaceful, the accumulated tensions seeping slowly out of them.

"Is that it?" Angie said tremulously. "Is it over now?"

She realised Dominic still had his arm around her and

moved away from him. He quickly lowered his arm and stepped back. Martin unclenched his fists, scowling about him for any sign the phenomena might be about to start up again. The professor started to say something; and then his voice broke off as all four students suddenly sat down hard, their bodies slumping bonelessly, until they were all sitting on the carpet around the coffee table. Their faces were horribly slack: empty of all expression, or awareness. Their mouths dropped open, and their unblinking eyes saw nothing at all. They sat still, barely breathing, completely silent, all trace of personality gone from their faces. The professor called out to them, saying their names increasingly urgently; but none of them responded. He came out from behind the camera at last, appearing on the screen for the first time. He shook the students by the shoulder and shouted into their empty faces, his voice rising hysterically as he realised there was no-one left to hear him.

|||||||||||||||||||||||||||

Professor Volke buried his face in his hands. Melody stopped the recording, and the television screen went blank. Volke breathed deeply a few times, then raised his head to look desperately at JC.

"Do you understand what happened here? Nothing like that was supposed to happen! It was a stupid séance, a parlour game! You've got to help me wake them up!"

"They're not asleep," said Happy. "They're gone."

"Are you sure?" said JC.

"Their heads are empty," said Happy. "I'm not picking up a single thought or impulse, on the conscious or unconscious level. Everything they were has been ripped right out of them. Nobody's home."

Melody looked up from her equipment. She'd finished setting up her equipment in its usual semi-circular formation, while everyone else was concentrating on the television. Her fingers darted from one keyboard to the next, bringing everything on-line. Monitor screens glowed brightly, information flowing in endless rows across her various displays.

"This room is a good twenty degrees colder than it should be," she said calmly. "And I'm getting some really weird electromagnetic readings."

"What sort of weird?" said JC.

"Like you'd understand even if I did explain it to you," said Melody. "All you need to know is, they are way off the scale. Happy was right; this room is soaked with information, old and new. And . . . I'm getting signs of something that might be an interdimensional doorway."

"What?" said the professor. "What are you talking about?"

"There are places in the world where the hard and certain can become soft and malleable," JC said carefully. "Places where different worlds, or dimensions, can rub up against each other; and the walls of reality get worn thin. Sometimes, local operating conditions . . . break down, overwhelmed and replaced by the natural laws of other dimensions. And then you get an opening, a door between realities. Between here, and Somewhere Else. And then . . . Something Else can break through, from There into Here. This is rarely a good thing."

"You really expect me to believe such unscientific nonsense?" the professor said angrily. "This isn't what I called you people for! I need practical help, not . . . pseudo-scientific bullshit!"

"If the doorway opens again, it will make a believer out of you in one hell of a hurry," said JC. "Happy, take another look at what's going on inside the students' heads. Dig deep. See if there's any trace of them left that we can use to call them home."

"Sorry, JC," said Happy. "When I said their heads were empty, I meant completely cleaned out. Nothing left but the autonomous nervous system, to keep the body going. We're not only talking about their minds; their souls have been snatched, too."

"What can you tell us about the room, Happy?" said Melody, her gaze darting from one monitor screen to another. "I'm picking up all kinds of readings, but none of them make any sense."

Happy frowned, concentrating; and then he winced. "This room is supersaturated with information. Layer upon layer, from recent events to the far past. Going back . . . decades. This isn't the first time something bad has happened here."

JC looked thoughtfully at the professor, who suddenly didn't want to meet his gaze. JC walked right up to him, and the professor started to back away, only to find Happy suddenly standing behind him, blocking his way.

"Tell me, Professor Volke," said JC. "Why choose this particular location for your little psychological experiment? Is this your home? Or perhaps the home of one of your students?"

"Martin leased this house, a few months back," said the professor, reluctantly. "And when he told me about it, I remembered I'd heard of this address before. I remembered a story . . . of a haunting, or some kind of supernatural disturbance, from years ago. Back in the early eighties, when I was a child. There was a report on the local news about it. Scared the crap out of me at the time. That's what gave me the idea to hold my séance here. But I checked! I did my research! This house has been quiet for years. Decades . . . No reports of anything out of the ordinary. Nothing since that original story from the eighties."

"Did you tell your students about any of this?" said JC.

"No," said the professor. "I didn't think it necessary. They didn't need to know. It might have affected their responses and reactions, compromised the experiment. Look! We have to get the students back! Something like this could lay me open to all kinds of lawsuits! Ruin my career!"

"I'm more concerned about helping your students," said JC.

"What? Oh, yes, of course." The professor nodded quickly. "Can they be helped?"

"We'll give it our best shot," said JC.

He deliberately turned his back on the professor and walked slowly round the lounge, looking at everything. Happy and Melody watched him patiently.

"Okay!" JC said finally. "I think the best thing to do . . . is restart the séance. Recreate the conditions that affected the students. They clearly made contact with Something. Let's see if it's still hanging around."

"That is like jumping in the deep end when you've already been told it's full of sharks," said Happy. "Rabid sharks, with really big teeth. Séances are always dangerous. It's like kicking open a door when you've no idea who or what might be waiting on the other side."

"The door's already open," said JC. "We're going to take a quick peek through the opening, hopefully locate our missing students in whatever new place they've been taken to, then either persuade or haul them back through the door by main force."

"And then shut and lock the door," said Happy.

"Well, obviously," replied JC.

"Just like that?" said Melody.

"Of course," JC said mildly. "We are, after all, professionals."

"What if we have to push the door all the way open, to get to the students; and Something Big and Nasty comes crashing through from the other side?" said Happy.

"Then we deal with it," said JC.

"I want to go home," said Happy.

"Race you to the Land Rover," said Melody.

"Oh ye of little faith," said JC.

"Wait; wait just a minute," said the professor. "Are you saying this . . . rescue, could be dangerous? To us?"

"Grow a pair, Prof," said JC.

"I think I have a right to . . ."

"No you don't," said JC, his voice suddenly very cold. "Not when this is all your fault. So sit down at the coffee table and keep quiet, like a good little professor."

He glared at the professor until he sat down, very reluctantly, beside the coffee table, and JC sat down with him, squeezing in among the motionless students. JC then glared at Happy until he also came over and sat down with them. The professor stuck both his hands in his lap and hunched in his shoulders, so he wouldn't have to touch Elspeth and Dominic, sitting very still on either side of him. JC looked over at Melody; and she smiled briefly.

"I've got all my sensors cracked wide open. All systems are green, all readings coming in sharp and clear. Ghost Finders are Go!"

JC picked up one of the plastic cups the students had been drinking their wine from. He emptied out the last of the contents onto the carpet, turned the cup upside down, and placed it carefully in the middle of the Ouija board. The professor frowned.

"Doesn't it have to be . . ."

"No it doesn't have to be," JC said firmly. "The board and everything else are symbols, to put people in the right frame of mind. It's the participants who do the hard work, the psychic heavy lifting, and make things happen."

He placed a forefinger on the upturned plastic cup, then stared firmly at Happy and the professor until they did, too. The professor's touch was so unsteady, the cup rattled back and forth for a moment until he settled down. They all sat and looked at the cup. It didn't move.

"Come on," JC said encouragingly to the cup. "Let's see a little action, hmm? Move it! We haven't got all night . . ."

Happy's head came up sharply, and he looked quickly round the lounge. "We're not alone here, JC. There's a definite presence, right here in the room with us. Can't quite . . . pin it down . . ."

"Friendly?" said JC.

"What do you think?" Happy winced. "Ooh, this feels bad. Really bad."

The professor snatched his hand back from the plastic cup and scrambled to his feet. JC grabbed him by an arm and hauled him back down again.

"Don't draw attention to yourself, Prof," he murmured. "Might not be healthy. Melody? You getting anything?"

"Nothing useful," said Melody, her gaze jumping from one display to the next. "Nothing's showing up on the

motion trackers . . . Or the short-range sensors. But the
temperature in here has dropped another seven degrees.     •
Could be an energy sink—draining power out of the world
to fuel some kind of manifestation . . ."

"It's here," said Happy. His face was pale, and wet with
sweat. His eyes were very bright. "I can feel it, moving
around us. Watching us."

"Could it be one of the students, trying to get home?"
said JC.

"It's not human," said Happy.

The professor yanked his arm free of JC's grasp and
tried to get to his feet again. He was breathing hard, his
gaze fixed on the exit. JC grabbed him again, his fingers
sinking deep into the professor's arm muscle, until Volke
cried out. JC pulled him back down again.

"Let me go!" said the professor, struggling to break
free. He was breathing so fast now, he was almost panting,
borderline hysterical. "I have to get out of here!"

"You are not running out on your students," said JC.
"You got them into this; you are going to help bring them
back."

"I'm leaving! You can't stop me!"

"Bet I can," said JC.

He let go of the professor, smiled briefly, and took off
his sunglasses. Bright golden light shone fiercely from his
eyes. The professor stared at him: fascinated and horrified,
all at once.

"Dear God, man; what happened to you?"

"I was touched inappropriately by forces from Outside," JC said calmly.

"What are you . . . ?" whispered the professor.

"Professional," said JC. "So sit tight and don't be a distraction, so the rest of us can clean up the mess you've made."

The professor subsided. JC looked at him with his glowing eyes until he placed his finger back on the upturned cup; and then JC put his sunglasses back on.

The single bulb lighting the room began to dim, steadily losing its light, until the room was full of gloom and shadows. Melody kicked in the spotlights built into her equipment array. The harsh lights illuminated the group sitting around the coffee table, as the light bulb gave up the ghost and shut down completely. Drifting shadows moved slowly round the lounge, large and shapeless, twisting and coiling like fog, unconnected to anything that might have cast them. The professor made a low, whimpering sound but didn't move. JC ignored the shadows with magnificent disdain. He kept his gaze fixed on the upturned plastic cup and his finger firmly in place, along with Happy's and the professor's. They sat almost as still as the four students mixed in with them—breathing slowly and steadily, concentrating on the cup.

And, slowly, it began to move. Edging forward a few inches at a time, in sudden jerks and rushes, dragging the three arms after it. The cup moved faster and faster, shooting round and round the Ouija board, not even trying to spell out a message. JC had a sudden strong feeling there was someone standing right behind him. He didn't turn to look. He knew there wouldn't be anything there he could see. He looked across the table at Happy, who nodded quickly.

"We've definitely got Something's attention, JC."

"I've locked onto the spatial coordinates of the dimensional door," Melody said quietly. "It's there at the table, with you."

"Department of no surprises," said JC.

"Oh God," whispered the professor. "Please. I don't want to be here. I don't want to do this. Please let me go!"

"Don't move your finger, Prof," said JC. "It wouldn't be safe."

"I'm picking up new information from the room," Happy said suddenly. "Old impressions, rising to the surface. Something to do with . . . a family that used to live here, some years back. Could be the family you were talking about, Professor; back in the eighties."

"On it," said Melody. "My computers are tapping into all the local-history sources . . . Yes. Here we go. I've got an old local television news report, from 1983. All about this house and the supposedly supernatural troubles the family had been having, ever since they moved in. Probably the same report you saw as a kid, Professor Volke."

"How did you find it so quickly?" said the professor.

Melody smirked. "With these computers, I can find anything, anywhere. There isn't a security system on this planet strong enough to keep me out."

"Yes, yes, we're all very impressed," said JC. "Can you show us this old report, on the television?"

"Of course," said Melody.

"The cup has stopped moving," said Happy.

They all looked back at the Ouija board. The upturned cup had come to a rest, standing motionless at the NO station. JC sniffed loudly.

"We don't take no orders from stinking boards!" he said grandly. "Play the report, Melody."

The television set snapped on again, pumping out light

to push back the general gloom. A local news report began, with a tag line at the bottom of the screen, saying it was from September 17, 1983. Fronted by a young, female reporter with a bright, enthusiastic smile, big hair, and barely restrained eighties fashion. She was standing in front of the house, beaming cheerfully into the lens.

"Hello! This is Isobel Hardestry, from Thames News, bringing you a fascinating story of things that go bump in the night, from an estate in South-East London. The house behind me looks like any other house; but strange things have been happening here. According to the family who moved in last month. I have with me Mrs. Katy Perrin, the mother of the family."

The camera pulled back a little, to show a woman who probably wasn't much older than the reporter but looked prematurely aged. She was dressed in rough, respectable clothes. Her face was drawn, with dark, deep-set eyes. She looked like she hadn't been getting a lot of sleep recently. Her arms were tightly crossed, and she kept her back firmly turned on the house behind her. She barely glanced at the reporter, or the camera, as she was asked a series of quiet, respectful questions. Yes, bad things had been happening in the house. No, they hadn't seen any ghosts. Yes, there had been . . . manifestations.

"We were so happy there, at first," said Mrs. Perrin. Her voice was flat, almost unemotional. As though she'd given up caring whether she was believed or not. "This was the first house that was really ours. We'd only ever been renters, before. It took everything we had to make the deposit. But then the kids started fooling around with this Ouija board their uncle Paul found at a jumble sale. We all thought it was only a toy, something to keep them occupied. But then the kids started talking about this new friend they'd made through the board. At first, we all thought it was just another Imaginary Friend. But it wasn't imaginary; and it wasn't a friend.

"It started playing tricks. Opening and closing doors, moving things around, hiding things . . . The kitchen got flooded, the fuses kept blowing . . . and then something tripped my husband, at the top of the stairs. He fell all the way down. Broke both his legs.

"Finally, some of next door's children came round, to play with my kids and keep them company while I was off visiting their dad at the hospital. When I got back, my kids were crying, hysterical. There was no trace of the neighbour's children. They'd just . . . vanished. We never did find out what happened to them. We had the police around, and everything, but it did no good. They were gone."

She had to stop for a moment, on the verge of tears. Exhaustion, as much as horror. The reporter, who'd been nodding and smiling encouragingly all through this, waited patiently for Mrs. Perrin to continue. She finally shook her head slowly and looked straight into the camera for the first time.

"We've moved," she said, almost defiantly. "Had no choice. Got out, while we still could. I burned the Ouija board before we left. Apparently, it's been quiet in the house ever since. But I wouldn't trust it. And God help whatever family moves in."

She disappeared from the screen, replaced by a tight shot on Isobel Hardestry. From the change of light behind her, it was obvious some time had passed.

"I also talked to the local priest, Father Callahan."

He turned out to be a surprisingly young man, barely

into his twenties. Calm and relaxed, not obviously concerned.

"Yes," he said. "I was called in, by the family. To examine the house and the situation. Nothing happened while I was there."

"Did you perform an exorcism, Father Callahan?"

"No," said the priest, a little condescendingly. "I would have to ask permission from my bishop first, before I could take on such a thing. And there really wasn't anything I could take to him to justify such an extreme response."

"And you didn't . . . feel anything?" said the reporter, clearly doing her best to encourage him without leading him.

"I didn't say that," said the priest. "I did feel a certain . . . presence, in the house."

"What kind of presence, Father Callahan?"

"Malignant."

The two-shot disappeared, replaced by a close-up of the reporter's face. She smiled bravely into the camera.

"The Perrins are gone. A new family lives in the house now, and they . . . have nothing disturbing to report. What really happened here? I don't suppose we'll ever know, for sure. But whatever it was, I think we can safely say, it's over."

The television screen went blank. Happy sniffed loudly.

"Just as well they didn't try an exorcism. Would have been like trying to put out a raging inferno with a water-pistol."

"Whatever came through the dimensional door must have retreated back to its own world, once the house was empty, and there was no-one left to play with," said JC.

"But the door didn't close completely. It stayed a little ajar; perhaps merely the potential of a door . . . Until the professor's séance blasted it wide open again. And now, I think Something that has been waiting on the other side of that door for all these years . . . has come through again."

"What sort of Something?" asked the professor. "And why did it take my students' . . . minds?"

He couldn't bring himself to say the word *souls*.

"Because it could," said JC. "Because it's hungry. Perhaps because it likes to play. Depends on what it is we're dealing with here."

"Are we talking about some kind of ghost?" said the professor.

"If we're lucky," said JC.

"And if we're not?"

"It's a Beast," said Happy.

"Something from the Outer Rim," said Melody. "The furthest reaches of existence, the most extreme dimensions, where Life, or something like it, takes on powerful and disturbing forms. Spiritual monsters; terrible abstracts given shape and form and appalling appetites."

The professor looked like he wanted to say something scathing but couldn't bring himself to. The atmosphere in the room wouldn't let him.

JC looked steadily at the upturned plastic cup, still holding resolutely still on the Ouija board. He prodded the cup carefully with one fingertip; and it scraped noisily across the wooden board, unresisting. JC raised his head, and addressed the room outside the circle of Melody's spotlights.

"Hello!" he said loudly. "We are the pros from the Carnacki Institute! Who are you?"

The television turned itself back on. A thick grey fog filled the screen, twisting and curling; while a heavy buzzing static blasted from the speakers.

"Okay," said Melody. "That wasn't me. Did any of you touch the remote? Of course you didn't. Ah, that's interesting . . . According to my instruments, there's no incoming signal. That television shouldn't be showing anything."

"Somebody wants to talk to us," said JC.

"You say that like it's a good thing," said Happy. "I can't believe there's anything our interdimensional intruder would want to say that we would want to hear. Any sane person, with working survival instincts, would be sprinting for the horizon right now."

The professor looked hopefully at the door; but one glance from JC was all it took to hold him in place. JC looked thoughtfully at the television screen.

"All right," he said. "What do you want?"

The screen cleared to show shifting, disturbing images from some awful hellish place. Another world, another reality, where everything was alive. Horribly alive. Lit by a flaring, blood-red light, everything in this terrible new world seemed to be made of flesh. The ground had skin. Corpse white and blue-veined, it pulsed and heaved, sweating fiercely. Great trees rose to make a fleshy jungle, with thick meat trunks and flailing branches, lashing the air like boneless tentacles, grabbing hungrily at distorted, malformed creatures than ran and leapt and scuttled through the dark shadows between the trees. Alien shapes, moving in inhuman ways, pursuing and eating each other; every living thing attacking and feasting on every other living thing. A world of endless appetite, of ravenous hunger, without any trace of conscience or regret to hold them back from every appalling thing they did.

It rained blood. And the fleshy ground drank it up with vicious glee.

The professor vomited, noisily and messily. JC patted him absently on the shoulder, his gaze fixed on the other world.

"It's showing us where it comes from," he said quietly. "It's not giving us a name, or even showing what it is, because it doesn't want us to have any information we could use against it. I don't recognise this . . . place. Melody?"

"My computers are coming up blank," Melody said steadily. "Nothing even like this, in all the Institute's records. This must be way out in the Outer Reaches. The Shoals, perhaps, where the material meets the immaterial."

"It's playing with us," said JC. "Taunting us . . ."

"Wait," said Happy. "What's that?"

The image on the screen had zoomed in on the meat forest, to show four human figures running desperately through the swaying trees. They lurched and stumbled, avoiding the lashing branches and the leaping creatures. They looked worn-down and exhausted, as though they'd been running for some time. But the huge and horrible thing lunging through the forest after them, snapping at their heels, was enough to keep them moving. And though the dark presence was half-hidden among the trees, it was still stunningly repulsive and horribly powerful. The only reason it hadn't already caught and consumed its human prey . . . was that it was having too much fun chasing them.

"I don't understand," the professor said plaintively, wiping his mouth with the back of his hand. "Is that their . . . souls? If those are their souls, how can they be in any danger?"

"A world made of psychoplasm; psychogeography," Happy said unexpectedly. "A world made physical by the thoughts and desires of those who live there. It looks like that because that's what they want. The immaterial made real and solid by the intents of its inhabitants. Your students' souls are real and solid, there, because that's what the thing chasing them wants. They might not be able to die, or at least die permanently; but they can certainly be made to suffer."

The professor looked like he wanted to vomit again. He made a high, keening sound, his eyes stretched painfully wide. JC had seen that look before—on the faces of people forced to understand and believe too much, too quickly.

"You were right, Happy," said Melody. "It's a Beast. And it's hungry."

"*Shit,*" said Happy.

"Why is he looking so scared?" demanded the professor.

"That's his normal condition," said JC. "I wouldn't worry about it."

"Why is he taking those pills?" said the professor.

"He does that," said JC.

Happy dry-swallowed hard and put his pill box away. "Ah! Yes! That's the stuff to give the troops! If I were any more aware, I'd be twins. The doorway's shifted position, JC; I can tell. It's moved away from the coffee table, to the television set. The Beast is forcing the door all the way open, from the other side. It wants in. It wants . . . Oh dear God, it's so hungry, JC! It wants to eat us all up, the whole damned world, body and soul." He laughed suddenly; a sound with no real humour in it. "Let it come through! I'll kick its head right off."

"Might have overdone the dosage a bit there, Happy," murmured JC.

"Can it do that?" demanded the professor. "Can it break through? Actually appear, here, in our world?"

"That's what doors are all about, Prof," said JC.

"It wants to come here and . . . eat our souls, as well as our bodies?"

"That's what Beasts do," said JC.

"I think I'm going to be sick again," said the professor.

"Perfectly normal response," said JC. "Try to keep some of it off my shoes, this time."

The professor swallowed hard and looked beseechingly at JC. "Can you stop it? Can you get my students back? Bring them home?"

"We can try," said JC. "But if we're to successfully pull off this increasingly unlikely long shot . . . I'm going to have to bring in the fourth member of our little team. The real expert on all things ghostly. Come in, Kim."

The ghost girl Kim Sterling walked through the far wall to join them. She stood beside the television set, glowing, and smiling sweetly on one and all. A beautiful, pre-Raphaelite dream of a woman, with a great mane of glorious red hair tumbling down to her shoulders, framing a high-boned, sharply defined face with vivid green eyes and a wide, happy smile. She was in her twenties and had been ever since she was murdered down in the London Underground. She wore a long black dress with white piping and a neat little hat pushed well back on her head.

Kim Sterling, the only working ghost in the Ghost Finders.

"Hello, darlings," she said. "Don't I look divine? Is no-one going to applaud? It isn't easy, you know, looking this glamorous on no budget."

The professor almost jumped out of his skin when she walked through the wall. He looked very much like he wanted to run again, but JC had a hand ready to clamp down should it prove necessary; so he settled for hiding behind JC and peering at the ghost girl over his shoulder.

"Why didn't you ride down with us, in the Land Rover?" asked Melody, entirely unmoved by Kim's dramatic arrival.

"She probably heard about your driving," said Happy.

Kim smiled easily about her. "Sorry I'm a bit late. I came by the low road, the paths the dead walk. It's very scenic, this time of year."

She smiled disarmingly at the professor, who was still refusing to come out from behind JC.

"I don't believe in ghosts!" he said loudly. "I don't!"

"Really?" said Kim. "I don't believe there are people as stupid as you, but I keep being proved wrong."

She hadn't even finished speaking when suddenly everything that wasn't actually nailed in place or bolted down went flying round the room. Heavy objects shot through the air, seeking out living targets. Porcelain figures flashed past ducking heads, to crash and shatter against the walls. Clocks exploded, sending metal fragments flying through the air like shrapnel. Every piece of furniture went tumbling end over end, in a major outbreak of poltergeist activity. The only things not to move were the coffee table and the television set. A shard of broken mirror-glass almost took the professor's head off as he sat there gawping; but JC dragged him down at the last moment. The professor pulled away from him.

"I have to get this on camera!" he said desperately. "No-one will ever believe me unless I can record this!"

The camera burst into flames. The professor moaned miserably and hit the floor, hugging the carpet. Melody crouched behind her array of equipment, her fingers still darting across the keyboards, pumping out psionic chaff to fill the room and block the activity. Happy scrambled rapidly across the floor on all fours, to huddle at her feet, behind the equipment. Kim stood where she was. Large and bulky objects went hurtling through her insubstantial form without disturbing her in the least. She walked forward to stand before JC. He stood up abruptly and stepped forward, so that he occupied exactly the same space as she did.

She seemed to disappear within him, his form overlapping and enveloping hers; but her ghostly glow now surrounded JC. And nothing in the room could touch him. Flying objects actually changed direction in mid air, to go around him. He took off his sunglasses again; and his golden eyes glowed fiercely in the gloom. JC wore his ghost girl like spiritual armour, and wherever he turned his glowing gaze, objects fell out of the air, crashed to the floor, and did not move again. The poltergeist activity stopped as suddenly as it had begun.

JC and Kim, melded and merged together on many levels, turned slowly to look at the television screen. It still showed the four missing students running desperately through the living jungle, pursued by Something too horrible to look at that was slowly but steadily drawing nearer. JC and Kim looked at the screen with JC's glowing eyes, and the image suddenly grew larger, until it was the size of the room. Like looking through a window into that awful other place. JC and Kim strode forward, through the enlarged television screen, out of this world, and into the other.

\*\*\*\*\*\*\*\*\*\*\*\*\*\*\*\*\*\*\*\*\*\*\*

The blood-red light was almost too fierce, even for JC's altered eyes. The falling rain-drops hit him with the impact of bullets. The skin-covered ground heaved sickly under his feet, flushed and sweaty. The meat trees stank of carrion and the exposed guts of things. The air was full of screams and howls, of living things endlessly eating and being eaten. Nothing could touch or affect JC while he wore Kim like armour; but the terrible grinding oppression of the place was a burden on his thoughts, breaking his heart and cutting into his soul.

Dominic ran past, not even seeing JC in his panic. JC grabbed him by an arm, and hauled him to a halt. The student tried to break free, but JC made him stand.

"Dominic; it's all right," he said. "I'm the rescue party."

One by one he grabbed the other students as they came to him, brought them to a stop and made them listen to his calming voice. They were all half-out of their minds, clinging to each other like traumatised children, barely able to grasp where they were or that their nightmare might finally be over. But they all slowly responded to a human face, and the firmness of his voice. Rotten, revolting creatures leapt and surged and postured all around them, menacing them with teeth and claws and other things; but none of the awful things wanted to get too close to the new arrival, with his potent aura. And not one of them could face his glowing, golden gaze.

The huge dark thing came crashing through the last few trees and halted abruptly, towering over the humans. It was a horrid mixture of a dozen different creatures, slapped haphazardly together, as though it had chosen all its favourite bits and pieces, then clapped them together. Its shape made no sense, an affront to all logic and reason. It stank of blood and guts and death. It had too many limbs, and far too many eyes, and it wore the entrails of its previous victims as clothing and trophies. It looked down on its human prey and smiled suddenly, its long face splitting open to reveal row upon row of jagged teeth.

"Hello, JC," it said, on a waft of breath like a charnel-house. It had a voice like screaming women and troubled children, like a blade slicing through yielding flesh. "The infamous JC Chance himself. Well, well. I am honoured. Have you come to lead me back to your world, like the good little Judas goat you are?"

"Dream on," said JC. "Kim, we are going!"

The ghostly aura leapt suddenly out to surround not only him but the four students as well. And suddenly they were all back in the lounge, on the other side of a normal-sized television screen.

·······················

The aura shrank back to cover just JC again; and four confused and dazed spirits stumbled back to their bodies, still sitting round the coffee table. Kim stepped out of JC, to stand before him; and they smiled contentedly at each other. Dominic's spirit stopped suddenly and looked back at JC.

"It knew your name," he said. "How did that thing know your name?"

"I get around," said JC.

Dominic went to join his friends as they clustered confusedly round the coffee table. Happy and Melody stood behind the equipment array, looking thoughtfully at JC and Kim.

"How . . . ?" said Melody.

"Hold everything!" said Happy. "Look at the television!"

They all turned to look. Blood-red light was blasting out of the screen as it bulged away from the set. The screen stretched impossibly wide, pushing forward, as though being forced out by some unbearable pressure from the other side. The television screen stretched and stretched, like a soap-bubble that wouldn't break. Something huge and dark pressed up against it from the other side, the other place.

"It knows we're here!" said Happy. "It's coming through! You showed it the way, and it followed you! I can feel it . . . So hungry . . . *Get out of my head!*"

Melody worked her keyboards fiercely, then glared at JC. "It's coming through; and I haven't anything here that can stop it!"

"I can't stand it!" said Happy, his eyes screwed tightly shut. "It's inside my head, and it's too big, too powerful. I can't contain it . . ."

He scrabbled desperately in his pockets, pulling out a dozen pill boxes at once. He fumbled and dropped them, and they hit the floor and burst open, spilling multi-coloured pills everywhere. Happy cried out and dropped to his knees, scrabbling for his pills with both hands.

"You don't need your damned pills, Happy!" said Melody. "Just stop that bloody thing coming through!"

"I'm sorry, I'm sorry," said Happy. But he didn't look up from his precious pills.

JC looked at Kim, and she nodded quickly. She strode back into him again, and he glowed fiercely in the gloom. JC made a gun with his right hand and pointed the finger barrel at the bulging television screen.

"Bang," he said.

The television exploded, throwing its insides across the carpet. The set was suddenly normal again; the screen nothing more than so many broken bits on the floor. The light fixture overhead snapped back on, filling the lounge with perfectly ordinary light. All the oppressive atmosphere was gone in a moment. Kim stepped out of JC. His glow flickered and went out, and he put his sunglasses back on.

"According to my instruments, everything here is back to normal," said Melody, in an only slightly brittle voice. "No dimensional door, no strange energy readings; even the temperature is climbing back to what it should be."

She left her array of equipment and knelt down beside Happy, to help him gather up his scattered pills. She didn't say anything to him.

"Is it over?" asked the professor, looking dazedly around him. "Is it finally over?"

"For now," said JC. "There's a good chance the dimensional door has made a permanent weak spot here; but I'll send you some Institute technicians to put in a patch. To be on the safe side."

He stopped, as he realised Melody and Happy were back on their feet again and looking at him and Kim.

"Nice trick, the two of you working together," said Melody. "How long have you been able to do that?"

"Not long," said JC.

"We were . . . experimenting," Kim said lightly. "And we discovered we could do all sorts of things, together. It's the closest we can come to touching."

"And you didn't tell us about this before because?" said Melody.

"Didn't think it was any of your business," JC said steadily. "We weren't sure it had any practical value. Until now."

"We don't keep secrets from each other!" said Melody.

"Since when?" said JC.

He looked at Happy, who nodded guiltily.

"Sorry," he said. "Sorry about that. I sort of . . . lost it, for a moment there."

"You could have got us all killed," said JC.

"I know!" said Happy. "But, please, JC. Not now, okay?"

"We will talk about this," said JC. "Later."

And then they all looked round sharply, at a babble of raised voices from the four returned students at the coffee table. They were all up on their feet, waving their hands around and shouting excitedly at each other. It quickly became clear, from listening to the voices coming out of the faces, that something quite extraordinary had happened. The four spirits had been so dazed and confused when they returned, that somehow . . . they'd all ended up in the wrong bodies. And they really weren't too pleased about it.

JC turned to smile at the increasingly horrified Professor Volke. "Well, Prof," he said. "You wanted a psychological experiment . . ."

# TWO

......................................

## JUST A WALK IN THE PARK

JC Chance and Catherine Latimer, field team leader and Boss of the Carnacki Institute, went walking together in the open air, in London's Hyde Park. It was a bright, sunny day, and the venerable park was packed full of people making the most of the good weather, in a calm and easy blue-skied summer's afternoon. Green lawns, neatly-turned-out paths, wide-branching trees . . . and happy, smiling faces everywhere. Most of whom paid little or no attention to the two very significant persons walking among them, strolling casually through the park.

JC's rich white suit seemed almost to glow in the bright sunlight, and his good looks, rock-star hair, and very dark sunglasses, did draw the occasional admiring glance. Catherine Latimer was well into her nineties now, but she still went striding along with almost unnatural strength and vitality. Medium height and unrepentantly stocky, her grey hair cropped in a severe bowl cut, she wore a smartly tailored grey suit with sensible shoes. Catherine's face was all hard edges and unflinching lines, but there were still traces left of what had once been handsome, even striking, features. Her cold grey eyes regarded the sunny day with open suspicion, as though expecting it to disappear suddenly and without warning, at any moment. Catherine Latimer was not a trusting person.

She smoked black Turkish cigarettes in a long ivory holder, apparently an affectation that went all the way back to her student days in Cambridge; and she ignored the occasional disapproving glance from passersby with magnificent disdain. She walked in a straight line, from one side of the park to the other, and it was up to everyone else to get out of her way. And they did. JC had to work hard to keep up with her.

"All right!" he said finally, feeling very strongly that he'd been quiet and courteous for as long as he could stand. "You called and said we had to meet urgently; so here I am. What are we supposed to be talking about? And why did we have to meet here, of all places?"

"There's a lot to be said for the great outdoors," said Catherine, not even glancing at him or slowing her pace. "Open spaces, and lots of people. Nothing like being part of a crowd to make you safely anonymous. And, there's nothing like a great open space to make it a lot easier to see your enemies coming for you. We are talking here, Mr. Chance, because it's safer and more secure than anywhere in the Carnacki Institute. Very definitely including my private office. It's harder for us to be overheard here, amidst the clamour of so many other voices and minds, by anyone or anything. Besides . . . it does people like us good, to get out among the ordinary, everyday people. In the everyday world. We spend too much time operating in the dark and in the shadowy places. This world, and these people, are what the Carnacki Institute was established to protect. They are the important ones, the ones who really matter. And we forget that at our peril, Mr. Chance."

"I'm in trouble, aren't I?" said JC. "I always know it's going to be really bad once you start lecturing me."

"We're all in trouble," said Catherine. "That's why I can't trust my office any more."

"I don't think I've ever seen you outside the Institute, before this," said JC. "It's occurred to me, more than once, that you live in your office."

"Does feel like that, sometimes," said Catherine. "I have a cot out the back, for emergencies. When there's a real flap on, and I don't dare leave for fear of missing something . . . But no; I do have a home, and a life, outside the Institute. Even if I can't always give them as much time and attention as I would like."

"Do you have . . . a family?" asked JC, tentatively. Because it felt like he was dipping a toe into unfamiliar and possibly very murky waters.

"This is an official discussion, about official Institute business," Catherine said firmly. "Not a pleasant personal chat."

"You know all there is to know about my life," said JC, defensively.

"Which is as it should be." Catherine allowed herself a small smile. "It is necessary that I know everything about you if I am to protect you properly."

JC gave her a calm and easy smile of his own. "You only think you know everything about me."

"Go on feeling that way," said Catherine. "If it makes you feel better."

JC looked around, taking his time, considering the wide-open space and the people milling around everywhere.

"Don't you feel . . . vulnerable, out here on your own? Without your usual personal bodyguards and special protections?"

"I am perfectly capable of looking after myself," Catherine said sternly. "I am quite possibly the most dangerous person you will ever meet, Mr. Chance, and have been for most of my life. Certainly long before I joined the Carnacki Institute. And anyway, I am always guarded and protected. Even if you can't see who's doing it. Especially if you can't see them. In fact, if you could spot any of my people, I would have no choice but to fire them for seriously underperforming."

JC fought down a suicidal urge to slap her round the back of the head, just to see what would happen. Some impulses should be suppressed immediately—as long as you still have any working self-preservation instincts.

Catherine Latimer stopped abruptly, and JC stumbled to a halt beside her. He looked quickly about him, but they didn't seem to have reached any particular destination, anywhere special or significant. He let his gaze drift casually over the nearest people passing by, but they all gave every appearance of being ordinary people, going about their everyday business. Men in city suits, out for a brisk walk between important meetings. Families with loud and raucous children: picnicking and sunbathing, or throwing Frisbees for dogs who clearly hoped the afternoon would never end. Young lovers reclining on towels and blankets,

wearing as little as they could get away with, casually en-
twined. And tourists of every stamp and nationality, come
to see what there was to be seen and take photos of it. JC
turned back to Catherine and gave her his full attention.

"Who do you trust to protect you, in these uncertain
times?" he said, carefully. "When you know absolutely
anyone in the Carnacki Institute could be a traitor or a
double agent, or a servant of the Flesh Undying? Who can
you rely on to have your back? Old friends, perhaps?"

"In our business, you learn never to rely on friends,"
said Catherine. "They're the ones you have to keep an eye
on. You always know where you are with your enemies."

"I don't think I ever want to learn to think that way,"
said JC.

"I used to feel the same, once upon a time," said Catherine, surprisingly. "But it comes with the job, and the
territory."

She turned to face JC and considered him thoughtfully.
And then, quite suddenly, her eyes blazed with a fierce,
golden glow. A very familiar golden light, much like the
one that issued from JC's eyes when they weren't hidden behind very dark sunglasses. The glare was only there
for a moment, then the golden light snapped off, leaving
Catherine Latimer regarding JC with her usual cool grey
gaze. JC realised his mouth was hanging open and closed
it abruptly. He swallowed hard, his mind trying to race off
in a dozen different directions at once. A quick glance
around was enough to confirm none of the people hurrying
by had seen anything out of the ordinary. The golden glare
had been meant for him alone.

"But . . . You . . . What the hell?" said JC.

"I learned long ago how to conceal my altered gaze,"

said Catherine. "You will, too. You can't go around in sunglasses all the time. It draws far too much attention. Suppressing the glare is quite a simple discipline. Even you could master it."

"When were you touched by forces from Outside?" said JC, honestly shocked.

"That is a story for another time," said Catherine.

"How many are there?" said JC. "I mean, how many, like us?"

"More than you'd think," said Catherine. "Scattered across the world, in all kinds of organisations. The forces from Outside do so love to meddle. They hang around outside our reality like drunks outside a wine lodge. Drawn to Humanity like moths to a flame. Except we're the ones who get burned."

"Why did you want to speak to just me?" JC said suddenly. "And not the rest of my team? Don't you trust them? Am I supposed to keep this from them?"

"You can tell your associates as much as you feel is safe," said Catherine. "I'm sure you already keep some secrets from them, and vice versa. You are here, Mr. Chance, because since you have been touched and altered by Outside forces, certain others will find it harder to get inside your head and see what's there. So I can tell you things, in the certainty that they are unlikely to go any further. Like my true nature. That puts you on a very short short list. You should feel honoured."

"Oh, I do," said JC. "Really. You have no idea how honoured. And more scared and less safe than I did before I entered this park to talk with you."

"Good," said Catherine, approvingly. "You see, you're learning. It's not that I don't trust Miss Chambers and Mr.

Palmer, or at least I don't distrust them any more than anyone else who works for me; it's that I can't be as sure of their personal security as I can be with you." She stopped, and her mouth pursed in a brief moue of distaste, as though she'd thought of something unpleasant. "The telepath—is he still . . ."

"Yes," said JC. "Even more than before. I did think he was getting better; but apparently that was wishful thinking on my part."

"Drugs are no substitute for proper mental discipline," said Catherine. "He must learn to control himself or the drugs will control him. You do realise, the path he has chosen will not lead him anywhere good."

"There's nothing I can do!" JC protested. "I can see what the damned pills are doing to him. I'm not blind. But . . . he can't function without them."

"We all have the right to go to Hell in our own way," said Catherine. "And one of the hardest things to learn is that you can't help people who are determined not to be helped."

"The pills are killing him by inches," said JC. "I know that. So does he, and so does Melody. But I think taking them away . . . would be cruel. He sees so much more of the world than we do, even with our altered eyes. If we could see the world he's forced to live in, we'd probably reach for the chemical lobotomy, too."

"I see more than enough," said Catherine. She raised her voice; urgently and imperatively. "*Ghost girl, come forth.*"

And the ghost of Kim Sterling, who had merged with JC to hide within him before he entered Hyde Park . . . so she could listen and watch over him unobserved, had no

choice but to step forward out of him and stand revealed
before Catherine Latimer. Kim held her head high and
glared right back at Catherine. The ghost girl glowed
faintly in the bright sunshine. JC would have liked to glare
at Catherine, too, but he was frankly flummoxed by the
sheer power in Catherine's voice. He could still feel it,
ringing and reverberating on the air around them. A voice
and a power that could not be disobeyed. JC looked quickly
about him, again, but it was clear no-one else was reacting
to Kim's sudden appearance. No-one else could see her.
Kim had learned to hide her presence from the world.

It had been her idea to hide inside JC during his meeting with the Boss. She hadn't explained why she felt it
was so important; and he hadn't pressed her. Partly because he trusted her, and partly because there were a lot of
things JC and Kim kept from each other. For their mutual
comfort and protection. JC hoped that her reasons for
keeping some things secret were as good as his.

Kim glowered at Catherine. "How did you know I was
there?"

Catherine let her eyes flare briefly golden again.
"There's not much in this world that can hide from me,
young lady. It's the things I can't see that I have to worry
about." She looked briefly about her. "It's not only a bigger world than most people comprehend; it's bigger than
most people *can* comprehend. That's why we exist; to protect them from all the things they don't know they need
protecting from."

"You see almost as much as Happy, don't you?" said
JC. "How do you cope?"

"By seeing the beauty as well as the horror," said Catherine, surprisingly. "There are amazing things sharing the

world with us. Marvellous vistas and beautiful creatures, wonders and marvels, miracles and joys. All around us, every day. It's not all monsters."

"Will I be able to see these things someday?" said JC.

"If you last that long," said Catherine. She turned her attention back to Kim. "You've made a good start, though. You're not just another ghost, are you?"

"How did you know she was merged with me?" demanded JC. "I have a right to know!"

"Kim has been working directly for me, covertly, for some time now," said Catherine, entirely unmoved by the obvious anger in JC's voice. "Very much on the quiet: my own special secret agent, searching out the things I need to know, in the places only the dead can go. Searching for the identity of the main traitor working inside the Carnacki Institute."

There were a great many things JC wanted to say about that, but in the end he settled for the most practical. "You trust Kim to do that?"

"I have to trust someone," said Catherine. "I've always found the dead so much easier to deal with than the living. The dead may have their own agendas, but they do tend to be much less complicated. And far more biddable. You can make the dead do what you tell them."

"My girl-friend is not your servant," said JC; and his voice was very cold and very dangerous.

Catherine smiled calmly at him. "You both work for me, Mr. Chance. You are all my servants until I tell you otherwise. In the name of a greater good, of course."

"Whose greater good?" said JC.

"You see?" said Catherine. "You're learning."

"It's all right, JC," Kim said quickly. "I went into this

with my eyes wide open. I wanted to help. By helping her uncover the traitor, I'm helping you. I'm protecting her so she can protect you, and Happy and Melody, from the Flesh Undying and its agents."

"The main traitor has to be someone high up in the organisation," said Catherine. "And it bothers me that I can't tell who. That I can't see it for myself, for all my knowledge and expertise and altered sight. It has to be someone I know, someone close to me. Someone I think I can trust. Working against me, undermining my decisions and sabotaging my operations . . . Trying to get me removed, so I can be replaced by someone who serves the Flesh Undying. Not only to stop me interfering with . . . whatever it is it's trying to do, but because it knows I will eventually locate and destroy it. The Flesh Undying sees our world, our whole reality, as a prison. A cage. And it is perfectly ready to destroy everything if that's what it takes for it to break free."

"Why do people serve it, knowing that?" said Kim. "I've never understood that."

"Presumably they have some plan to control the Flesh Undying; or at the very least make some kind of deal with it," said Catherine. "Damned fools . . ."

JC looked at Kim. "And you didn't tell me about any of this because?"

"You were safer not knowing," Kim said steadily. "You couldn't accidentally give away what you didn't know."

"We don't keep things as important as this from each other!" said JC.

"Really?" said Kim. "Since when?"

JC nodded, stiffly. Some conversations you know aren't

going to go anywhere good. "All right," he said. "How's it going, being the Boss's superspy?"

"Nothing useful, so far," said Kim.

JC wasn't sure she was telling him the truth, or even part of the truth, but he didn't want to challenge her in front of Catherine Latimer. So he turned back to the Boss and folded his arms tightly across his chest in a way he hoped suggested he'd put up with quite enough and had no intention of being pushed any further.

"Talk to me," he said. "Why are we here? What did you bring me all the way here, to tell me?"

"I've been feeling . . . troubled," said Catherine, meeting his gaze unflinchingly. "How do you think I've lived so long and stayed so vital? Because that's what the forces from Outside wanted. They altered me for their own reasons because they have a purpose in mind for me. Just as they do for you, and probably all the others like us."

"But who, or what, are these Outside forces?" said JC. "What is it they want from us? What do they need us to do that's so important and so dangerous we had to be . . . changed, transformed, so we could achieve it? And how do we know these forces are any better, any more trustworthy, than the Flesh Undying?"

"I've spent most of my life trying to work out the answer to those questions," said Catherine Latimer. "And I'm no wiser. Or at least, no better informed. Maybe you'll have better luck."

"Have they ever . . . contacted you?" said JC. "Asked you to do things, for them?"

"No. I think I might feel happier if they had. At least then I might have some clue as to their wishes. Or true nature. That's why I joined the Carnacki Institute in the first place, all those years ago. Why I worked so hard to become the one in charge of everything. So I could have access to all of the Institute's records. All its official and unofficial resources. And much good that has done me."

"Then why have you stayed on as Boss for so long?" said Kim.

"Because I decided it was a job that needed doing," said Catherine. "A job important enough, and necessary enough, that I wouldn't have felt right leaving it to anyone else."

"Maybe that's what They wanted," said JC. "For you to become head of the Carnacki Institute. The right person, in the right place."

"I don't think They think that small," said Catherine Latimer. "And besides, I'm still waiting to find out what the price will be. There's always a price to be paid, for every gift. And the greater the gift, the greater the price."

She set off again, striding briskly along, and JC and Kim had to hurry to catch up with her. Kim was careful to walk in the space between JC and Catherine, so the people coming and going all around them wouldn't bump into her unknowing, and walk right through her. She hated that. It made her feel . . . unreal. Occasionally, someone would walk right at them, clearly intending to walk through the apparent open space between JC and Catherine; but somehow they always stopped, at the last moment, and decided to walk around them instead. Even though it was clear from the look on their faces that they had no idea why. Kim carefully linked her insubstantial arm through JC's, so they could at least seem to be walking arm in arm. JC kept his arm carefully crooked, so that she could, and pretended not to notice Kim was walking an inch or so above the ground.

The people passing by still didn't pay JC or Catherine much attention. They had no idea that very important matters were being discussed, right in their midst. JC looked at all the happy, shiny people, in their happy, normal world; and almost envied them. Almost. JC liked knowing things other people didn't know, even if most of the things he knew weren't particularly nice, or comforting. And he definitely liked being able to Do Something about the things he knew. And, of course, if he hadn't been a Ghost Finder . . . he would never have met Kim. The one and only true love of his life. Now and again, he peered over the top of his sunglasses, concentrating on seeing the park and its visitors through his golden eyes; but he couldn't detect anyone or anything threatening. Or even out of place. He said as much to Catherine, and she nodded briskly.

"I know. People have no idea what's really going on; and they're better off that way. It's our job to keep them in happy ignorance of all the things that threaten them, so they at least can sleep soundly at night."

"But maybe, if we trusted them . . ." said JC, "they could learn to defend themselves?"

"Look at them," said Catherine. "Do any of them look like they could cope with that kind of knowledge? With knowing that their world is nothing but a fragile thing, under constant assault by forces beyond human comprehension? Do you really think they could stand the extensive training it would take before they could even hope to fight back successfully? No. They're better off not knowing. We carry the burden, so they don't have to."

The three of them walked on a while, in silence. Catherine stared straight ahead, while JC kept a watchful eye on anyone who got too close, or even looked like they might. And Kim smiled happily at everyone even though they couldn't see her, because . . . she was that sort of girl. Finally, JC broke the silence, which made him uncomfortable.

"I thought you didn't approve of me and Kim, boss?"

"I don't," said Catherine, still not looking at either of them. "The living and the dead are not supposed to fall in love for any number of perfectly good reasons. You must know, both of you . . . there is no way your relationship can end well."

"Come on," said JC. "I have been altered by otherworldly forces, and she is mortally challenged. We have so much in common!"

"I think we're a very post-modern couple," Kim said cheerfully. "Opposites attract and complement each other. By being together, JC and I are making a positive statement!"

Catherine Latimer shook her head. "I have been head of the Carnacki Institute for too long. The world has changed so much . . . and I haven't. Sometimes I'll find myself watching some old black-and-white film, on late-night television; something from the forties or fifties . . . And that world looks more familiar, more comfortable to me, than the world I live in now. So many things I miss . . . and so few I value, now. I really think I would step down tomorrow if I thought there were anybody ready to take over. Or at least anyone I thought I could trust. But I can't go . . . Not until I've put a name to the main traitor and made sure how deep the rot goes. Not until I can be sure of how badly the Carnacki Institute has been compromised. I have to stay in charge. I know I can trust me."

"You know you can trust me," said JC.

"Yes, I can," said Catherine. "But not as head of the Carnacki Institute."

"What?" said JC, bristling. "Why not?"

"Because you don't have enough iron in your soul," said Catherine Latimer. "Not yet, anyway."

"Well," said JC. "That's something to look forward to . . ."

They walked on. Such a perfect summer's day. Not a cloud in the sky, not a shadow out of place. Nothing to worry about . . . Except . . .

"Why did you want me to come here?" said JC. "What was so important that I had to drop everything and come all the way across London, and you had to leave your very safe and protected private office . . . so we could have this conversation? Was it only to tell me about what you've had Kim doing for you? Or to lecture us about our unnatural relationship again?"

"No," said Catherine. She glanced at him; and her eyes flashed briefly golden again. "I wanted you to know you're not alone."

She increased her pace suddenly, leaving JC and Kim behind. JC stumbled to a halt and watched her go. Kim stayed with him, her arm still linked carefully through his. JC couldn't help noticing that everyone in Catherine Latimer's way seemed to step aside for her, without even noticing they were doing it.

"I can't see anyone protecting her," said JC, after a while. "Can you see anyone protecting her, Kim?"

"No," said the girl ghost. "That's sort of the point, isn't it?"

JC looked at her steadily. "How long has this spying business been going on, Kim? How long have you been working exclusively for the Boss?"

"A while," said Kim, looking back at him as steadily. "Ever since she promised me she could find me a body. A proper physical form, so I could be human and alive, again. So you and I could be together, properly."

"She can do that?"

"She says she knows someone who can."

"So you're saying; you did this for me?"

"For us!"

JC smiled, tiredly. "Typical Boss. Using our own needs to control us . . ."

"Of course," said Kim. "That's why she's the Boss."

"But when did all this start?" said JC. "Exactly?"

"When she summoned me to her office," said Kim. "Against my will. She called me, and I had to go even though I fought her all the way. She had this old and very powerful device . . . There was nothing I could do."

"The rotten cow," said JC; and his voice was very cold.

"Hush, hush, sweetie," Kim said quickly. "It's all right; really it is! It doesn't matter! Not if she can deliver on her promise, so we can be a man and a woman, together. You don't know how hard it is for me, not to be able to hold you, touch you . . ."

"I know," said JC. "I feel the same way. You know I do. How . . . dangerous, is this? What she has you doing for her?"

"Dangerous?" said Kim. "I'm dead, darling!"

"I could still lose you," said JC. "If something were to

happen; if someone broke your contact with the world, and me."

"I could still lose you," said Kim. "If one of your Ghost Finder cases went really wrong."

"I don't think I could live without you," said JC.

"I couldn't die without you," said Kim. "JC . . . You mustn't ask me questions I'm not allowed to answer. For both our sakes. We both have to do what we have to do."

JC looked suddenly about him, concerned that people were looking at him oddly. "Can any of these people see you, Kim?"

"Of course not, sweetie," said Kim. "I'd know. Unless I decide otherwise, only you can see me, JC. Only you."

"So," said JC. "All of these people around us, right now . . ."

"Think you're taking to yourself; yes!" Kim said brightly.

"Wonderful," said JC.

# THREE

## DEAD AIR

*Some places you know are going to be bad
for you. Bad for everybody. Because
there's something in the air . . .*

JC mooched aimlessly around the car park, outside the
sprawling old country house that was currently home to
Radio Free Albion. Local radio, serving (parts of) South-
West England. The setting was calm and peaceful, pleasantly bucolic. Wild woods surrounded the house and car
park, providing a natural buffer between the house and the
civilised world, very definitely including the main road
beyond the woods that only existed to connect two far
more important destinations. It was a warm and sunny
afternoon. Perhaps a bit humid. Not a cloud to be seen
anywhere in the perfect blue sky and not even a hint of a
passing breeze. Although it did seem to JC that the scene
was almost unnaturally quiet. Not a bird singing anywhere,
in all the dark and shadowy woods. Not an insect buzzing,

on the heavy summer air. Only the most muffled sounds of traffic passing by on the distant main road. The world seemed to be holding its breath, as though waiting for something important to happen.

JC had been standing in Radio Free Albion's car park for more than half an hour now, increasingly impatiently, ever since the taxi dropped him off from the railway station. But as yet, no-one had come out to ask who he was or what he was doing there. He could have walked up to the front door. Could have knocked loudly, or rung the bell, or marched right in and announced himself. He could have thrown handfuls of gravel at the downstairs windows, or given the handful of parked cars a good kicking, to see if any of them came equipped with a car alarm. But for some reason he couldn't quite put a finger on, JC felt strangely reluctant to do any of these things. He preferred to wait until the rest of his team arrived. If only because there was safety in numbers; or at least, someone to hide behind.

Interestingly enough, he'd had a lot of trouble at the railway station, finding a taxi driver willing to drive him to Murdock House. He couldn't get anyone to say why; they pretended they already had a fare, or that they weren't going in that direction. Some even locked themselves in their taxis and pretended they couldn't hear him. Still, when in doubt, there's always bribery and corruption. JC loudly proclaimed he was ready and willing to pay double the going rate; and one driver got out of his taxi and considered JC for a long moment, scowling deeply.

"Triple fare," he said finally. "Take it or leave it."

"I'll take it," said JC. "May I ask why?"

"Danger money," said the driver.

And that was the last thing he had to say, all the way to Murdock House. JC sat thoughtfully in the back, enjoying the marvellous scenery and wondering how he was going to justify the fare for this trip on his expenses. When they finally reached their destination, the taxi slammed to a halt, right at the entrance to the car park. And the driver sat there, stubbornly silent, while JC got out. He announced the fare, in an entirely unrepentant tone, and JC paid the man the exact amount. The driver looked directly at JC, for the first time.

"No tip?"

"You've got a nerve," said JC.

"Not enough to hang around here," said the driver. "You want someone to take you back to the station, call another company."

He revved his engine hard, swung the taxi round in a sharp arc, and departed the car park at speed, in a spray of gravel.

That had been the last sign of life in that car park, for some time. JC thrust both hands deep into his trouser pockets, glared at the old house, and sighed loudly. In a much put-upon way. Still no sign of the rest of his team. Melody had phoned him half an hour ago to say they were almost there . . . then nothing. JC could have called her; but he had his pride. He was, after all, team leader. Reluctantly, he gave the house his full attention again. If only because a large part of him didn't want to.

Most of Murdock House was crumbling old stone, pock-marked with the accumulated damage of time, weather, and many years of basic neglect. A series of protruding bay windows punctuated the length of the ground floor, with glass that needed cleaning, paintwork that needed

redoing, and heavy curtains whose dull, ugly colours were
an affront to civilisation. The windows on the upper floor
were hidden behind closed wooden shutters—all cracks
and gaps and peeling paint. The sloping, grey-tiled roof
looked like a bunch of determined thieves had been at it,
assuming there was a market for broken old tiles. JC was
pretty sure he wouldn't like to be anywhere on the top
floor when it rained. But then, he didn't think he'd feel
particularly comfortable anywhere inside Murdock House.
It should have had a cosy, comfortable air, the feel of a
place much lived in and cared for. But it didn't.

There was definitely something . . . about the house.
The blank bay windows of the ground floor seemed to
regard JC with dark, accusing eyes. Warning him off; de-
fying him to come inside and hunt for answers the house
had no intention of providing. JC suddenly felt very cold
and shivered, violently, as though someone had danced on
his grave. He pushed his very dark sunglasses down to the
end of his nose and looked over them at the house. And
saw, for a moment, the house disappear; behind a blast of
blazing light. So fierce and spiteful and overwhelming, he
cried out in shock despite himself. He had to close his
eyes, in self-defence. When he opened them and looked
again, it was only a house. Nothing strange or unusual
about it at all. He concentrated, with his glowing, altered
eyes, trying to see through the facade Murdock House presented to the world. But the house remained stubbornly
ordinary. JC pushed his sunglasses back into place with
one finger. The day was warm; but he still felt cold. Bone-
deep, soul-deep, cold.

No-one in the house seemed to have heard him cry out.
No-one came out to investigate. He was alone in the car

park, face-to-face with a mystery he wasn't sure he wanted
to solve.

He deliberately turned his back on Murdock House and
wandered over to the handful of parked cars, four of them,
huddled together in one small corner of the car park. None
of them new. Nothing especially distinctive about them,
apart from the oldest. A powder blue Hillman Super Minx
convertible, from the late sixties. Well preserved, apart
from several dints and dings in the bodywork. It looked
like it hadn't been cleaned, let alone waxed and polished,
since the late sixties. The rear bumper sticker proclaimed:
WARNING! I BRAKE FOR UFOS!

JC glowered at the house again and wondered what the
hell he was doing there. Catherine Latimer had phoned
him that morning, and told him to go pay a visit to Radio
Free Albion and sort it out. As a matter of urgency. No
details; only directions. And then she put the phone down
before he could ask any questions. After their recent
encounter in Hyde Park, JC didn't feel like pushing his
luck. Now that he was here, though, he did wonder what
it was he was supposed to be sorting out. Was this a haunting? Poltergeist activity? Nasty things crawling out of the
woodwork? Apart from the somewhat disturbing ambi-
ence, it seemed a normal enough setting.

The front door to Murdock House slammed open, and
JC looked sharply round in time to see himself stagger
out of the open door and into the car park. His other self's
white suit was tattered and torn, ripped apart and soaked
in fresh blood. So fresh, it was still dripping. JC stood
where he was, frozen in place, transfixed by the sight.
Staring at himself, and the blood, and the awful wounds
and injuries that produced it. The other man stumbled for-

ward, out into the open. His sunglasses were missing; and his eyes were gone. Instead, there were two empty eye-sockets, with thick crimson trails running down his cheeks.

The man who looked like JC stopped and almost fell. JC ran forward, sprinting across the gravel. His heart was pounding fast, his breathing ragged and harsh. He got there in time to catch the other man as the last of his strength ran out, and he collapsed. JC held on to him tightly, holding him up, supporting him. The weight of the body was very real in his arms. This was no ghost, no vision, and not any kind of hallucination.

JC lowered his other self carefully to the ground, the gravel crunching loudly under their combined weight. He sat down hard, holding his other self cradled in his arms. He knew a dying man when he saw one. The other JC raised his ruined face. His mouth worked, and blood spilled out of it. He swallowed, with difficulty, and forced words out past his tortured breathing.

"It's you, isn't it?" he said hoarsely. "It's me. Me, from the past. I remember this; from when I first arrived here."

"Are you saying . . . you're me, from the future?" said JC. "What the hell happened here? What's happened to you?"

"It all went wrong," said the future JC. "There was nothing I could do . . ."

"What happened to your eyes?" said JC.

"They took them back."

His voice faded away. JC held on to him tightly. "Tell me! What happened . . . What's going to happen?"

"You should have listened . . . You should have paid attention, to the warnings." He coughed hard, spraying blood on the air. He grabbed a handful of JC's jacket, pulled him close. "It's all going to Hell."

"What is?" said JC.

"Everything. We're all going to die. The world's going to die. And it's all our fault . . ."

"There must be something I can do!" JC said desperately.

His future self's blind head rolled back. "Kim . . . ?"

The last of his breath went out of him, and he died. Right there, in his past self's arms. JC sat there, on the ground, holding the body tightly. He didn't cry. He didn't feel right about crying for himself. He was still trying desperately to think of something, anything, he could do, when the dead man vanished. JC was left sitting alone, on the ground, cradling empty air. He looked slowly around him, but the car park was still empty, still quiet. As though nothing had happened. JC would have liked to deny it all; but the bloody handprint remained on the front of his white jacket, from where his future self's dying hand had grabbed it. He touched the blood, carefully. It was still wet. JC scrambled to his feet, breathing harshly. Cold beads of sweat stood out on his face, his head swimming as his thoughts raced madly in all directions.

*There is no single, fixed future. Events to come are not carved in stone. There are multiple timelines, with all kinds of potential futures. Which one we end up in depends on the choices we make. Everyone knows that. What I saw . . . was only a possibility. Not fixed, or certain; not inevitable . . .*

But standing there, with his future self's blood still wet on his fingertips, JC wasn't sure he believed that.

He heard a car engine approaching, and the sound of

squealing tyres. He turned around quickly, to see a very familiar Land Rover finally arrive at Murdock House. It roared into the car park and slammed to a halt a few yards short of JC. It rocked back and forth for a moment, settling itself, then the engine shut down. There was a long, ominous pause, then both front doors flew open. Melody and Happy got out, deliberately not looking at each other. They both advanced on JC, each clearly determined to get their version in first. JC thought quietly to himself, *When did I agree to become the referee in their relationship?* But he had to admit; he found their familiar problems something of a relief, even comforting, after what he'd just been through.

He surreptitiously wiped blood off his fingertips, against his hips; and if he looked a little more closely at Happy and Melody, to be sure they were exactly who they seemed to be, they were both too preoccupied with their own problems to notice.

*"Let's drive down together!"* Happy said viciously. *"It'll be fun!* Never again . . ." He appealed to JC. "Sorry we're late, boss; but it wasn't my fault, honest! She didn't trust the sat nav. I swear, we already drove past this entrance road twice!"

"I can't believe an actual adult could say, *Are we there yet?* so many times!"

"You drove over a speed camera!" said Happy.

"You set fire to the map!" said Melody.

"It was an accident!"

"Why? What were you intending to set fire to?"

"Children, children," JC said soothingly. "Please calm the fuck down, right now, or I swear to the spiritual provider of your choice that I will inject you both with an industrial-strength dose of Ritalin!"

Happy smiled, briefly. "I already tried that. I think I've developed an immunity."

"I wish I thought you were joking," said Melody.

JC nodded solemnly to her. "At least this time you can be sure you've got all your equipment with you. Isn't that nice? Doesn't that make you feel so much better? Why don't you go and unload it all and check that everything's still working properly? You know you always enjoy that."

Melody was looking at the front of his jacket. "Is that blood, JC? Are you hurt?"

"I don't want to talk about it," said JC.

"You're not hurt," said Happy, frowning. "But . . ."

"I said I don't want to talk about it!"

Happy and Melody looked at each other.

"Ah . . ." said Happy. "It's going to be one of those cases, is it?"

"I'll go sort out my tech," said Melody. "And my gun."

She marched away, to open up the back of the Land Rover and have a good rummage around. Happy stood uncertainly before JC, trying to decide what to say.

"Don't," said JC. "Just . . . don't."

"I've been there," said Happy.

"I will talk about it, later. But not now."

"All right."

"I am now going to change the subject," said JC.

"Go for it," said Happy.

"There's a reason why I don't travel to cases with the two of you any more," said JC. "It's so I'm not trapped in a confined space with you and Melody waiting for my ears to start bleeding."

Happy couldn't even be bothered to shrug. He looked at Murdock House and sniffed loudly. "What a dump. I've crapped more-impressive-looking things than that."

"Far too much information, Happy," murmured JC. "Do you get any . . . feelings, from the house?"

Happy looked the place over carefully, taking his time. "No," he said finally. "Not a thing. Why? Am I supposed to be picking up something?"

"I don't want to talk about it," said JC.

"All right. Can I ask instead, why are we here, JC?"

"Didn't you read the case file?" JC said innocently.

"What bloody case file? There is no case file! Just a phone call from the Boss, at far too early an hour of the morning, instructing Mel and me to get our arses down to Murdock House and Radio Free Bloody Albion, and do something about it!"

"Same here," said JC.

"You really don't know why we're here?"

"Haven't a clue."

Happy grinned. "So, essentially, we've gone ghost finding by accident . . . That's kind of cool, in a weird and creeping-me-out sort of way."

"I think the Boss wanted us out of London for a while," said JC. "And chose the first case that came to hand."

"Ah," Happy said wisely. "Something's come up at the Carnacki Institute HQ, hasn't it? Something to do with the Flesh Undying and the main traitor?"

"You are addressing your questions to entirely the wrong person," said JC. "No-one tells me anything."

"Where's Kim?" said Happy. "Didn't she come down with you?"

"She's making her own way here," JC said carefully. "She had a few things she needed to do, first."

"There are far too many secrets in this team," said Happy.

"Or not enough," said JC.

Melody came back to join them, followed by a huge, piled-up assortment of her technological toys, balanced precariously on a squat, motorised trolley that puttered noisily along behind her. Under its own power, and apparently without any need for instructions. It stuck close behind Melody, following her every movement like a faithful dog. Melody stopped before JC and Happy, and the trolley stopped with her. JC looked at the trolley and shook his head resignedly.

"I suppose it was only a matter of time . . ."

Something appeared abruptly, out of nowhere, hanging on the air right in front of Melody. Huge and dark and horribly distorted—something that might have been human once but was now ugly beyond bearing. So powerful, so wrong, that its presence alone beat on the air like a thunderclap. Its mouth stretched impossibly wide, but when it tried to speak, no sound came out. The long, bony face seemed to scream silently. The shape reached out to Melody with one long-clawed hand. She stood frozen in place, caught by surprise and transfixed by shock. Happy lunged forward, putting himself between Melody and the thing that towered over her.

"Don't you dare touch her!" he roared, right into the thing's face.

The apparition looked at him and stopped. It hung on the air before him, motionless and silent. It seemed . . . to recognise him. It reached out a hand to Happy, almost imploringly. And then it vanished. Gone, as suddenly as it had arrived. Happy let out a long, shaky breath. Melody put a gentle hand on his shoulder.

"My brave boy. Always there when I need you. I know I can always depend on you."

"We both know that's not true," said Happy, not turning round to look at her.

"Well," said Melody. "Let's pretend it is."

Happy finally turned to look at her; and they shared a quick smile. Happy turned to look at JC.

"So? Was the thing you didn't see anything like the thing we just saw?"

"No," said JC.

"Fair enough," said Happy.

They all looked round sharply as the front door to Murdock House suddenly opened. JC actually jumped, despite himself. He quickly recovered, but not before Happy and Melody both noticed his reaction. JC didn't say anything, so neither did they. All three moved to stand together, to face the approaching newcomer. The Ghost Finders believed in presenting a united front in the face of the enemy. Or civilians. The man who came through the door crashed to a halt before them and looked from one face to another, almost imploringly.

He was middle-aged, with a lion's mane of long grey hair and a neatly trimmed grey goatee beard. His face was basically bland, as though he'd used up all his character and individuality in his hair. He wore a smart three-piece suit in a sloppy way, as though he didn't have the energy to do it justice. He looked tired, and flustered, and quite definitely relieved to see them. Which made a nice change. He started to speak, then broke off abruptly. He looked quickly around, to make sure there was no-one else in the car park, and leaned forward to address them, lowering his voice conspiratorially.

"You are . . . *them*? Aren't you?"

"Almost certainly," said JC.

"Who did you have in mind?" said Happy.

The new arrival took in the bloody handprint on the front of JC's white jacket. He started to say something.

"Don't ask," said Melody.

"He doesn't like to talk about it," said Happy.

"Who were you expecting?" said JC. "Exactly?"

If anything, the man became even more furtive. "You are . . . the Ghost Finders? Yes?"

"That's us!" JC said brightly. "Licensed to kick supernatural arse and glad to do it. You are . . . ?"

"Oh; yes! Sorry. I'm Jonathan Hardy. I run this radio station. For my sins."

"So," said JC, "what's the problem? What's been happening here?"

Jonathan looked shocked. "You don't know?"

"We always prefer to hear the details first-hand, from the people directly affected," JC said smoothly. "Less misunderstandings that way."

"Say *Aargh!* and tell us why you're scared," said Happy. "We have the medicine for what ails you."

Melody punched him hard in the arm. "You keep your medicines to yourself."

"Ow!" said Happy, pouting and sulking simultaneously, with the ease of long practice. "That hurt!"

"It was meant to," said Melody.

JC smiled winningly at Jonathan. "Don't mind them. They're being themselves. You have to make allowances for them; because it's either that or shoot them. And don't think that hasn't been seriously discussed. All appearances to the contrary, we are professionals. We are the Ghost Finders! We don't take any shit from the Hereafter."

Surprisingly, Jonathan smiled and nodded, understandingly. "You should see some of the staff I have to work with. I'm glad you're here. Things have been . . . pretty intense. We'll take all the help we can get."

JC performed the introductions for his team, and Jonathan insisted on shaking everyone by the hand. But then his good humour disappeared quite suddenly, as he glanced back over his shoulder at Murdock House. He seemed scared, and something else, too. JC wasn't sure what. Guilt, perhaps. Jonathan quickly pulled himself back together again and looked quickly from one team member to another. As though trying to make up his mind as to whether they were going to be up to the job. Whatever that turned out to be.

"You are . . . real professionals?" he said. "You've dealt with this kind of thing before?"

"We've dealt with everything before," said Happy. "Suddenly and violently and all over the place. We are the pros from Dover, and we have all the best toys."

"Exactly!" said Melody. "You think I'm humping this equipment around for the fun of it?"

JC looked at Happy. "Please tell me she hasn't actually started humping her equipment."

Happy shrugged. "It was only a matter of time . . ."

"Funny," said Melody. "Funny men . . ."

"Oh God," said Jonathan. "Look . . . you'd better come in. Before somebody sees you."

He hurried back to the open front door, not looking round to see if they were following. JC strolled unhurriedly after him, Happy slouched along, and Melody and her worryingly independent trolley brought up the rear. Jonathan held the door open for them. JC only hesitated a moment, before squaring his shoulders and striding through the doorway. The same doorway his dying self had emerged from. He could feel all the hairs standing up on the back of his neck and a cold hand gripping his heart. He looked suddenly back, to catch Happy and Melody looking at him. He met their curious stares unflinchingly, then turned away to give Jonathan his best casual, confident, smile. It was always best to look like you knew what you were doing, in front of civilians. It helped calm them down. JC strode into the reception area with his head held high, doing his best to give the impression he was doing everyone a favour by showing up. Happy and Melody followed him in. Fortunately, there was a handicap ramp to accommodate Melody's trolley. It still managed to drop a few things, and Melody's language made all three men blush for a moment.

\*\*\*\*\*\*\*\*\*\*\*\*\*\*\*\*\*\*\*\*\*\*\*

JC looked thoughtfully around the large, open, and fairly airy lobby that served as Radio Free Albion's reception area. He was quickly relieved to discover it all looked reassuringly normal. No obvious dangers and not a sign anywhere of his future self. JC realised Jonathan was looking at him and flashed the man his best meaningless smile before turning to Happy. Who was staring around in a vague, unfocused way.

"Still not picking up anything?" JC said quietly.

"Not a thing," said Happy, as quietly. "Why? What am I supposed to be . . . All right, I know, you don't want to talk about it . . ." He frowned. "You know, come to think of it, this whole place is unusually quiet. I mean, I should be getting something. A house this old, you'd expect it to be packed with history. Layer upon layer of laid-down psychic impressions. And given that there's supposed to be a group of people working here every day; why am I not getting anything from them? It's like something is suppressing all the local mental chatter and preserved images. Something big enough and powerful enough to hide itself completely from me. And there isn't much, in or out of this world, that can do that."

"Do you feel any danger?" said JC.

"Always," said Happy. He looked again at the bloody handprint on the front of JC's jacket. "You're going to have to come clean about that, eventually. If it's a part of what's happening here . . ."

"I know," said JC. "Really, I know. But I'm not ready yet."

"We're here, for when you are. Was it really that bad?"

"Worse," said JC.

"Shit . . ." said Happy. "You want a few of my little helpers?"

"My head's in a bad enough place as it is," said JC.

"Sit!" Melody said loudly. And everyone turned to see her trolley come to a sudden halt, almost spilling its entire load. Melody glared at it, then at everyone else.

"It's learning!" she said.

"Maybe we should hire you a pack-mule," said JC. "Less hard on the nerves . . ."

He beckoned her to him with a quick jerk of the head, and the three Ghost Finders stood together, looking the reception area over carefully, taking their time. Refusing to be hurried . . . even though it was obvious Jonathan wanted very much to move them along. Never let civilians set the pace. They never know what's really important. Because first impressions always matter when you're looking for things that don't belong.

The entrance lobby had probably been quite impressive, once upon a time, but now it was seedy and ratty and run-down. The walls hadn't been repainted or replastered in a long time, the carpet had been worn thin in more places than it hadn't, and while there was a large reception desk at the rear of the room, complete with a great many telephones, there was no-one there to run it. There were no photos on the walls, no publicity shots of the various radio personalities, nothing to impress the casual visitor with how important Radio Free Albion was. Only a single large poster on the wall behind the reception desk, saying WELCOME TO RADIO FREE ALBION—YOUR LOCAL RADIO STATION! They all turned to look at Jonathan, who had the grace to shrug and look embarrassed.

"Cost cutting," he said bluntly. "New owners. Since taking over, they have made their attitude very plain. They paid for a radio station, not a country house. If we want to make necessary repairs and improvements, it's up to us to find the money. They don't want to know. We're doing what we can, but . . . Well, when I say we, I mostly mean me. I bought Murdock House and turned it into a radio station, all those years ago. I had such hopes, then . . . But, bit by bit, I lost control, giving up point after percentage point, to keep the place going; and now . . . I just run the station.

"The new owners are determined Radio Free Albion should turn a profit as soon as humanly possible. So they can get their investment back, bring in new advertisers, and turn the station into a cash cow. None of which is going to happen anytime soon. Advertisers have been running for the hills like rats from a sinking ship. Pardon my metaphors. The new owners don't know about our . . . current problems. Or why the old owners were so keen to sell."

"Why were the new owners so keen to buy?" said JC.

"I may have . . . slightly exaggerated the financial possibilities," said Jonathan, smiling slightly. "They're not local, so they don't know about . . . I was desperate to find someone, to keep the station going! I liked the old owners. They ran us as a tax loss and left us alone." He looked almost pleadingly at each of the Ghost Finders in turn. "You have to find an answer to this . . . mess. Before the new owners find out!"

"Who are these new owners?" said Happy. "Anyone we might have heard of?"

Jonathan winced and looked away. He couldn't have seemed any more embarrassed if his trousers had suddenly dropped down around his ankles. When he finally spoke, his voice was barely audible. "Seriously Substitute Sausages."

"What?" said Melody.

"Seriously Substitute Sausages!" Jonathan said loudly. "All right? They're made of soya! And, other things. They're very big in their field. So I'm told."

"Taste good, do they?" JC said innocently.

"Like chewing on a towel," said Jonathan. "And the new

owners can't be doing that well, or they wouldn't need us as a cash cow."

"Excuse me for pointing out the obvious," said Happy. "But why isn't there a receptionist, behind the reception desk?"

"She's on a break," said Jonathan. "She takes a lot of breaks. Sally Walsh; only temporary. Because we can't get anyone to stay. Not since . . . You know, we used to broadcast right around the clock, twenty-four hours a day. Our coverage was exemplary. Advertisers were fighting each other for space. Now it's all we can do to manage eight hours. Most of the announcers and technical staff are gone. We're struggling to keep the station going with a skeleton staff."

"How many, exactly?" said JC.

Jonathan met JC's gaze almost defiantly. "There are four of us left, now. The ones with nowhere else to go."

"All right," said JC. "Let's get down to what matters. What is the problem here?"

Jonathan looked around the reception area, as though afraid someone else might be listening. He hesitated, searching for the right words.

"Officially," he said finally, "as far as the staff are concerned, you're here as guests. To be interviewed on air, as experts in the supernatural. You have my authority to ask the others anything you like, but *please* . . . tread carefully. We're all a bit . . . on edge after everything that's happened. We've all been through a lot. So please don't do anything to upset anyone. I can't afford to lose more people."

JC stepped forward and thrust his face right into Hardy's. "Enough! *What is the problem?*"

Jonathan took a deep breath, swallowed hard, and braced himself. All at once he looked older. Tired, and beaten down by circumstances beyond his control. But at the same time, he looked almost relieved. As though he could finally put down a weight he'd been carrying for far too long. He looked carefully at each Ghost Finder in turn, willing them to understand.

"Over the last few months, we've been having problems with . . . voices. Voices from outside, from nowhere. At first it was the odd sound, breaking into our transmissions. We didn't know what it was. The sounds became words, and the words began to form sentences. To begin with, they only appeared during unanticipated moments of radio silence. When for one reason or another, there was no music, no chat, what's known in the business as dead air. Then these . . . voices started to appear more often. Harsh, raw; shouting and screaming. Desperate to be heard. Some sounded barely human . . . unnatural. Hearing them was enough to make your blood run cold.

"At first, the engineering staff tried to explain it away as Electronic Voice Phenomena. The radio equivalent of Rorschach ink-blots. The brain imposing patterns on random sounds. Hearing things that weren't actually there. But what started out as gibberish became increasingly clear. Complete sentences, making more and more sense. Human voices, shouting and pleading, trying desperately to warn us about . . . something. Like the voices we hear in nightmares, full of dreadful significance.

"They weren't limited to dead air, any more. They started appearing in the middle of broadcasts, breaking into shows, overriding on-air voices. All across the schedule, at every hour of the day and night. No pattern to it, no obvious scheme or agenda . . .

"And then they began appearing on the phone lines. On the phone-in shows. The engineers thought they sounded like genuine callers, and let them through. These . . . voices started having actual conversations with the show hosts. Spooked the hell out of them and their audiences. The conversations didn't make much sense, but the intent was clearly there. We did everything we could to track down where the voices were coming from. Whether they were signals from some other station, some more powerful signal overriding our own. Or some independent operator, with illegally powerful equipment . . . But the engineers couldn't identify the sources or keep the voices out. They shut everything down; and the voices still kept coming in . . .

"It was one of our listeners, calling in, who first suggested . . . that what we were all hearing were the voices of the dead. She said she thought she recognised one of the voices as her uncle Paul. Who'd been dead for seventeen years. After that, the floodgates opened. More and more people phoning in, saying they were hearing familiar voices, from their dear departed. They pleaded with us to stop them because they didn't want to hear what the voices were saying. Some even accused us of perpetrating a vicious hoax . . . Professional psychics and would-be mediums started turning up here, at reception. Offering their services. And I was so desperate by then, I tried some of the more plausible ones. But they ran like hell once they were exposed to the actual voices. Our engineering staff ran off, too. You can't blame them . . ."

"You said, these voices were trying to warn you," JC said carefully. "Warn you about what, exactly?"

"It's never clear!" said Jonathan. "The voices are clear enough, but what they're saying makes no sense at all. Whoever they are, they sound genuinely desperate. Desperate to warn us about something that's coming."

The front door slammed shut behind them, and they all spun round. Something about Jonathan, and his story, had got to all of them. Even the very professional Ghost Finders. Standing in front of the closed front door was a sturdy young woman with a scowling face, spiky crimson hair, extremely distressed jeans, and a T-shirt bearing the message DON'T WASTE MY TIME. One of her grubby white sneakers was held together with a lot of black duct tape. Her round, sulky face held enough metal piercings to make her dangerous to stand near during thunderstorms, along with enough garish make-up to stun an Avon Lady at twenty paces. She glared at them all, impartially.

"I don't care who you are, the answer's no!" she said loudly. "And feel free to throw in a few *Go to hells* and *Over my dead bodies* while you're about it. Now go away and stop bothering me or I'll drop-kick you through the nearest window."

"Our receptionist, Sally Walsh," said Jonathan, resignedly. "Welcome back, Sally. How was your break?"

Sally growled, loudly, and studied each of the Ghost Finders carefully, in turn, paying particular attention to the bloody hand-print on the front of JC's jacket.

"You're not reporters? Good. I have had a gut load of local hacks, coming here to poke fun. You're the ghost experts, aren't you? About bloody time you got here. You've got to do something! Sort this mess out! I do not want it on my résumé that I had to quit my last position because the bloody place was haunted! Things like that do not go down well at interviews."

"You've seen a ghost?" said Melody, entirely unmoved by all the sound and fury.

Sally started to say something, then shook her head, almost reluctantly. She glowered at Jonathan, as though daring him to say something, then looked back at the Ghost Finders.

"No," she said. "Not actually seen anything. But I've heard them. Everyone here has. And most of our audience, the poor bastards. Half of them have stopped listening, and the other half are scared not to. In case they miss something vital . . . A lot of them have been turning up here at reception, barging in like they own the place, cursing and complaining and shouting at me, convinced it's all some new publicity stunt. You wouldn't believe some of the things I've been called . . . Heartless. That one comes up a lot. Taking advantage of the bereaved . . . that comes a close second. Cruel, vicious, playing with people's emotions . . . The ones who think it's real are even worse. They're really upset. And the phones never stop ringing! Some people ring up just to cry down the phone at me . . ."

She broke off and scowled meaningfully at Jonathan. "Why don't you shut down the phones? Give me a few moments' peace?"

"Because it's against regulations," Jonathan said tiredly.

"Then why don't you at least put some security guards at the door, to keep the headcases out?"

"Because we haven't got the money."

"Getting really tired of hearing that," said Sally.

"Not half as tired as I am of saying it," said Jonathan.

"Why do you keep taking breaks, Sally?" said JC.

"To get away from this place," the receptionist said immediately. She looked round the large, open room, and some of the brash confidence seemed to go out of her. "I don't like it here. Not only this room; the whole house feels . . . tainted. Spoiled. Place used to be okay. Before all this started. But now the atmosphere's gone bad. Rancid. Malignant. It feels like something's watching me all the time."

"Have you heard any of the voices . . . in here?" said Melody.

"No. Not yet. But sitting behind that desk gets on my nerves! I stand it here as long as I can, I really do . . . and then I have to get out. Go outside, walk around in the fresh air. Until I can work up enough courage to come back in. Because this is my job."

"Why don't you leave?" said Happy.

Sally's scowl deepened. "Because I can't. I've already quit too many jobs, for perfectly good reasons. Social Security said they'd stop my benefits if I walked out on one more job. I keep hoping Hardy will fire me. I've tried all kinds of things, including offering to sleep with him, but he keeps saying I'm needed here. That I'm irreplaceable. Hah! The only thing this place needs is a direct hit."

"The station does need you, Sally," said Jonathan. "You're our first line of defence . . ."

"Then why did you take away my nunchucks?"

"Regulations . . ."

Sally said something very rude concerning the regulations, then strode past everyone to take up her position behind the reception desk. She dropped heavily into the waiting chair and glared at the phones, daring them to ring. Melody turned to Jonathan.

"Do you have any recordings of these unauthorised scary voices?"

"Hell yes," said Jonathan. "Tons of the things. We record everything, here."

"Have you listened to these recordings?" said JC. "Studied them?"

"No," Jonathan said flatly. "They upset me too much."

"I'll need to listen to them," said Melody.

"Of course," said Jonathan. "Though I don't know what good it'll do you. Even when the voices are clear, they're not exactly coherent."

"But what kinds of things have these voices been saying?" JC said patiently. "What is it that they're trying to warn you about?"

"I think it's best you listen to the recordings," said Jonathan. "I'm not trying to be evasive . . . You need to hear them yourself, to understand. I'll see that everything is made available to you. Perhaps you can work out why whoever this is is doing it to us. And it is just us. No other radio station, local or otherwise, is hearing anything."

"No-one else?" said Melody. "That's not possible."

Jonathan shrugged. "It was one of the first things our engineers checked. Before they all ran away. Only we receive these voices. Only we've been selected. Or targeted."

"I'll run the recordings through my equipment," Melody said briskly. "There are all kinds of things I can try. Special filters, diagnostics . . ."

"Best of luck," said Jonathan.

"You must have some idea of what it is they're trying to warn you about," JC insisted.

Jonathan and Sally looked at each other. Neither of them wanted to say anything. Finally, reluctantly, Jonathan nodded.

"They're trying to warn us about the end."

"Of what?" said JC.

"Everything," said Jonathan.

"Listeners phone in constantly, saying they're hearing all kinds of dreadful things," said Sally. "But not everyone seems to hear the same voice, or the same message, at the same time. Different people hear different things, during the same broadcasts. That's why some people claim to recognise some voices as particular dead relatives or loved ones. It's like people hear . . . what scares them the most."

"What do you hear, Sally?" said JC.

"We're all going to die," Sally said quietly.

"Sally . . ." said Jonathan.

"I'm not the only one who believes that!" Sally said fiercely. "The suicide rate in this whole area is way up! You know that!"

"That's only a rumour!" said Jonathan. He gave JC his full attention. "You have to stop this. Before the new owners find out how bad things have got and shut us down!"

One of the reception phones rang. The sudden harsh sound was very loud, and very insistent. Sally shook her head firmly and sat back in her chair with her arms folded tightly.

"No. No way. I am not answering that! I have had it up to here with being yelled at. Or cried at. Or . . ."

"It's your job, Sally," said Jonathan. "You never know. It might be important . . ."

Happy looked at them, puzzled. "What is it? What are you all hearing?"

"It's the phone," said Melody. "Can't you hear it ringing?"

"No," said Happy. "None of those phones are ringing."

They all looked at each other, for a long moment. The phone rang on and on. Happy moved over to the reception desk and looked carefully at each phone in turn before shaking his head firmly. Sally indicated one particular phone with a quick jerk of her head, refusing to uncross her arms long enough even to point at it. Happy picked up the receiver and hit the button to put it on speaker. He laid the receiver down on the desk, looked at it for a moment, then raised his voice.

"Hello? Is there anybody there?"

A voice came out of the speaker immediately; harsh but distant, as though it had travelled some impossible distance, to get to them.

"Hello, Happy. It's coming for you. Across the worlds, it's coming, dragging its broken chains behind it, and, oh, it's so hungry!"

"Did you hear that, Happy?" said Melody.

"Yes," said Happy. He addressed the speaker, his voice calm and uninflected. "Be specific. What is it that's coming for us? And how do you know my name?"

"How do you think?" said the voice. "It's getting closer all the time. It's coming for all of you: like a baby crucified inside the womb; like a young mother tearing out her heart and eating it; like Death herself in fuck-me shoes. Why won't you listen?"

Happy turned away from the phone and smiled at JC. "It's for you."

JC moved forward, and bent over the reception desk. "Hello?"

"Hello, JC," said the voice. "How hard do you have to be hit to get your attention?"

"Who is this?"

"You know who this is," said the voice.

The line went dead. JC picked up the receiver, put it to his ear, shrugged, and replaced it. He smiled engagingly at the others. "Wrong number."

"Weird . . ." said Happy.

Melody looked at him thoughtfully. "Why couldn't you hear the phone ringing?"

"Because it didn't," Happy said firmly. "None of those phones made a sound."

"But we all heard it," said Jonathan.

"You did," said Happy. "But that doesn't mean the phone was ringing."

"You heard the voice," said JC.

"Because someone wanted me to," said Happy. It was his turn to look thoughtfully at JC. "Whoever that was, they seemed to think you should know them."

"I didn't recognise the voice," JC said immediately. "How did they know my name? And yours? How did they even know we were here?"

"Because the voice wasn't coming from the phone," said Happy.

"What?" said Jonathan. "I'm sorry, I don't . . ."

JC gave him his best professional smile. "I think you need to give us the grand tour of Radio Free Albion. Show us everything. Introduce us to everyone who's still here. And then we'll see . . . what we can do."

# FOUR

## TALK RADIO

After a certain amount of dithering and being pressured on all sides to make up his mind, Jonathan led JC and Happy to a door at the back of the reception area, marked STRICTLY NO ADMITTANCE; AUTHORISED PERSONNEL ONLY. This immediately cheered Happy up. He always liked going places he wasn't supposed to go. Especially if it was the kind of place he knew would never normally lower itself to admit the likes of him. Jonathan held the door open, and Happy strode through with his nose in the air. JC started to follow him, then stopped and looked back as he realised Melody wasn't with them. She was still standing beside her overloaded trolley, with her arms firmly folded. JC raised an eyebrow.

"Not joining us, Melody?"

"You go on," she said. "I've got work to do, right here."

"Suit yourself," said JC. "Do you have your . . . ?"

"Yes," said Melody. "Easily to hand, locked and

loaded." She looked past him to Happy, who had poked his head back through the door to see what the hold-up was. Melody shot him a meaningful look. "Have you got . . . everything you need?"

"No," said Happy. "But I've got enough about me to be going on with." He caught JC considering him thoughtfully. "Something on your mind, JC?"

"More than you could possibly imagine," said JC. "Let's go. We have people to question and ghosts to interrogate. What more could you want?"

"I've got a list if you're interested," said Happy.

"Excuse me," said Jonathan. "But, was I supposed to understand any of that?"

"No," said JC.

"Ah. Well, that's all right then, I suppose," said Jonathan. "This way, please."

Melody waited till they were all gone, and the rear door had closed and locked itself behind them; then she relaxed a little and nodded amiably to Sally, still sitting stiffly behind her desk.

"Right! The boys are gone, so girl to girl, fill me in on what's really going on here. I want facts, I want guesses, I want down-and-dirty gossip. I want atmosphere and all the things you know for a fact you're not supposed to know about. Start anywhere, and I'll tell you when to stop."

Sally looked at Melody for a long moment, making up her mind. So as not to place undue pressure on the receptionist, Melody deliberately turned away and started unloading her equipment from the trolley. Which bobbed up and down a few times in a hopeful sort of way, realised it wasn't going anywhere anytime soon, and settled down for a sustained sulk. Melody set about assembling her various pieces of scientific equipment into their usual semi-circular configuration. Everything slotted neatly together, as she'd designed it to. And then she looked around, unhurriedly, as Sally cleared her throat.

"Can I trust you?"

"I can keep a secret," said Melody. "Except for when I choose not to."

"God knows I need to talk to somebody," said Sally. "And since the only other girl in this hellhole is our leading presenter and personality, Ms. *I am so far up myself I can see out my own nostrils* Felicity bloody Legrand . . . you'll have to do."

"I haven't met Ms. Legrand yet," said Melody.

"You won't like her," said Sally. "No-one does, apart from her fanatical fanboy audience. Look, do you want to stop working while I'm talking, and pay attention?"

"Almost certainly not," said Melody. "I can listen and work at the same time. I have raised multi-tasking to an art-form. If it helps, whatever you have to say will be kept in strict confidence between us. Right up to the point I decide otherwise."

"Fair enough," said Sally. She watched Melody bully her computers for a while but made no move to come out from behind her reception desk and help. "Don't you need somewhere to plug in all that stuff? Only we're a bit short of sockets in here."

"Not a problem," said Melody, bending over a recalcitrant monitor screen. She hit it hard a few times, to remind it which one of them was in charge. "My glorious high-tech installation comes complete with its own very powerful built-in generator. Because it's safer that way. I won't risk my information-gathering being compromised by local conditions. And since you can't always depend on an uninterrupted power supply from a local source, I don't."

"You're very . . . professional," said Sally.

"You don't last long in this game if you're not," said Melody. "The only things that aren't out to kill you want to do even worse things to you. Which is why my lovely assemblage here contains a self-destruct mechanism big enough to blow up this entire house, and most of the land surrounding it. Best to be thorough about such things."

"You're joking . . ." said Sally.

Melody looked up. "Not even a little bit," she said. And then went back to work.

"Cool!" said Sally, punching the air with one fist and grinning openly for the first time. "Are you guys really experts in the supernatural?"

"We know what we're doing," said Melody.

Sally sniffed loudly. "If that's true, you're the only ones here who do. I think . . . if I really understood what was going on here, I'd run away, like everyone else. Hell, I'd be a blur through that door, legging it for the nearest horizon. I can't escape the feeling . . . that the really bad shit hasn't even started yet."

"Wouldn't surprise me at all," Melody said briskly. "One thing you can always be sure of, in the kind of cases we get thrown . . . It's always darkest before all the lights go out, and you can bet it's going to get a lot worse before it even starts getting better."

"You're not big on comfort and reassurance, are you?" said Sally.

"It doesn't come naturally, no," said Melody. "And anyway, that's not my department. Would you prefer a comforting lie?"

"Yes! Definitely!"

Melody looked up and smiled briefly. "Everything's going to be fine." And then she went back to work again.

Sally slouched down in her chair and glared balefully around the large open reception area. "I don't like it here. Really don't like it. Can't you feel the atmosphere?"

"No," said Melody. "But then, I've been told on many occasions that I am not the sensitive type. Which is why I surround myself with these excellent toys. They supply me with all the facts and figures I need to properly understand what's happening. For everything else, I rely on people like you. So tell me, Sally, why did you come here in the first place? What lured you to the bright lights and scintillating possibilities of Radio Free Albion?"

"Wasn't the money; I'll tell you that for free." Sally slumped even lower in her chair and tugged pensively at the heaviest of the steel rings piercing her lower lip. "We might as well talk. Helps me keep my mind off . . . things."

"All part of the Ghost Finder service," said Melody. "Feel free to unburden your soul."

Sally looked at her, frowning hard. "Why would anyone in their right mind want to find a ghost?"

"So we can do something about it," said Melody. "Can't kick ectoplasmic arse until you've located it. And be sure you understand exactly what it is, so you can kick it right where it hurts most. Or at the very least, where you can do the most damage."

Sally considered her for a long moment. "There are different kinds of ghosts?"

"Lots and lots," Melody said cheerfully. "Everything from your basic apparition, to manifestations from the

Outer Reaches to Beasts. Don't ask about them. You really don't want to know. I know, and I wish I didn't."

"Are any of these ghosts . . . safe? Harmless?"

"Hardly ever," said Melody.

"I am changing the subject," Sally said firmly. "On the grounds that if I actually believed what you are saying, I'd be freaking out big time. So why did I end up here? In this unholy mess? Radio Free Albion may be small-time local radio, with few pretensions, but I saw it as a stepping-stone. A way in and a way up, to bigger and better things."

"You wanted a career in radio?" said Melody.

"No! In show business! Everyone has to start some-where . . . I thought I could make useful contacts here, use the station as a launching pad . . . That was the plan, any-way. Before all the scary shit started happening. Just my luck; I had to choose the one haunted local radio station in England."

Melody was about to smile and say something snarky when she realised Sally had stopped talking. She looked up and saw that the receptionist was crying, quietly. Big fat tears rolled slowly down Sally's cheeks, even as she tried to sniff them back. She produced a grubby handker-chief from somewhere and dabbed angrily at her face.

"Sorry. Sorry . . . This isn't me, really. I don't do this normally. Being here, having to tough it out every day, it wears you down . . ."

Melody nodded. She didn't leave her tech to go to Sally. She was pretty sure that wasn't what the reception-ist wanted. So Melody carried on working, assembling the last of her equipment, giving Sally time to pull herself together. After a while, Melody started talking again, care-ful to keep her tone calm and professional.

"When you're faced with the supernatural, in all its unearthly and upsetting aspects, being a bit scared is the only sane response."

"You still get scared?" said Sally. "After everything you've seen?" She blew her nose loudly into her handkerchief and tucked it away again.

"Of course," said Melody. "All the time. Being a little scared is good; it keeps you sharp, and on your toes. But you have to learn not to let it get to you."

"I was never scared of anything, before I came here," said Sally. "Not really scared. This place has turned me into a coward. Because I can't stand to stay in this room, for long. Because I keep having to run away."

"You've got it wrong, Sally," said Melody. "You're not a coward because you leave; you're brave because you keep coming back."

Sally thought about that for a while. "Can you fix things here? Really fix them?"

"If we can't, no-one can," said Melody.

"That isn't what I asked."

"I know." Melody looked up from her work long enough to smile briefly at Sally. "Talk to me, about Jonathan Hardy. What's he like? As a person, as well as a boss."

Sally shrugged. "Efficient enough, I suppose. Does his job, keeps the station afloat. He deals with the advertisers, and the lawyers, and all the everyday business stuff; so the rest of us don't have to. But outside of that? Wimp city. He doesn't want any trouble, doesn't want any of us to make waves. He's desperate to keep in with the new bosses. Lives in fear that they'll fire him, in favour of someone younger because he hasn't anywhere else to go. So he puts up with all the shit the new bosses hand down and won't let any of us say a word." Sally stopped and looked thoughtful. "And, I'm pretty sure he's gay."

Melody looked at her. "What makes you say that?"

"Because he's never once made a pass at me, all the time I've been here. I mean, it's not like he'd get anywhere, but you do sort of expect it . . ."

"Ah," said Melody. "I see." And she went back to her work.

"That JC . . ." said Sally. "He's a bit of all right. Is he . . . ?"

"He's in a very committed relationship," said Melody.

Sally shrugged. "I never do the chasing. I don't need to. Treat them mean to keep them keen. That's what I always say."

"Oh yes?" said Melody. "And how is that working out for you?"

Sally scowled. "Not so good. I'm too feminine, that's what it is. I intimidate men, put them off. Are you and Happy . . . ?"

"Yes."

"Just asking! Are you and Happy . . . all right, together?"

"Sometimes," said Melody. "It's complicated. Talk to me about the rest of the staff here, Sally. Who's still working at Radio Free Albion?"

"Only five of us now," said Sally. "Everyone else took off long ago. Including all the technical-support guys. In fact, they were the first to leave. When they were finally forced to admit they couldn't explain what was happening here. One by one, they did a runner, or stopped turning up; and I wish I'd gone with them . . . It gets harder and harder to come in, every morning. I only have to wake up at home, and my stomach starts hurting. And my head. I know it's tension, pressure . . . but knowing doesn't help. I think the hardest part of being here . . . is that there's nothing for me to get my hands on. I'm sure I'd feel so much better if I could find someone responsible and punch them out. A little personal pay-back for what they've put me through."

"I know," said Melody. "I often feel that way. That's why I have all this equipment. To help me find those responsible."

"Could you find me somebody to hit?" said Sally. "I'd be ever so grateful."

"I'll see what I can do," said Melody. She slammed her hand down on top of a computer. "Work, you bastard! Do what you're supposed to do . . . Yes. That's better . . . Sometimes I think I'd be better off with a trained dog."

Sally's head came up suddenly, and she looked sharply about her. "Hey! Did you hear that?"

Melody looked up from her computer and peered quickly around the open reception area. Everything was still and quiet. No new arrivals, nothing moving anywhere.

"No. I didn't hear anything. What did you hear?"

Sally looked longingly at the front door, but she didn't stand up and she didn't try to leave. Her face had gone pale, her garish make-up standing out starkly; and her eyes were haunted. She glanced across at Melody as though only her presence and support was keeping her there.

"It's like every instinct I've got is yelling at me," Sally said steadily. "Telling me to get the hell out while there's still time. That something in this room has changed, for the worst."

"Instincts are good," said Melody. "Science is better."

She looked quickly round her semi-circular arrange-ment of display readouts and monitor screens, and fired up all her computers. Lights glowed brightly, and screens snapped on, one after the other. Information flowed in steady streams before her watchful eyes. Her machines studied the reception area in minute detail, on levels most people didn't even know existed, searching for clues and give-aways and other hidden things.

"Okay . . ." said Melody, her eyes darting back and forth, her fingers flitting lightly across several keyboards. "Energy levels are all in the normal ranges. No spikes, no fluctuations . . . Room temperature is normal. No unusual radiations, all quiet on the electromagnetic front . . . Nothing showing up on the motion trackers or the short-range sensors. All the evidence says; it's only us here."

"Very good," said Sally. "Very scientific. Now what does all that mean? Really?"

"It means, nothing out of the ordinary is happening in this room," said Melody. "Which is pretty much what I expected. One of the reasons we're called Ghost Finders, is that the really bad stuff loves to try to hide from us. We're going to have to wait for something to kick off, so my instruments can measure and interpret and hopefully identify it."

"What if nothing happens?" said Sally.

Melody smiled an unpleasant smile. "Not very likely under the current conditions. The bigger the bad thing, the more it loves to show off. But if it is smart enough to keep its head down, tries to hide out until we're gone . . . then I'll have to hit it really hard with the science stick until something does happen." She looked steadily at Sally. "What did you hear; just now? Exactly?"

"You really didn't hear anything?" said Sally.

"No. And neither did my machines."

"It sounded . . . like a woman crying," Sally said. "Sobbing, really hard, like her heart was breaking. It didn't last long . . ."

"Did it sound like . . . anyone you recognised?" said Melody, carefully. "Someone who might have worked here?"

"I don't know! Maybe . . . I've never heard anybody cry like that." Sally looked intently at Melody. "Do you think this . . . means something?"

"Probably," said Melody. "Concentrate. Can you still hear the crying, maybe far away now . . . ?"

"No. I told you; it stopped, almost immediately."

"Pity," said Melody. "All right, back to the girly-chat stuff. You were telling me how you first came to Radio Free Albion."

"How can you switch back and forth so easily?" said Sally. "From the weird shit, to the regular stuff?"

"Practice," said Melody. "Go on."

"It seemed like a good idea at the time, all right? The station was on its way up, with a good regular audience, growing steadily. It was starting to pick up the really big advertising accounts . . . I was hoping to put the pressure on someone to give me a better job, get my voice on the air . . . I'd have made everyone sit up and take notice! And then it all went to Hell in a hand-cart. So damned quickly . . . And now Jonathan has to run the place with a skeleton staff. Yes, I know, very appropriate. Ho ho ho. Ghost Finder humour . . ."

"Who else is left?" said Melody.

"Captain Sunshine," said Sally, pulling a face. "That's

his radio handle. Don't ask me what his real name is; I get the impression he's had a lot of names, and a lot of handles, down the years. Old-time hippie, brain-damaged fallout from the Summer of Love. Still likes to talk about the rock-and-roll revolution, and the mind's true liberation, and all that mystical tree-hugging crap. Like that ship didn't sail long ago. I think he changes his handle with every new job, so his current boss can't check on what happened at his last job. He's got a Past; but he never talks about it. Though I'm not sure he really remembers. Or cares. He fried a lot of brain cells at Haight Ashbury, back in the day. Now he's too mellow to be scared."

"He and Happy will probably find lots to talk about," Melody said solemnly.

Sally looked at her uncertainly, then decided to press on. "Tom Foreman is our engineer and general handyman. He's keeping everything going with patches and baling wire and frantic improvisation. And because there isn't anybody else, he also presents Sports, and Weather, and Traffic News. Though I'm pretty sure he makes that last one up as he goes along."

"Is he any good as an engineer?" said Melody.

Sally shrugged. "Like I could tell the difference. It doesn't matter; he's all we've got. Whatever he does, it never lasts long. Something's always threatening to break down, at the worst possible moment."

"I could take a look," said Melody. "If you like. Never met a machine I couldn't intimidate."

"Someone should take a look," Sally said darkly. "Wouldn't surprise me to discover this whole place is run off a steam engine and held together with elastic bands."

"Why do you think Tom stayed while so many others have left?" said Melody.

"He may be a good engineer," said Sally, "but I think it would be fair to say no-one has ever accused him of being the brightest button in the box. He stays because Jonathan stays. That's it. He and Jonathan go way back. Tom's been working at this station ever since Jonathan founded it, over twenty years ago."

"Do you think Tom's gay?" Melody said innocently.

Sally smirked. "I know for a fact that he isn't . . . I backed him into a store cupboard, one boring afternoon. A bit old for me, but if you can't have the boss, have the second in command . . . Tom's okay. Though not nearly as good in the clinch as he likes to think he is."

"Few men are," said Melody. And the two of them shared a smile of girlish mischief.

"Finally," said Sally, "we come to our very own star in the making—Felicity Legrand. Presenter, journalist, chat-show host, and living goddess to the far-too-impressionable young men in our audience. Oh, she thinks she's so big time! I mean, I'm ambitious; but she's so confident and accomplished, it's downright sickening. She thinks she's doing all of us a favour by starting her brilliant career with us. *Stick close,* she likes to say. *Maybe some of my destiny will rub off on you.* I locked her in the women's toilet once, to bring her down a peg; and she had the lock picked with a hairpin in under two minutes. I'd love to give her a good slap, on general principles. Except I'm pretty sure she could take me."

"But is she really any good at her job?" said Melody.

"Yes! That's what's so infuriating! She's the only reason some people are still listening to us. You know what really bugs me about her? She isn't scared. The only person in this shit-hole who genuinely isn't freaked out of their wits by what's going on. She even argues with the voices when they break in to her shows!"

"Has she ever seen anything?"

Sally shook her head, reluctantly. "No. And she's been very vocal about that. She doesn't believe in the supernatural. At all."

"That can't be easy, with everything you people have experienced," said Melody. "How does she explain . . ."

"She can't," said Sally, smiling with cold satisfaction. "She keeps insisting it will all turn out to have some sane and rational explanation, in the end, but . . ." Sally's smile widened. "I can't wait for something really unnatural to blow her out of the water. Preferably live on-air, so everyone can hear it happen. And I'm really looking forward to hearing her interview you guys. Give her a good kicking; she deserves it!"

"JC and Happy can do that," said Melody. "I don't do the public face of the Ghost Finders bit. Apparently, I upset people. I stick with the science. You know where you are, with the science."

"You know, it just occurred to me," said Sally. "The voices first started becoming clearer on her shows . . . She's the one they talk to most. As though they're attracted to her. Don't know if that means anything . . . I'll tell you this for free; she'd love to leave. Walk out of here and never look back. If only because she finds all this supernatural stuff an affront to her precious, rational mind."

"Then why doesn't she go?" said Melody.

"Because this is her first big break, her first real success. She doesn't want it on her résumé that she had to quit because she couldn't take the pressure. And she doesn't want to be forced to admit there's anything happening here bad enough to justify her running away."

"But she hasn't *seen* anything?" said Melody.

"No-one's *seen* anything!" said Sally. "Not as such. But we've all felt things . . . Especially on the top floor. That feeling you get, when you know you're not alone, even though you can see there's no-one else in the room with you. We've all heard footsteps, and sounds of people moving about, in places where we know nobody should be. Whatever room you're in, you can always hear someone moving in the room next door. Walking up and down, talking quietly, saying things you can never quite make out or make sense of. But when you go in, there's never anyone there. Sometimes there are loud bangings, in the walls. In the floor and the ceiling. Like someone trying to get out or get in. Lights turn themselves on and off. Doors swing open on their own. Once, I had to go up to the top floor with a message, and I swear someone put a hand on my shoulder from behind. And when I spun round, there was nobody there."

She broke off, looking quickly at the Ghost Finder to see how she was taking it. Melody nodded. Sally laughed shakily.

"I'm spooking myself, now, talking about it . . . I don't talk about it, usually. I try not to even think about it . . ."

"This is all pretty standard stuff," Melody said carefully. "Low-level manifestations. Is there any particular place where the scary stuff seems worse? More threatening, or more common?"

Sally shuddered suddenly. "I don't go upstairs any

more. It's bad enough down here . . . at least I can leave reception and go outside for a while."

"What about the other rooms on the ground floor?"

"I don't go into them, either," Sally said firmly. "They're mostly living quarters for Jonathan and Tom, and the Captain." She shuddered again, and hugged herself tightly. "They actually live here! Can you believe that? In Murdock House! After everything that's happened . . . Though how they can stand it is beyond me . . . Probably keep their doors locked and the lights burning all night. I know I would. I'll tell you right now, there isn't enough money in the world to keep me here one minute after quitting time. Let alone after it gets dark. No; the minute my shift is over, I am out that door and gone! I stay out of all the other rooms. No matter what I hear. Sometimes . . . I get the feeling that if I were to concentrate hard enough, and long enough . . . I would see something. But not anything I'd want to see. So I don't."

"What about outside?" said Melody. "How does it feel out in the House's grounds?"

"Oh, outside is fine! Quiet and peaceful and . . . I spend as much time in the back gardens as I can. Leaving this room and going out there is like . . . putting down a heavy weight. And coming back in again is like picking the weight back up. And finding it gets heavier and heavier, all the time. The day will come when I won't be able to lift it, then . . . No. I feel safer outside."

"So it's Murdock House itself that feels bad?" said Melody. "Not the general area?"

"It's the house," said Sally. "It's gone bad. Feral."

"Do you know of anything . . . bad, that happened inside the house?" said Melody. "Ever?"

"Jonathan says not." Sally looked at Melody, who was still bent over her display screens. "Tell me; be honest. Is any of that technological shit really going to help?"

"Yes," said Melody, not looking up from her various readings. Her fingers flitted back and forth across her keyboards, and occasionally she would pause to pat the top of a particular machine as though it were an old friend or a favoured pet. "This is state-of-the-art equipment, some of it from advanced research labs who haven't even noticed it's gone missing yet. The best tech there is at what they do. My machines can dig up information, uncover hidden things, interpret data, and offer good advice. Information is ammunition when it comes to kicking the crap out of supernatural entities."

And then Melody's head came up sharply as she heard a woman scream. Close at hand, it went on and on—a terrible sound, loud and raw and harsh. A single human voice, racked with unbearable agony and unspeakable horror. To hear it was to feel it claw at your heart. Melody's first thought was that something had happened to Sally; but when she looked across the room to the reception desk, Sally was still sitting there, looking straight back at her. It was clear from the expression on Sally's face that she wasn't hearing what Melody was hearing. She checked her instruments again; but there was nothing. No changes in any of the readouts, no reactions to any of her scans. Her machines weren't hearing anything either.

The screaming went on and on, filling the room with pain and grief long after a human voice should have collapsed, unable to sustain it. An awful sound . . . Melody had to grit her teeth against it. She would have liked to put her hands over her ears, to keep the screaming out; but she knew that wouldn't help. This wasn't the kind of sound you heard with your ears.

Whoever it was, Melody wanted desperately to help; but she couldn't. She couldn't even tell where the scream was coming from. Melody stabbed at her keyboards with stiff fingers, increasingly angrily, trying to force her machines to reveal what was going on . . . And then the screaming broke off. Melody stopped what she was doing, and realised for the first time how badly her hands were shaking. The sound had got to her. Not least because Melody thought she knew who it was; who had been screaming so loudly. There were no words in the sound; but somehow Melody was still sure she recognised the voice. Somehow she knew—Sally.

She looked again at the reception desk; and Sally wasn't there. Her chair was empty. All that remained of Sally was her severed head, floating in mid air above the desk. Which was covered in blood, swimming with blood, dripping thickly off the edges. Sally's head hadn't been cut off; the raggedness of the wound, the torn stump, made it clear the head had been torn off. There were bloody wounds all over Sally's face that made Melody think of an animal attack.

Sally's eyes were still moving; and her mouth was still working though no sounds came out. She was still alive, still conscious and suffering. The eyes saw Melody looking at her and knew her. Recognised her. She didn't try to call out to Melody for help. She just looked sad . . . for Melody. As though she knew something . . . And then the head was gone. The vision was gone. And Sally was back behind her desk again. Everything looked perfectly normal.

"What the hell is the matter with you?" said Sally.

"Why are you looking at me like that? I mean, really! Cut it out, right now! You are freaking me out, big time!"

"Sorry," said Melody. "Sorry. I . . ."

"Why are you so pale? Why are you breathing so hard?"

"I said I was sorry!"

"You saw something, didn't you?" said Sally. She seemed almost . . . jealous. "What did you see?"

"You don't want to know," said Melody.

She tore her gaze away from the receptionist and made herself concentrate on the information flowing across the various screens before her. Still nothing; or at least, nothing that made any sense. Melody shook her head hard, to clear it. It didn't help. She glared at her instruments.

Come on, guys! Get your act together! You are seriously letting the side down here . . .

......................................

Jonathan led JC and Happy up the narrow back stairs to the top floor of Murdock House, chatting loudly and inconsequentially, almost as though he didn't like the quiet and felt a need to fill it with friendly, human sounds. JC looked around him carefully; but nothing seemed out of place, out of the ordinary. When the top of the stairs finally spilled them out onto a long, wide landing that seemed to stretch the whole length of the house, it all seemed very still. Even peaceful—now that Jonathan had finally stopped talking. The station manager looked down the landing, holding himself tensely, as though prepared for something to happen. But nothing did.

"It's quiet," said Happy. "Too quiet . . ." And then he spoiled it by giggling.

"Sound-proofing," said Jonathan, looking disapprovingly at Happy. "Our two main studios stand side by side. Can't have any stray sounds getting out. Are you really a telepath?"

"Usually," said Happy. "Something in this old house seems to be suppressing my talent. Holding it down, stifling it. Like having a blanket wrapped around my head, keeping the rest of the world out. I like it."

"So you're not . . . receiving anything?" said Jonathan.

Happy struck a dramatic pose. "I sense . . . unease!"

"Knock it off, Happy," said JC. "You've been watching those *Star Trek: Next Generation* box sets again, haven't you?"

"Everyone's a critic," said Happy.

JC looked down the length of the landing. Slats of light spilled in past the closed window-shutters. Electric lights burned reassuringly steadily, at regular intervals. And what shadows there were looked like just shadows. It was all very bare and basic, no frills. But Happy was right; even allowing for sound-proofed studios, it was too quiet. As though the whole upper floor were holding its breath, trying not to attract attention. JC looked to Happy and raised an interrogative eyebrow. Happy sighed, in his best and most practised put-upon way, and concentrated. Scowling fiercely. And then he relaxed suddenly, shrugged, and shook his head firmly.

"Not a thing, JC. And that is definitely not natural. I should be getting something . . ."

JC turned his gaze back to Jonathan, who stirred uncomfortably. The station manager looked like he wanted to be ushering JC and Happy along the landing, to the studios. Showing them things, getting the show on the road . . . But he couldn't because JC was making it very clear he had no intention of moving yet.

"What was Murdock House like before you came here, Jonathan?" said JC. "Any history of hauntings or psychic phenomena? Any stories of bad things, from out of the Past?"

"It was an old family home!" said Jonathan. "No bad back-history, nothing out of the ordinary. I checked. All part of the due diligence before I bought the place. After all this started, I checked the archives in the local papers. There's never been a murder here, no-one's ever died here . . . Not even a bad accident!"

"How did you end up here?" Happy said suddenly. "At Radio Free Albion?"

"I had to come here," Jonathan said steadily, "because I screwed up my previous life, very thoroughly, at the BBC. I had a drinking problem, back then. The problem was, I couldn't get enough of it. I quit before they could fire me; and then I burned any number of bridges at a great many other places before I finally stopped blaming everyone else for my problems and stopped drinking. I used the last of my savings to buy Murdock House and refit it as a local radio station. My last chance to do the kind of work I'd always believed I was capable of. I used the last of my reputation to attract old friends and new talents, by promising them a chance to do something different, something that mattered. A chance to build a reputation, without the usual editorial interference. You have to understand: Radio Free Albion is my last chance. If I lose this station, I lose everything."

By the time he finished talking, his voice was shaking, and he couldn't meet their eyes. Happy looked at JC. This was usually when JC would say something kind and re-assuring, to put the civilian at their ease. Except JC didn't say anything. His attention seemed far away, lost in his own thoughts. Happy wondered if he should say something and quickly decided against it. He didn't have the touch.

"There's more to the history of radio than most people realise," JC said finally. Not looking at anyone in particular. "It has been said, by people in a position to know, that the first people to build working radio sets weren't interested in long-distance communication. They were pursuing something quite different. They were trying to build machines . . . that would allow them to talk with the dead."

Jonathan cleared his throat, uncomfortably. "Well, that's news to me. Did anyone ever succeed?"

"Depends on who you talk to," said JC.

"I think I'd better take you to the first studio," said Jonathan. "So you can talk to Captain Sunshine. He's very interested in . . . things like that. You'll like the Captain. Everyone does."

He led the way down the landing, not looking to the left or the right, finally stopping before a door with a red light burning fiercely over it. Jonathan opened the door carefully and eased inside, gesturing urgently for JC and Happy to follow him in. They pretty much filled the crowded outer room, looking through a sound-proofed window at Captain Sunshine, busy at his work. Jonathan closed the door quietly. JC and Happy studied the Captain as he talked easily into his microphone. He seemed normal enough. There was no sign of a support engineer or an editor. The Captain had clearly been left to his own resources.

"That's Malcolm Blackwood," Jonathan said quietly. "Captain Sunshine when he's on the air."

The Captain was clearly an old-time hippie. He had the look and the clothes, and had to be at least in his late sixties. He wore his thinning grey hair pulled back in a long ponytail, hanging half-way down his back; but while his face was heavily wrinkled, it still possessed a certain cheerful, childlike quality. He wore a battered old Grateful Dead T-shirt, with the legend FORCE FEED YOUR HEAD, over extremely faded blue jeans. He sat relaxed before his microphone, talking easily and fluently. Jonathan knocked twice on the dividing window. The Captain looked round, nodded briefly, and flashed a smile and the peace sign to JC and Happy. All without interrupting his monologue. Jonathan hit a switch, so they could all hear what he was saying.

"Okay, okay, oh my brothers and sisters, that was the Doors, with 'Riders on the Storm.' Next up we have the ever-youthful Beach Boys, with their hymn to sun and sand and bright young things, 'I wish they all could be California girls.' Stick with the Captain, for the best music and the best feelings. This is Captain Sunshine, the Sixties Survivor, bringing you what you want, what you need, all sixties all the time, joyful sounds to get you through the dark days of this grim grey world they made for us to live in. I'll be back, right after this . . ."

He cued up the Beach Boys, letting the needle drop lightly onto the album with the ease of long practice, then he sank back in his chair and gestured easily for the others to come in and join him. Jonathan led the way. The Captain smiled beatifically at his new visitors but made no move to get up or shake hands.

"I see you still prefer vinyl in this digital age," said JC.

"Vinyl is cool," said Captain Sunshine. "It has warmth, and soul, unlike the digital stuff. Vinyl gives a damn."

He smiled and nodded sagely, and waited for JC to pick up the conversation again. Jonathan stood back and let JC get on with it.

"All sixties, all the time?" said JC. "Don't you like anything more recent, Captain?"

"Welcome, oh my best beloveds, to the sounds of the sixties," said Captain Sunshine. "The best music from that best of times. Balm for the soul in these troubled times."

"We're the Ghost Finders," said JC, deciding to cut to the chase. Because somebody had to, and it clearly wasn't going to be the Captain. "We're here to help you with your supernatural problems."

Captain Sunshine nodded wisely. His eyes didn't seem to track all the time, and his attention faded in and out, even while he was talking. His gaze wandered round the studio, passing lightly over the other people in it; and then they came to JC and seemed to snap suddenly into focus.

"You're here to do something; about the Voices from Beyond? Good. If you could keep them from butting in while I'm playing a classic, I'd be grateful."

"You don't seem too bothered by the . . . phenomena," said JC.

"I'm not," said the Captain. "Ghosts are groovy . . . a blast from the past! Perhaps it takes one survivor to appreciate another. I'm fascinated by the otherworldly. The natural and the supernatural are two sides of the same coin—the great groovy ride that is the life trip. But you have to do something because a lot of what's been happening here is not good, man. Definite negative karma, baby." He switched his knowing gaze to Happy. "You're the mind-reader, aren't you, man? I can tell. We all shine on . . . Are you here to help these poor lost souls find their way home, back to the Light? Lay the unquiet spirits to rest, at last?"

"I don't think that's what these voices want," said Happy. "But we'll do what we can."

"That's cool," said the Captain. He looked at the bloody hand-print on the front of JC's jacket, started to say something, found it all too much of an effort, and turned away. His gaze drifted off, lost on some far horizon. "You'll have to excuse me, good people. My children are waiting. The Captain has a show to do."

He cut back in just as the Beach Boys were finishing, with impeccable timing, and started talking quietly and confidently into his microphone again. Jonathan ushered JC and Happy out of the studio.

||||||||||||||||||||||

In the studio next door, Tom Foreman was immersed in the preparation for his upcoming Traffic report. This seemed to consist mostly of looking up at the ceiling with his mouth open and doodling on a note-pad. He stood up quickly when Jonathan brought in the Ghost Finders. Tom nodded and smiled, in a professional and uninvolved sort of way, a middle-aged man carrying rather more weight than was good for him. A worn-out man in a well-worn business suit. Jonathan made the introductions, and Tom insisted on shaking hands in a brisk, business-like way. He had a round face, hardly any hair left, and a sense that he was only talking to you out of the goodness of his heart. Because you were obviously keeping him from something far more important. He did his best to appear calm and at ease but didn't fool anyone. He was jumpy, on guard, his gaze moving quickly from JC to Happy and back again, his professional smile flickering on and off like a faulty light bulb.

"You're them, aren't you? You're the ghost-busting guys, the spiritual advisors. Good! Good . . . I really hope they can help you, Jonathan, because if they can't, I am out of here. Please! Don't say it. I've heard everything you have to say, several times; and I don't care any more. Tonight is my last night. I've had enough. My nerves are shredded, my ulcers have ulcers, and the sleeping pills don't work any longer."

"Please, Tom," said Jonathan. "Do you want me to beg? Because I'll do it if that's what it'll take. Give me a little more time. These people are from the Carnacki Institute; they're the real deal. They can fix this mess."

Tom shrugged quickly. "Then they've got tonight to show what they can do. Because after we've shut down for the evening, I am out of here. Whatever it is that's in this house with us, it doesn't want us here. I'm hearing the voices everywhere now. I even hear them in my dreams."

JC stepped forward, immediately intrigued. "Dreams can be significant in cases like these. Can you remember anything that seemed . . . out of the ordinary, in these dreams?"

"A sense of Time passing," Tom said reluctantly. "A growing urgency; a feeling that we're all running out of time. That someone's trying desperately to warn us; and we're not listening."

They all waited; but he had nothing more to say. In fact, he seemed to feel that he'd said more than enough already.

"Have you seen anything, Tom?" said JC.

"No. And I don't want to. That's why I'm leaving."

"You can't go, Tom!" said Jonathan.

"Watch me."

"Where would you go?" said Jonathan; and there was a sudden anger in his voice, almost spiteful.

"Anywhere would be good as long as I wouldn't have to be scared all the time," Tom said levelly, not rising to the emotional bait. "I mean it, Jonathan; I really can't stand this place one day longer."

"Well, before you run off like all the others, to join their Get a Backbone Club, I need you to do something for me," said Jonathan. "There's a young lady downstairs, very scientific, name of Melody Chambers. She's with the Ghost Finders. I need you to sort out the voice recordings we made and take them down to her, for analysis. Think you can manage that?"

"I can do that," said Tom. "Though what she thinks she can do with the recordings that I haven't already tried . . ."

"She has a lot of equipment," said JC.

"Loads and loads," said Happy. "She could dig the secrets out of a sphinx, then ride it bareback up and down the street . . . Sorry. My metaphor kind of broke loose there. But she really is very good. Very scientific."

"All right. Leave it to me," said Tom. He looked steadily at JC. "You've met the Captain? He can cope with this shit because he isn't all here, and I wish I wasn't. But you've still got a treat in store. Meeting Felicity Legrand. If you're looking for something really scary . . ."

⁙⁙⁙⁙⁙⁙⁙⁙⁙⁙⁙⁙⁙⁙

Jonathan led JC and Happy almost to the end of the long landing, to the lounge, which turned out to be a reasonably comfortable setting with big chairs, heavy tables covered with piled-up newspapers and magazines, all kinds of junk food, and an assortment of energy drinks. A woman who had to be Felicity Legrand stood up quickly as they entered, springing up out of her chair, half-spilling the drink in her hand. She almost jumped out of her skin, then tried very hard to look like she hadn't. She slammed her plastic cup down on the nearest table and glared at Jonathan.

"Next time, knock first!"

"Sorry," said Jonathan, holding up both hands defensively, as though afraid she might attack him. "Allow me to present JC, and Happy; the Ghost Finders. You're interviewing them later, for your show. Remember?"

"Of course I remember!" Felicity turned a cold glare on JC and Happy. "So; you're the *experts*, are you?"

"Got it in one!" JC said cheerfully. "You must be psychic."

Felicity sniffed, loudly. A good-looking woman in her mid twenties, fashionably dressed, with a cold, detached air. She wore her hair in a fashionable style and used only minimal make-up. She had the look of someone determined that everyone else should take her very seriously. Felicity didn't smile at either of the Ghost Finders and didn't offer to shake hands. JC didn't think he'd offer her his on the grounds he wasn't sure he'd get it back in one piece. He had a strong feeling Felicity Legrand would only ever reveal those aspects of her personality that she believed would get her the things she needed. And she didn't need anything from him or Happy.

"You caught me by surprise," she said, almost defiantly. "I was reading, doing my research."

"I saw the papers," said JC. "And the glossy magazines."

"I need to concentrate on what matters," said Felicity. "I go through all the dailies, and the most popular magazines, as background for my shows. You have to keep up with what people are interested in. What they think is important; what everyone is talking about. Though of course right now my listeners only seem to want to talk about the one thing."

"The voices," said JC.

"Exactly!" said Felicity. "You must be psychic, too."

"No; that's me," said Happy.

Felicity shot him a quick look, then turned all her attention back to JC as a more interesting target. "So what kind of an *expert* are you, really?"

"The experienced kind," said JC. "The sort who knows what he's doing. You're not impressed by us at all, are you?"

"Should I be?" said Felicity.

"Yes," said JC.

"Why have you got blood-stains on the front of your jacket?"

"He doesn't like to talk about it," said Happy.

"Why are you wearing such dark sunglasses, indoors?" said Felicity, ignoring Happy.

"Because I'm cool," said JC.

Felicity looked at him dubiously but decided to let that one pass. She gestured vaguely at a pile of handwritten pages on the table beside the chair she'd just jumped up out of.

"I've been making notes on you, for my show. For when I interview you. The Ghost Finders . . . such an intriguing name."

"It's what we do," said JC.

"You've heard of us?" said Happy.

"It's amazing what you can find on the Net," said Felicity smugly. "Particularly on the more rabid conspiracy sites, which led me to some very interesting stories about the organisation you work for. The Carnacki Institute. That is right, isn't it?"

"Yes," said JC. "A charitable institution that funds investigations into supernatural events and other things of related interest."

Happy looked at JC. "Really?"

"It's a public-face, private-face thing," said JC. "It's complicated."

"Oh . . ." said Happy. "No-one ever tells me anything."

"Yes we do," JC said crushingly. "But you never listen." He turned back to Felicity. "You don't want to believe everything you find on conspiracy sites. The clue is in the name."

Felicity deliberately turned away from him to fix Jonathan with her fierce, predatory gaze. "How did you find out about the Carnacki Institute, Jonathan? How did you know to call them for help?"

"There was an . . . incident, on a BBC programme, some years back," Jonathan said carefully. "A televised séance got out of hand, and the presenter ended up . . . apparently possessed. Someone there knew whom to call. I was only an assistant producer, but I stood my ground when everyone else ran, so I got to see what happened when the Carnacki representative turned up. He was very . . . professional."

"Don't suppose you remember his name . . . ?" said JC.

"Hadleigh . . . something," said Jonathan. "Look, I need

you people to go on Felicity's show. So you can say calm and comforting things, in a reasonable and professional tone of voice, to stop our audience freaking out. We have to calm them down before they turn up here as a panicking mob, complete with pitchforks and flaming torches, and copies of *Exorcism for Dummies*." He glared at Felicity. "So please, for the good of all, everyone play nice."

Felicity frowned. She turned away from JC to glare at Happy. "So then, you're the so-called team telepath . . ."

"That's me," said Happy. "Think of your pin number! Go on; I dare you . . ."

"Go ahead," said Felicity. "Impress me. What am I thinking, right now?"

"Oh, this can only end well," murmured JC.

"Yes, your bum does look big in that," Happy said to Felicity. "And why are you thinking about having Botox, when you're only on the radio and no-one sees you anyway?"

"Not even close," said Felicity, smiling triumphantly.

"All right, all right," said Happy. "I'll admit that, right now, it's hard for me to pick up anything. Something inside Murdock House has shut everything down."

"How very convenient," said Felicity.

"No it bloody isn't," said Happy. "Makes the job so much harder . . . Though I will say, I do find the psychic peace and quiet rather relaxing, now I'm cut off from the world's babble . . . It does mean there's a limit to what I can do, to help with this investigation, which I can't help feeling is probably the point."

"You're the first person to find Murdock House relaxing in a long time," said Jonathan. "I haven't been able to get a good night's sleep in months. I hate living here."

"Then why don't you move out?" said JC.

"Because this is my home, and I won't be driven out of it," Jonathan said steadily. "And because I've nowhere else to go."

Happy moved forward suddenly, planting himself right in front of Felicity. She jumped again, but refused to retreat a single step. Happy stared at her thoughtfully, and she met his gaze unflinchingly.

"Sorry," said Happy, after a moment. "Still not getting anything. Are you sure you're not some kind of machine?"

"Play nicely, Happy," murmured JC.

"Oh . . ." said Happy, smiling suddenly. It wasn't a very nice smile. "Proximity really does make a difference. Oh, Felicity . . . you gave the boy up for adoption. Because you were only eighteen and had no idea how to be a mother. And because you knew you couldn't raise a child and have the career you wanted. You had to choose. So you gave him up and moved on. But sometimes, when you're lying alone in your bed in the early hours of the morning and sleep won't come . . . Sometimes you think to yourself, *Is he doing well? Is he happy?* You could find out. You have the contacts. But you always end up deciding . . . it wouldn't be fair to either of you."

"You piece of shit," said Felicity. "You rotten little piece of shit! Who told you?" She turned on Jonathan. "Did you tell him?"

"You told me," said Happy. "I wonder what else you're holding back that you don't want to tell me . . ."

Felicity pushed roughly past him and strode out of the room, not looking back once. Jonathan started to go after her, then stopped himself.

"We'll need to talk to all your people," said JC. "Separately and together."

"The Captain will be off the air in a few minutes," said Jonathan. "Then he's all yours. You can talk to Tom after he's done his piece. Then it's your interview with Felicity . . . After that, I'm shutting the station down for the day. And we will all be available. But I need you to do the interview first. That's the deal I made with Felicity to get her cooperation."

"You know she's planning to do a hatchet job on us," said JC. "And on you, for bringing us in. So when she finally leaves the station, she can point at you and say, *It was all his fault . . . Nothing to do with me.*"

"Of course I know. That's what she always does," said Jonathan. He smiled, briefly. "I'm sure you can handle her. You are professionals, after all."

"Once Radio Free Albion has shut down, I'll need free access to everywhere in Murdock House," said JC. "And everyone. Including your receptionist. In situations like this, it's the people who matter most. Either as victims or instigators."

Jonathan nodded. He looked more tired than anything.

‖‖‖‖‖‖‖‖‖‖‖‖‖‖‖‖‖‖‖‖‖‖‖

They all went back out onto the landing and bumped into Tom Foreman, carrying a large cardboard box full of digital recordings of the voices from beyond. Happy immediately volunteered to take them down to Melody, and Tom was happy to let him do it. He handed over the box and hurried back to his studio. Jonathan offered to show JC the rest of the upper floor. Happy was left alone, heading for the top of the stairs, carrying a box that was a lot heavier than he'd expected.

Something appeared before him, manifesting suddenly out of nowhere. It was the thing he'd seen in the car park earlier, the apparition that had towered over Melody. It hung on the air, huge and dark, twisted and malformed. Monstrous but still, somehow, human. Happy put down his box, carefully, then straightened up to glare at the apparition.

"Well?" he said. "What do you want?"

The thing rose and fell slowly before him. It was hard to look at directly; its details seemed to flow and change and merge. It was a horrible thing, and Happy knew he should have felt scared . . . but somehow he didn't. He didn't feel threatened or in any immediate danger. Happy looked the thing over carefully.

"All right," he said. "I'm here. You're here. I assume there's some purpose to this. Talk to me. I'll listen. What do you want?"

Still no answer. Happy scowled, trying to reach out with his mind, force it through the interference that was shutting his Sight down. And for the first time since he'd entered Murdock House, the clouds seemed to clear a little. Sometimes it's not all about the Seeing; it's about listening. The thing hanging on the air spoke to him, only to him. It said his name. Happy's heart lurched in his chest. He knew that voice. He'd heard that voice say his name, so many times before.

"Oh my God," he said. "Melody? Is that you, Mel? What happened? What happened to you?"

It hasn't happened yet, said the familiar voice inside

his head. But it will. And there's nothing you can do to stop it.

"You're Melody from the future?" said Happy. "No . . . No! I won't let this happen to you! I won't! How long, before . . ."

Tomorrow. It all happens tomorrow.

And then the awful thing was gone. The air before him was open and empty, with nothing remaining to show there had ever been anything there. Except that Happy's heart was hammering painfully fast; and his face was covered with a cold sweat. He swallowed hard and breathed slowly and deeply, trying to calm himself. He crouched, picked up the cardboard box, and started down the stairs. Wondering what, if anything, he should say to Melody. And also thinking; *What did you see in the car park, JC? Why do you have a bloody hand-print on your jacket? What's going to happen—to all of us?*

He carried on down the stairs, one step at a time, hugging the box to his chest.

That's not going to happen to you, Mel. I'll die before I let that happen. I promised you, and I promised myself; I will stand between you and all evil. Even if I have to take every pill I have on me.

# FIVE

## SOMETIMES THE SKY REALLY IS FALLING

When Happy went back into the reception area, he was relieved to find Melody right where she belonged, working away at her semi-circular array of watchful machines. He stood inside the rear door for a while and watched her while his heart and breathing slowly returned to normal. She was currently busy cursing out one of her computers because it wasn't giving her the answers she wanted. Machines disappointed Melody at their peril. Happy glanced over at the reception desk and wasn't all that surprised to see that Sally wasn't there. He started across the room towards Melody and she addressed him immediately, without even looking up.

"You took your time, Happy. What were you doing up there? Collecting autographs? And before you ask, Sally's outside, taking another break."

"How could you be so sure it was me?" said Happy.

"I know your walk. I know everything about you, te-lepathy boy; and don't you ever forget it."

Happy smiled. He liked that. He liked being such a familiar part of Melody's life that she could immediately recognise even the smallest thing about him. But his smile quickly vanished as the image of the awful thing he'd seen at the top of the stairs refused to leave his mind. The terrible thing that was going to happen unless he could prevent it. He stopped walking and shuddered suddenly. Melody looked up to see why he'd stopped and caught the expression on his face. Love and horror; misery and des-peration. It took her a moment to realise that he was look-ing that way because he was looking at her.

"What happened?" she said. "Something's happened. It's no good trying to hide it from me; you know I'll get it out of you. I always do. You can't hide anything from me."

"I can," said Happy. "When it's to protect you. This is a bad place, Mel. Dangerous. We should drop everything and get the hell out of here. While we still can."

"Well, we can't, can we?" said Melody, not even trying to hide the puzzlement in her voice. "What's got into you? We have a job to do here. We can't run out on these people until we've figured out how to clean up this mess."

"Is the job really that important?" said Happy, walking slowly towards her. "More important than us?"

"Mostly, yes," said Melody. "We knew that when we signed up. We gave our lives, and maybe our deaths, to the Institute because we believed it was a job worth doing."

"Really?" said Happy. "I joined up to get my hands on medications I couldn't hope to find anywhere else. And I'm pretty sure you told me, you only joined because the Institute had the very best toys."

"That was then," said Melody. "This is now. Things change, in time."

She caught the way his face twisted painfully at her words; and a sudden chill ran down her spine. For the first time, she realised that when he'd said the place was dangerous, he meant dangerous to them.

"What happened to you upstairs, Happy? Did you see something?"

Happy looked away. He couldn't say anything without blurting out everything. He had to be strong, for her. He couldn't escape the feeling that by putting his experience into words, he would be making it real, and fixed, immutable. And, anyway, how do you tell the woman you love that you've seen her dead, and worse than dead? Melody started to move out from behind her machines, leaving them for him; and then they both looked round sharply as JC came striding confidently into the reception area, and the moment was broken. Melody moved back behind her machines again.

"Talk to Happy, JC!" she said loudly. "He's hiding something from me!"

"Good for you, Happy," JC said briskly. "Keeping secrets from each other is all part of maintaining a successful relationship."

Happy realised he was still holding on to the cardboard box full of voice recordings and that it was growing increasingly heavy. He marched forward and slammed the box down, right in front of Melody's array. When in doubt, you could always distract Melody by giving her something new to play with. He straightened up, pressed both hands into the small of his back, and stretched slowly and dramatically.

"The voice recordings you ordered," he said. "Hours and hours of the things. I swear, humping them down the stairs has done serious damage to my spine. Can I get a nice back rub?"

Melody ignored him, hurrying out from behind her array to crouch beside the cardboard box and rummage through its contents.

"I see Sally's wandered off again . . ." said JC.

"She really doesn't like it in here," said Melody, not looking up from the box. "And I'm starting to agree with her. The atmosphere in this room is . . . unhealthy."

JC looked at her thoughtfully. "Could you be more specific?"

"Not yet," said Melody. "My machines are still working on it. But you don't need to be psychic to know when you've been dropped into shark-infested waters. Spiritually speaking."

"Hold everything!" said Happy. "I am team telepath; it's my job to say things like that!"

"Then get on with it," Melody said ruthlessly. "What is it that's got you so rattled? What's it like, upstairs?"

"Nothing obviously out of the ordinary," said JC, after it became clear Happy wasn't going to answer. "If it wasn't for the voices, and the way everyone here is acting so damned twitchy, I'd say this was an extreme case of Sick Building Syndrome."

"That would explain why Sally has to keep walking out," said Melody. "I could have made her stay here till you got back, so you could question her; but I didn't have the heart. Would have felt like kicking a puppy. Underneath all those piercings and the scary make-up, she's not nearly as grown-up as she likes to make out. And it's not like there's much work for her to do here. No-one's rung in on any of those phones in ages."

"Really?" said JC. He strode over to the reception desk, picked up the nearest phone, and listened for a while to make sure it was still connected.

"Anything?" said Happy.

"I can hear the sea," said JC. He put the phone down and looked back at Melody. "So what have you been up to while Happy and I were gadding about upstairs, making friends and influencing people?"

"Keeping busy," she said, then looked carefully at JC. "You didn't see anything, upstairs? Either of you?"

"An old hippie, a man desperate to leave, and a very scary woman heading straight for the top," said JC. "Have your machines turned up anything useful yet?"

Melody gave up on the voice recordings, straightened up, and marched back behind her array of instruments. She ran her gaze quickly over the various readouts and displays.

"I'm mostly getting all sorts of ordinary," she said grimly. "Nothing out of place, no unnatural phenomena or weird occurrences, down here or upstairs. Normal and everyday, right across the boards. But I don't think I trust these readings. It's like they're too normal, too ordinary. Almost text-book conditions. And you never get that, out in the real world. It's as though Something is interfering with my instruments, trying to hide the true state of affairs from me. Suppressing the evidence and distorting the data. Which I would have said was impossible before this . . ."

"Are we talking about the same Something that's shutting down Happy's E.S.P.?" said JC.

"Probably," said Melody.

"I am still here, you know!" Happy said loudly.

"Only just," said Melody.

"Would you care to make an educated guess as to what this Something might be?" said JC.

"Something very powerful," said Melody. She scowled at her monitor screens as though they'd let her down. "We'd have to be talking about a really Big Bad, and nasty with it. Powerful enough to hide every trace of its presence and true nature from us."

"If it's that powerful . . ." said Happy, "why does it need to hide from us?"

"Good question," said JC. "Melody?"

"I could elaborate further, but I'm already seriously worried," said Melody. "If we can't trust Happy's E.S.P., or my machines, or even our own senses . . . There's only one thing it can be. This isn't any standard haunting, or any of the expected phenomena. We're dealing with a Beast."

"Oh bloody hell," said Happy. "Not another one."

Melody was still looking steadily at JC. "Are you sure the Boss thought this was only another case? She didn't say anything to you?"

"No," said JC. "Not a damned thing. I am starting to wonder, though . . . She did say she didn't trust the people around her any more."

"So there is the possibility that she's being played, as well as us?" said Melody. "That all of this is bait to lure us into a trap?"

"Does feel that way, doesn't it?" said JC.

"I want to go home," said Happy. "Seriously. Right now."

"Life was so much simpler when you were merely paranoid," said Melody. "I could cope with that. Now it really does feel like the whole universe is out to get us."

"I should feel vindicated, or even triumphant," said Happy. "Oddly, it doesn't feel nearly as good as I thought it would."

"Let's concentrate on the job, people!" JC said sharply. "It's a bit early to be panicking when we're not even sure what's going on yet."

"It's never too early to panic!" said Happy.

"You're taking too many pills, Happy," JC said coldly. "Or not enough." He turned to Melody and gave her his full attention. "What can you tell me, Mel? There must be something . . ."

"I'm monitoring Radio Free Albion's output," said Melody. "And so far, all their transmissions seem normal enough. Not a single intruding voice. Here; listen."

She turned on the speakers built into her array, so they could all hear what the radio station was putting out. Captain Sunshine was wrapping up his show, his voice calm and professional and unhurried. He wished his audience love and peace, reminded them that flower power was still groovy, then handed over to Tom Foreman.

Tom introduced himself and launched straight into the Traffic News Update. Compared to the experienced Captain Sunshine, he sounded like an amateur. It quickly became clear he was simply reading from a prepared script, with no attempt to sound spontaneous or witty, or engage with his audience at all. He put no effort into it. None of the Traffic News sounded in the least interesting, let alone urgent. He finally ran out of things to say, introduced

Felicity Legrand making a trailer for her show, and got off the air with almost indecent speed.

Probably because he could tell he didn't belong there.

Felicity's voice was a pleasant relief: warm and soothing and almost confidential, as though she were talking directly to every individual member of her listening audience. She sounded friendly and inviting, a completely different personality to the woman JC and Happy had met in the upstairs lounge.

"Stay tuned, everyone, for a very special show!" said the dulcet tones of the on-air Felicity. "I have some really exciting guests lined up for the interview segment of my show, and you're not going to want to miss a single moment. Joining us shortly will be three of those famous, fabulous, ghost-busting types: JC Chance, Melody Chambers, and Happy Jack Palmer! Of the internationally renowned and only slightly secretive Carnacki Institute! Ghosts R Us; and all that. They've promised to shed a new and hopefully revealing light on the strange things that have been plaguing us here at Radio Free Albion; and you can be sure I'll be asking them all kinds of probing and pointed questions.

"And I'm sure they'll be only too happy to answer any questions you have! So put on your thinking caps, ring the regular number, and be ready to press them hard for the answers that satisfy! We'll be taking your calls, sharing your opinions, and talking about the things that concern you . . . And we won't give up till we've got some answers! I know you have some fascinating questions to put to our three Ghost Finders, so stand by your phones! Now back to Tom for the Weather."

"She's setting us up to take a fall," said JC. "Embarrass

us with awkward questions she doesn't believe we can answer."

"How much can we say?" said Melody. "I mean, the truth is out of the question. Isn't it?"

"Unless we want to start a mass panic, I would think so," said JC.

"I did not sign up to do public relations," said Melody.

"Don't want to go on her programme," Happy said sulkily. "I thought we'd agreed I don't have to do interviews?"

"It'll be fun!" said JC.

"No it won't," said Happy.

"All right, it'll be interesting," said JC. "You have to be there, Happy, now she's named you. Or she'll say we're trying to hide something."

"We are!" said Happy.

"Yes, but we don't want everyone else to know that," JC said patiently. "It's bad enough that Felicity is throwing the name of the Carnacki Institute around so casually; we can't have people taking too much of an interest in us. So we go on her show, spout a whole bunch of boring platitudes, speak a lot without actually saying much, and shut Miss Clever Mouth down. We don't need the publicity."

"Better let me and JC do most of the talking, Happy," said Melody.

"Suits me," said Happy.

Melody cut Felicity Legrand off in mid sentence, and a peaceful quiet settled over the reception area. She came back out to study the cardboard box again. JC had a look in the box, too, to keep her company. It did seem very full.

"How long will it take you, to work your way through all these recordings?" he said finally.

"God knows how many hours there are in this box," said Melody. "Maybe even days . . . But I think we can do better than that."

She flourished a long data wand and waved it briskly over the box. Then she went back behind her instruments, checked a few readings, and smiled smugly.

"There! Every single file is now stored in my marvellous machines. You have to love digital . . . Now I let the computers do the heavy lifting as they go through each file and sort out the wheat from the chaff, so I only need to listen to the significant material."

"All right," said JC. "How long is that going to take?"

"Depends," said Melody, not giving an inch.

"You don't know, do you?" said Happy.

"I've never actually tried this before, okay?" said Melody. She realised she was still holding the data wand and tossed it casually to one side. "It's new software. The theory is sound, but . . ."

"I always hate it when she says *but*," said Happy. "Don't you always hate it when she says *but*, JC?"

"Always," JC said solemnly.

Melody glared at both of them. "My computers are currently digging through mountains of detailed information, looking for hidden layers and levels, messages within messages, audio palimpsests . . . All the seriously weird shit that normal searches wouldn't pick up on."

"While they're doing all that," JC said calmly, "what do your highly experienced instruments have to tell us, about our current surroundings? Anything?"

"There are no suspicious gaps in the data," said Melody, peering dubiously from one monitor screen to another. "Nothing that should be there but isn't. All my sensor readings are well within acceptable ranges. The only thing I have found, that I didn't even think to look for at first because you so rarely encounter them out in the field . . . I'm picking up the occasional burst of tachyon radiations."

Happy blinked at her. "Okay, I have heard you use that word before, but . . ."

"You never listen when I talk, do you?" said Melody.

"I listen!" said Happy. "I just don't always understand every single word . . ."

"Tachyons!" Melody said loudly, "are theoretical particles that can't travel any slower than the speed of light. Often associated with temporal anomalies."

"If they're only theoretical," said JC, "how are you picking them up?"

"Because they're not really tachyons!"

"Back away slowly," Happy said to JC. "Try not to show fear."

"Look!" said Melody. "I am dumbing this right down, for the technically deficient and the scientifically illiterate. We call this tachyon radiation because it often appears when there's some kind of . . . disruption, in the flow of local Time."

JC and Happy looked at each other and shrugged pretty much simultaneously.

"Still not getting it," said JC.

"Something is very wrong with Time in Murdock House," said Melody.

"Yes," said Happy. "Got that. But what does it *mean*?"

"I don't know!" said Melody. "Not as yet . . . I'm looking into it, all right? You asked me if there was anything different or unusual here, JC, and that's what I've got!"

"Let me know if it starts to mean anything," said JC.

Happy walked away. He slumped heavily into the chair behind the reception desk and started searching through his many pockets. He produced a whole series of pill boxes, bottles, and phials and set them out on the desk-top before him. Some were labelled in his obsessively neat handwriting; some were colour-coded with bright stickers; and a few had been left ominously blank. He lined them all up in neat rows before him without opening any of them, then moved them back and forth, arranging them in groups and patterns that presumably meant something to him. Then he looked at them and set about rearranging them. As though searching for some particularly significant combination.

JC watched him do it; and said nothing.

After a while, Melody came quietly out from behind her machines and walked over to the reception desk. She dragged a chair into place beside Happy, sat down, and without looking at Happy or JC, she began sorting through the pill boxes and bottles. Putting some in front of Happy, and discarding others. Happy sat back in his chair and let her do it.

"How long has this been going on?" JC said finally. "When did you decide to become his nurse and his junkie muse, Melody?"

"I'm only sorting out what he needs to keep himself sharp," said Melody, not looking up. "The right mixtures and dosages, to keep him focused on the job. While still keeping him . . . balanced."

Happy nodded. He didn't interfere with any of her selections. He trusted her to know what he needed. What was best for him.

"I work out the proper doses for each pill, now," said Melody. "My computers calculate the exact combinations to give him what he needs, what his body can stand. Because at least this way I have some measure of control over what he's doing to himself. Chemicals are science. I can do science."

"Oh yes; it's all very scientific now," said Happy. "Or so she assures me. I hardly ever get muscle cramps or cold sweats these days. I used to follow my instincts, with a whole bunch of trial and error thrown in. I hardly ever collapse, now, or sit crying in the corner for hours. I'm doing so much better now she's here to help."

"Really?" said JC.

"Who can tell?" said Happy. "My body has become an alchemical work of art. I should be on display, in a Museum for the Terminally Strange. My brain cells are so soaked in experimental medicines, I'm amazed they're still talking to each other. But it's what I need—to stay sane. To keep the world out, to hold the supernatural at bay, so there's no-one inside my head but me. Never be a junkie, JC; it's hard work."

Melody finally assembled a richly coloured assortment of pills, mustered them into a neat pile, and set them before Happy. He sat up straight in his chair and looked at the drugs for a long moment, not even reaching out to touch them.

"Don't you want them?" Melody said carefully.

"You know I do," said Happy. "But given all the troubles I'm having with my E.S.P. right now; will they help?" He smiled briefly at Melody. "I should know better than to ask questions like that, shouldn't I? You know everything about the pills except what it feels like to take them. I can't live with them, can't function without them . . . Oh hell, girl. We all do what we have to do, when all the other options are worse."

Melody handed him a plastic bottle of water, and Happy knocked the pills back, one after the other. His hands were perfectly steady. Melody pushed back her chair and strode over to her array of instruments. So she wouldn't have to watch. JC let her get back into position, then strolled over to stand opposite her.

"You know that stuff is killing him by inches," he said quietly.

"Of course I know," she said. "But it's necessary. Sometimes, all that's left is to hold someone's hand while they put the gun to their head. You never cared before . . ."

"Of course I care," said JC. "He's no use to me dead."

Kim walked into the reception area, through the left-hand wall. She looked solid and real and not at all ghostly. She smiled sweetly at everyone.

"I'm dead, and I'm useful!" she said brightly. "Hello, everyone! Isn't it an absolutely super day? Hello, JC! How's my sweetie?"

JC smiled back at her and felt some of the tension ease out of him for the first time since he'd arrived at Murdock House. He walked over to the ghost girl, and the two of them stood face-to-face, as close as they could get without actually touching, so as not to spoil the illusion. In the background, Happy was singing quietly.

"Where do I begin, to tell the story . . ."

"Shut up, Happy," said JC.

Melody looked up from her instruments and glowered at Kim. "You're late!"

"Of course I'm late," Kim said cheerfully. "I'm the late

Kim Sterling!" She smiled demurely at JC. "Sorry it took me so long to get here, darling. I came by the low road; but I took the scenic route."

"I'm not even going to ask," said JC.

"Best not to," Kim agreed.

JC lowered his voice. "More private work for the Boss?"

"Don't," said Kim, quietly. "Don't even go there."

"What?" said JC. "I'm not even allowed to ask?"

"No," said Kim. "Because it's safer that way, for both of us. I am doing this for us, remember? So we can be together? I can't go on like this, being a ghost. There's no future in it—for me, or for you. It's not only the . . . not being able to touch each other. You're going to grow old, JC, and I'm not. You're going to die and move on; and I won't be able to go with you."

"Ah!" said Melody. "That's interesting . . ."

They all turned to look at her, then drifted across the room to join her.

"What?" said Happy, slouching even more than usual. His eyes were bright, his complexion decidedly unhealthy. "What's *interesting*? Do I really want to know; and if so, is it headed my way? Should I be looking round for the nearest escape route? Can any of you hear a cloister bell ringing?"

"Steady," said JC.

"None of my instruments detected Kim approaching," said Melody. "And they should have. A ghost anywhere in the vicinity is one of the first things my machines are calibrated to look out for, above and beyond anything else. But Kim isn't showing up on any of my very special sensors. Proof, if proof were needed, that Something is very definitely screwing around with my machines. Hiding from us in plain sight, behind a manifested appearance of normality."

"I love it when she talks dirty," said Happy.

Kim looked carefully around her. "I don't see anything . . ."

"Neither do I!" said Happy. "And I am so buzzed right now, I should be able to see dust motes gang-banging each other."

"Concentrate on the voice recordings, Melody," said JC. "They're the only hard evidence we've got to work with. Have your machines digested them all yet?"

"Oh yes," said Melody. "Ages ago. Let's see. Hmmm . . ."

"Oh God," said Happy. "I hate it when she goes *Hmmm* . . . It's even worse than when she says *but* . . . What have you found now, Melody, and can I please hide behind you?"

"For once, I think I'm with Happy," said JC. "He may be a junkie and a paranoid depressive; but his self-preservation instincts are second to none."

"Thank you, JC," said Happy. "Nicest thing you've ever said about me."

"What have your computers found, Melody?" JC said patiently.

"They have been scrutinising the recordings with an intense scrute," said Melody. "Sifting through the voices, contrasting and comparing them, searching for anything that might help us understand their true nature. From the very first basic sounds, to the most recent conversations. And it seems they all have one thing in common. None of them have an identifiable source."

JC looked at Happy and Kim and saw they were no wiser than he. Somewhat encouraged that it wasn't just him, he cleared his throat meaningfully and fixed his attention on Melody.

"Could you be a little more specific, please?"

"I mean, my instruments can't tell where any of these voices are coming from!" Melody said loudly. "They're not coming in over the radio waves or through the phones. No microwave transmissions, no electromagnetics, nothing! I can't even tell which direction they're coming from or how far they had to travel to get here! Hold on; wait a minute, wait a minute . . . This can't be right. The latest recordings of incoming voices seem to suggest they simply . . . appeared, here, in Murdock House! This place is the source inasmuch as anything is . . ."

"I think it's well past time we listened to some of these recordings for ourselves," said JC. "Line them up, Melody. Start with the earliest, then bring us up to the Present. A basic sampling, touching all the bases, so we can get the flavour of what everyone else has been hearing."

"I'll go get us some popcorn," said Happy.

"You stay right where you are," said JC.

Melody's hands moved swiftly over her keyboards; and a staccato series of distorted sounds issued from the speakers built into her array. Everyone cocked their heads, frowning intently as they concentrated, trying to make sense of what they were hearing. Just sounds at first. Quick bursts of raw, brutal noise, emerging briefly from heavy, hissing static, like fierce animals appearing and disappearing in the jungle shadows. Harsh, jagged sounds that might have been words, or might not.

"It's like the man said," Happy volunteered after a while. "It's noise that our minds are trying to turn into words because that's how we're programmed. To see patterns in things, whether they're really there or not. Like the shapes we see in clouds."

"I'm not hearing any actual words, as such," JC said carefully. "How about you, Kim?"

"No," said the ghost girl, frowning prettily. "If there was anything there, I should be able to hear it. There's nothing like being dead to help you experience the world more clearly. Fewer distractions, you see, without a body to get in the way. But . . . I'm not getting anything. Unless you count an increasing sense of unease."

"Oh, I do," said Happy. "I really do. Wait . . . Are those animal noises? Grunts, growls, squeals? Like . . . gigantic hogs, being herded into a slaughter-house?"

"Almost certainly not," said JC.

"Could be animals," said Melody. "Could be human . . ."

Kim wrinkled her nose, her mouth a flat line of distaste. "Nasty. All hunger and appetite. Things dying and feasting . . ."

"I'm not sure we're really hearing anything specific," said JC. "Just our minds imposing shape and substance on raw data. Move on, Melody, to when actual words and voices start to appear."

Melody made the adjustment, and the raw sounds cut off as more recent recordings kicked in. The sounds issuing from the speakers became bursts of gibberish, screams and howls, interrupted by occasional sounds that almost made sense. Now and again a discernable human voice could be heard through the babble: shouted words, full of emotion and desperation. Everyone leaned in close, listening intently. *Lost . . . Run . . . Help . . . God!* And on and on . . . Kim shuddered, suddenly.

"How can you be cold?" said Happy. "You don't have a body!"

Kim hugged herself tightly. "I'm not cold. It's how the voices make me feel. Like someone is digging up my grave. It's not a single voice we're hearing; can you all hear that? It's lots of voices . . . all of them clear and distinct."

"To you, maybe," said JC.

"You've got better ears than the rest of us, Kim," said Melody. "I'll put my computers on it, run the recordings through some more filters . . ."

"I really can't tell," said JC. "Are you sure, Kim? How many voices are you hearing, exactly?"

"Men and women," Kim said doubtfully. "Too many to count. I don't like the way they sound, JC."

"Move on, Melody," said JC. "Give us something more recent that we can get our teeth into. Whole sentences, if you can."

"Way ahead of you," said Melody. "I already had the computers sort us out some of the clearer messages, from when the voices started talking to people on the air, in the middle of programmes. Listen . . ."

The speakers fell silent for a moment. Even the heavy static stopped. And then voices burst out of the speakers—shouting, howling, desperate to be heard. *Can you hear me? Can anyone hear me? It's taken everything we have to force a door open, to send this message back. You have to listen, while there's still time. You have to stop it . . . Kill it before it kills us all! There is flesh, and there is blood; there is horror, and there is death . . . It's awful here! It's coming; across all the worlds there are it's coming, following the trail you left, and, oh, it's so hungry!* There was a pause, then a single voice was heard. *JC? Can you hear me, JC?*

The speakers went silent. Melody cursed and stabbed at her keyboards with stiff fingers. JC glared at her.

"Get that back!"

"I'm trying!" said Melody, her hands flying from one keyboard to another. "I can't find the recordings! Something's hiding them from me! Work, you bastards!"

"It knew your name already," said Happy, looking at JC with wide, unblinking eyes. "How could it know your name, JC? How could it know you'd be here? We didn't know we'd be here until this morning!"

"It's all starting to make sense," said Kim. "It's like the message starts out unclear because it's coming from so far away. It gets clearer, more understandable, the closer it gets. Or the closer we get to it. From sounds to words to sentences."

"But where are these messages coming from?" said Happy, almost angrily. "You heard Melody; they appeared out of nowhere, here in the house!"

"What is it they want?" said JC. "What is it they're trying to warn us about?"

"Something from . . . Out There, is desperately trying to make contact with people here," said Melody, giving up on her computers for the moment. "Someone is trying to . . . prepare us for something awful that's heading our way."

"Sometimes . . . different people in the listening audience heard different things, from the same voices," Happy said slowly. "But that doesn't seem to be happening here, with us. Perhaps because . . . these messages, these warnings, are meant for us."

"But what does it mean?" said Kim. "I don't understand! What's the point of all this?"

"Find the rest of those recordings, Melody!" said JC. "We need more information, more data. Where are the rest of the voices?"

"I don't know! My computers can't find them . . ." Melody slammed both hands down hard on her keyboard in sheer frustration. "The recordings are definitely still in here, but . . . Something is preventing me from getting at them."

"Something, or Someone," said Kim.

"Perhaps. Maybe! I can't tell!"

"Maybe . . ." said Happy, "Something doesn't want us to hear the warnings. Something is suppressing the voices, like it suppressed your instruments' readings and my E.S.P. because it doesn't want us to know. Can't afford for us to know. Which does seem to suggest that this Something . . . is either responsible, or is going to be responsible for, all the bad shit those voices are trying to warn us about!"

"Can't you sense anything, See anything?" said JC. "Now you've got a whole medicine cabinet running through your veins?"

Happy thought for a while, looking off into the distance, at something only he could see. "I'm getting . . . something. It's all messed up. Give me a while."

"I don't think we have a while, Happy," JC said steadily. "Talk to me. What did you See upstairs?"

Happy stared coldly back at him. "What did you see, JC, out in the car park? Why is there blood on your jacket?"

The two men looked at each other, unflinchingly. Neither of them wanting to talk about what they'd experienced but knowing they had to. Kim looked from one to the other, confused.

"I've missed something, haven't I? Something important happened before I got here. What could have been so bad that you can't tell me about it? After everything we've seen and been through together, what could possibly be that bad?"

Melody said. "Why can't you tell us where the blood on your jacket came from, JC?"

"You're not hurt," said Kim. "So whose blood is that, JC?"

"Talk to us!" said Melody. "We're a team! We don't keep important information from each other!"

"Since when?" said JC.

Happy turned suddenly to look at Melody. "It was you, Mel. I saw you, at the top of the stairs. It was you, and you were dead, and worse than dead. Something killed you and changed you horribly; but it was still you . . . From the future."

Melody looked at him. It never even occurred to her to doubt or challenge what he was saying. She could see the truth, and the pain, in his face.

"What . . . What did I look like?"

"You already know," Happy said miserably. "It was the awful thing we saw outside, in the car park. The thing I thought I was protecting you from."

They all looked at him. Trying to come to terms with this new information.

"It was me," said JC. "I saw myself, out in the car park.

My future self. He came stumbling out of the front door—horribly wounded, blinded, dying. I held him in my arms as he collapsed. He couldn't see me, but he knew it was me because he remembered its happening from the first time around. When he was me. He died in my arms, clutching at the front of my jacket."

They all looked at the bloody handprint on the front of his white suit. Kim moved in close beside him, trying to comfort him with her presence. Happy and JC nodded slowly to each other and even managed a small smile.

"The shit we go through in the Ghost Finders," said JC.

"I keep telling you, we need to unionise," said Happy.

"That's it!" said Melody. "I get it now! I know where the voices are coming from! They're messages from the future . . . That's why I kept picking up tachyon radiations! That's why the voices seem to appear here, out of nowhere. That's why they started out so hard to hear and understand because they were so far off in the future. As they moved closer, or we drew closer to the Time they come from, the messages became more distinct. Dear God, what's going to happen, so that bad warnings had to be sent back through Time to prepare us?"

"There is no single future," JC said stubbornly. "Nothing we do is fixed, inevitable."

"Yes, well; you would say that, wouldn't you?" said Happy.

"There are multiple timelines," JC said. "Which future we end up in is determined by the choices we make now. We can still avoid the things we've seen! That's the whole point of what's happening here!"

"You really believe that?" said Melody.

"I have to," said JC.

They all stood very still for a while, looking at each other. Wondering what to do, what to say, for the best.

"The future can't be fixed, or there wouldn't be any point in warning us," JC said finally. "So there's some hope right there. Whoever it is that's sending us these warnings, they're trying to change things that are happening now, or are going to happen, to prevent their future from coming into existence. So we must be able to do something!"

"But what do these voices want us to do?" said Kim. "The messages don't make any sense!"

"Maybe because we're not close enough to the actual events, yet," said JC. "Or possibly we're not getting the whole message . . . I assume it will all become clear. In Time."

"Something is trying to stop us from doing anything," said Happy. "That's why it's been interfering with my E.S.P. and Melody's machines. It must be afraid of something we can do . . ."

"Is this Something here, in the room with us now?" said Melody. "If it is, maybe my scanners can find it. Come on, babies, work for Mommy."

She set to work.

"Happy," said JC. "Can you See anything here, in this room?"

He looked around, turning slowly. "No . . . My E.S.P. is coming back, now I've supercharged my system, but I'm not running on all cylinders yet."

"I can't see anything," said Kim. "But this room hasn't felt right since I got here."

"Damn right," said Happy.

They all jumped and looked round sharply, as the door

at the back of the reception area slammed open, and Jonathan came hurrying in. He started to say something, then stopped to look at Kim. She gave him her best dazzling smile.

"A colleague of ours," JC said smoothly. "Kim Sterling. She knows more about ghosts than any of us."

"Hi!" said Kim.

Jonathan smiled at her, bowled over by her charm, like everyone else. He started towards her, extending a hand for her to shake.

"She doesn't like to be touched," JC said quickly.

"Ah, of course," said Jonathan, dropping his hand. "Listen! I came back down here because something has happened! Tom was taken short and had to nip out for an urgent bathroom break, so Captain Sunshine went back on the air to cover for him until Felicity appeared for her show. He was chatting away, minding the store, when the phone started ringing. He answered; and it was one of the voices! He's talking to it right now!"

"Melody!" said JC.

"On it!" She linked her speakers with the station's broadcast again, so they could all hear what was happening. Captain Sunshine's voice floated out into the reception area, calm and steady and reassuring.

"Take it easy, man. Be cool; the Captain is right here with you. I'm not going anywhere. Tell me what you need . . ."

A voice broke in the moment he paused, screaming desperately. Harsh and broken, full of unbearable pain and horror.

Get out of there! Oh God, please listen to me; get the hell out of there!

"Why, man?" said Captain Sunshine. "What's so important?"

You're all going to die . . . You're going to see everyone you know and care for die . . . Again and again . . . You don't want to die, Malcolm. It's horrible, here.

"How do you know my name?" asked the Captain. He sounded honestly shaken for the first time. "It's been years since anyone . . . Hello? Hello? Are you still there?"

"None of this is coming through the phones," Melody said quietly. "Still no source."

"We know where it's coming from," said Happy. "Or rather, we know when it's coming from."

"Do we have tachyons?" said JC.

"Spiking and bursting all over the place," said Melody. "As though a door is opening, then closing, again and again . . ."

Jonathan looked at Kim. "Did any of that mean anything to you?"

"Not a thing," Kim said innocently.

"Oh good," said Jonathan. "I'm glad it's not only me . . ."

The voice started shouting incoherently, interrupted by bursts of sobbing; a heart-breaking sound. And then it cut off abruptly, leaving the Captain talking to dead air. He tried to encourage the voice to return, but there was no response. The Captain put on Leonard Cohen's "Hallelujah." Melody shut down the speakers.

"Was that it?" JC said to Jonathan. "Was that the kind of thing you people have been hearing all this time?"

"Pretty much," said Jonathan. His face was pale. "Spooky; isn't it? Makes my hair stand on end, every time . . . That one was actually more coherent than most.

Made a kind of sense. Wanting us all to get the hell out of Dodge, before . . . Something."

Happy frowned. "That voice . . . sounded almost familiar. I'm sure I know it, from somewhere . . ."

"I thought that!" said Melody.

"Whoever it was, they sounded so sad," said Kim. "Wanting so much to save us . . ."

"Sally said she heard someone sobbing in here, earlier," said Melody. "Crying like their heart would break. I couldn't hear it. Do you suppose . . . some of these warnings are targeted to specific listeners? Which is why JC and Happy saw . . . what they saw."

"Why only some of us?" said Happy. "I mean, if we're all in danger . . . I still think Something's playing with us."

"If it is, it isn't always succeeding," JC said quickly. "Some of the warnings are getting through. That has to be a good thing. It proves this Something isn't as powerful as it would like us to believe. Which means it can be beaten."

"Bit of a stretch there, JC," Melody said carefully.

"I'm on a roll!" said JC. "Go with the flow . . ."

Kim beamed at Jonathan. "Isn't he marvellous? That's why he's our leader, you know. And not at all because we all voted, and he lost."

"Where's Sally?" said Jonathan, looking round the reception area. "She's not on another break already, is she?"

"She's outside, communing with the gardens," said Melody. "Want me to call her back in?"

"Oh hell," said Jonathan. "Leave the poor girl be. She's really quite highly strung, despite her . . . persona. She'll come back in when she's ready. I suppose it's just as well she wasn't here, to listen to . . . all that. She can get really upset when the crazy stuff starts happening."

"How very sensible," said Happy.

"The Captain didn't sound particularly freaked-out," observed Melody.

"He takes it all in his stride," said Jonathan. "Not much gets to him. It probably helps he doesn't think any of what's happening is real. But, then, he doesn't think much of anything is really real—not after everything he's put in his system down the years."

"I have got to get me some of what he's on," said Happy.

And then he stopped short, and his head came up, like a hound that's suddenly caught a scent. He moved away from Melody and her instruments, looking quickly around the room. Everyone else looked, too; but nothing obvious was happening. JC turned to Melody. She studied her sensors and shook her head.

"We are not alone here," Happy said quietly. "Something is in this room with us."

"Your E.S.P. is back?" said JC.

"Some of it," said Happy. "Enough . . . My mind is so expanded now, I can hear shadows banging together. I am so sharp, I could cut a sunbeam in half. And I am quite definitely Seeing something, out of the corner of my mind's eye."

Jonathan watched Happy move around the room, tracking something only he could follow. The station manager eased in beside JC, not taking his eyes off Happy.

"Is he a medium?"

"Oh, he's so much more than that," said Melody.

"Happy is our team telepath and tame mental marvel," said JC. "Talk to us, Happy! Describe what you're Seeing."

Happy walked slowly round the perimeter of the reception area, turning his head slowly this way and that. He was smiling—a cold, disturbing smile.

"I think . . . Either it's letting me catch glimpses of it, to try and scare me off . . . Or it's finally losing control of the situation, now we know it's here. Or, possibly, something or someone else is fighting the Something, to allow me to See it."

"Yes . . ." said JC. "Lots of interesting options there, Happy; but what it is you're Seeing?"

"Hush," said the telepath. "I'm trying to focus."

JC looked to Melody, standing helplessly before her tech, unable to assist Happy. She glared quickly from one monitor screen to another, then leaned forward abruptly.

"What?" JC said quietly.

"Major cold spot developing, JC. It's the size of this room! We are talking a massive energy sink. Something from Outside our world is draining all the energy out of this room, so it can manifest. If my machines weren't so thoroughly shielded, they'd be dead in the water by now. And I'm not sure how long even they can hold out against an energy drain this big . . ."

"Happy!" said JC. "Talk to me!"

"Faces!" said Happy, not looking round. "Screaming faces! So many of them . . . So many people dying! It's like the end of the world . . . Listening to them hurts so much . . . They're in so much pain, JC! Dying again and again . . ."

Then, to everyone's surprise, including Happy's, he channelled what he was Seeing, so everyone else could see it, too. He thrust the vision out of his head and into theirs; and the reception area vanished. Replaced by a whole new world. A terrible, horrible Other Place. They were still standing together; but everything else had changed. The sky was on fire. It was raining blood. The air stank of brimstone and sour milk, spilled blood and rotting flesh, curdling in their lungs. Voices screamed and howled all around them. Something huge beyond bearing came striding towards them, the ground shaking with every step. And then the vision snapped off; and they were all back in the reception area again.

Happy collapsed. Legs bending, eyes rolling up in his head, all his strength gone. Melody came sprinting out from behind her machines and was there to catch him as he fell. She lowered him carefully to the floor and sat there with him, holding him tightly to her. Murmuring reassuringly in his ear. Jonathan looked like he wanted to be sick. He staggered over to the reception desk and sat down behind it, shaking and shuddering. JC turned to Kim and had to swallow hard before he could speak.

"Did you see that, too? Did you hear that?"

"Yes! All of it . . . Where was that, JC? What was that place?"

"I think it's more when was that place," said JC. "That was a vision of things to come, of the future we're being warned about."

Jonathan made a low, distressed sound. His face was deathly pale, and his eyes were wild. He stared at the Ghost Finders, as though seeing them clearly for the first time.

"This is what you deal with all the time? How do you stand it? Who are you; what are you? *How was all that even possible?*"

"Steady," said JC, not unkindly. "Breathe . . . You've

had your first experience of the larger world. Takes some getting used to. Try not to think about it. I find that helps a lot. If it doesn't, feel free to ask Happy for some of his special little helpers."

Happy was back in control again. He nodded weakly to Melody, and she helped him back onto his feet. She didn't let go of him.

"Talk to me, Happy," said JC. "Did you get a sense of how far into the future that was? How long we've got, before our world turns into that?"

"Hard to be sure," said Happy. "Time . . . is all messed up, here." He turned suddenly to Jonathan. "That . . . was what your voices have been warning you about. No wonder they sounded so desperate . . ."

JC looked steadily at Happy. "You've never been able to share visions before."

"I've never been here before," said Happy. "Something wanted us to see that. Though whether it was the good guys or the bad guys . . . Take your pick. Could have been a warning or Something taunting us. All we can be sure of is that a terrible future is heading our way, at speed."

"Coming here? Right here? To this radio station?" said JC.

"Coming everywhere," Happy said steadily. "That really was the end of the world, JC. Our world, overwhelmed and replaced by the working conditions of another reality. The end of everything, or at least, everything we know and understand."

"But how long have we got?" said JC. "When does this happen?"

"Tomorrow," said Happy.

# SIX

## IT'S MY TURN

*"Tomorrow?"* Jonathan said loudly. "The whole damned world is going to end, tomorrow? *Really?"*

"Well, not necessarily," said Happy. "It could be later tonight . . . you have to allow for a certain amount of lee-way in these things . . ."

"Yes, yes; I get it!" Jonathan looked very upset. His eyes swept this way and that, and his hands clenched into fists at his sides, as though searching for someone to hit. JC understood how he felt. But, he was supposed to be the one in charge, so . . .

"It's all right, Jonathan," he said soothingly. "We can deal with this. It's only another deadline. We can do dead-lines."

Jonathan spun round and glared at JC. "Are you kid-ding me? I called you here to deal with a few spooky voices; and now one of your people looks me straight in the eye and says the world is going to end!"

"Not necessarily," said JC. "Not if we have anything to do with it. And we do. In situations like this, it's always important to pay attention to the small print. Look hard enough, and you can usually find a way out of anything. That's what we do. It's our job to deal with impossible situations; and we're very good at it."

"Mostly," said Happy.

JC gave him a hard look. "Really not helping, Happy."

"We could always take off and nuke the place from orbit," said Melody.

"Really not helping, Melody."

And then they all broke off and looked round sharply as one of the phones on the reception desk started to ring. Everyone stayed where they were, standing very still, partly because no-one wanted to draw attention to themselves and partly because everyone wanted someone else to answer it. The phone rang on and on, relentlessly, until finally JC strode over to the desk and snatched up the receiver.

"Hello?" he said. "Is this room service? I'd like to order a room . . ."

And then he stopped, listened for a moment, and turned to Jonathan, holding the phone out to him.

"Ah, Jonathan . . . It's for you."

The station manager came forward and gingerly took the receiver from JC. He put it carefully to his ear, as though afraid it might try to bite him, started to say something, then stood there and listened. They all saw the tension go out of him as he nodded several times, and said *All right* and *Yes, I understand*. And then he looked across at the Ghost Finders, almost apologetically.

"It's Felicity, from upstairs. She's in the studio, ready

to begin her show with its much-trailed and anticipated interview with the famous Ghost Finders, and she wants to know where the hell you all are, as she can't do the interview without you. There is more to the message, but I don't like to use language like that. Can I tell her you'll be right up? Please?"

"Oh sure," said JC. "I think we could all do with a little pleasant distraction."

Jonathan looked at him. "You've never heard Felicity skewer a guest in one of her interviews, have you? She performs interviews the way other people perform autopsies. If she's this keen to make a start, it can only be because she thinks she's got something she can use to nail you."

"We can look after ourselves," said JC.

"On your own heads be it," said Jonathan. He muttered briefly into the phone and replaced the receiver. He then moved quickly away from the desk, clearly worried one of the other phones might ring if he stayed too close for too long. Happy cleared his throat loudly.

"You don't need me for the interview, do you, JC? Really? You can speak for the Ghost Finders; you always give good public relations. You know all the right things to say. And you have, after all, been known to say, on many occasions, that I have very limited people skills."

"That is not what I say," JC said sternly. "I say that you have very distressing people skills, an uncanny ability to snatch defeat from the jaws of victory by saying exactly the wrong thing, and that in any public setting that involves up-close interaction with the public, you are a complete bloody liability."

"That does sound familiar," said Melody.

"Well, yes," said Happy. "I was paraphrasing. And I can't help but feel, JC, that you have made my point for me."

"If he doesn't have to do it, I don't have to do it!" said Melody, scowling fiercely. "People never want to hear what I have to say."

"He does have to do it, and so do you," JC said firmly. "Firstly, because we need to present a united front in the face of the enemy, which in this case might be Felicity Legrand or her audience or both; and secondly, this interview isn't about answering her questions. It's about reassuring and calming down the listening audience before they experience one shock too many and have one big collective coronary. So you, Melody, will baffle them with scientific bullshit, while I say calm, soothing, and possibly entirely misleading things. You, Happy, will sit quietly at the back and say *nothing*; because I want you ready to jump into action if one of the unnatural voices crashes the show. The recordings are interesting, but you can't talk back to a recording. I need to be sure these voices really are what we think they are."

"Suddenly I'm a ghostly lie-detector?" said Happy.

"Yes," said JC.

"Cool!" said Happy.

"Can I bring some of my equipment with me?" said Melody.

"No," said JC.

"How about my gun?"

"No!" said JC.

"I don't do radio interviews," said Kim. "I am a very private person; and I'm not even sure they'd be able to hear me."

"I know," said JC. "I don't like the idea of all of us cooped up in one place, anyway. You can sit this one out."

Jonathan looked confused. "Why wouldn't they be able to hear her? We have the very best equipment . . ."

JC smiled reassuringly at him. "It's a copyright thing."

Jonathan nodded slowly, pretending he understood because he could tell he probably wouldn't understand the real answer, even if it was explained to him. And that if he did, he almost certainly wouldn't like it. He pushed the thought aside, so he could concentrate on things he did understand. Like Felicity Legrand seething impatiently alone in her studio. He gave JC his best meaningful stare.

"You need to understand, JC, Felicity is renowned for the toughness and . . . thoroughness of her interviews. She does lots of research, digs up all the dirt, and never allows herself to be side-tracked from what she believes are the important questions. She reduced our local Member of Parliament to tears. Most popular show we've ever done. All she has to do is sense weakness, or blood in the water, and she'll go for the throat every time. But even so, JC, *I need you to go easy on her*. What's left of our listening audience adores Felicity Legrand. Can't get enough of her. She's the only reason we've still got anyone listening to us on a regular basis."

"Don't worry," said JC. "We've been trained to deal with worse things than her. We'll be very polite, and evasive, and Happy will quite definitely watch his language. Won't you, Happy?"

Happy nodded reassuringly to Jonathan. "You can rely on me. My Tourette's syndrome isn't anywhere near as bad as it used to be."

"Oh God," said Jonathan.

Melody stood in front of her machines, her arms folded firmly, her chin jutting forward. "I am not going anywhere until Sally gets back. I want her here, keeping a watchful eye on my machines while I'm away. I am not leaving them unprotected."

"You honestly think someone might walk in here and steal them?" said Jonathan.

"This doesn't strike me as one of the most secure locations I've worked in if I'm honest," said Melody. "No security staff, not even a doorman . . . My instruments have all been very carefully calibrated for maximum efficiency. I don't want anyone messing with them . . ."

"Couldn't Kim . . . ?" said Jonathan.

"No, Kim couldn't," Kim said firmly. "Machines and I do not get along. I think they're scared of me."

Jonathan looked very much as though he wanted to say something in response to that but decided against it. He knew there was more to Kim than met the eye and had a strong suspicion he didn't want to know what it was. JC gave the station manager one of his best winning smiles, and Jonathan sighed loudly. He walked over to the front door, opened it, stuck his head out, and yelled for the station's receptionist at the top of his voice.

"Sally! Get back in here! You're needed!"

There was a pause, then Jonathan backed quickly away from the open door as Sally came striding in, shoving her pierced and painted face right into his. She backed him all the way across the reception area, not even trying to hide her extreme displeasure. She drove Jonathan all the way back to the reception desk through sheer force of personality, battering him unmercifully with her raised voice.

"Don't you shout at me, Jonathan Hardy! You do not pay me enough to get to shout at me! And even if you did, I still wouldn't put up with it! Now what the hell is so important that you had to interrupt my very important private time, communing with nature and hiding from the weird shit? Have you forgotten your computer password again?" She realised she'd got him pressed up against the reception desk, and there was nowhere left for him to go, so she turned abruptly away to glare at the Ghost Finders. "Something happened here while I was gone, didn't it? I can feel it tingling in my piercings. Like someone else was here and only just stepped out. And maybe hasn't left completely . . ."

"Are you sure you're not psychic?" said Happy.

"It's all right, Sally," JC said quickly. "If something did happen, it's over. It's perfectly safe in here now."

"You're wrong," said Sally. "It's never safe in here."

"Everything's fine," JC said firmly. He looked across at Happy. "You tell her . . ."

"I will if you like," said Happy, "but you know I can never lie convincingly."

"I can feel another break coming on," Sally said loudly. "Listen! The back garden is calling to me . . ."

"I need you to stay here," said Melody. "Keep a close watch on my machines, while the rest of us are upstairs being interviewed by Felicity. You don't have to do anything except raise the alarm if anyone even looks at my stuff wrong. Don't worry; the machines will protect you."

Sally smiled, slowly. It wasn't a particularly pleasant smile. "You're going to be interviewed by Ms. Smug Bitch Scary Trousers Legrand? Okay; I think I will hang around, so I can listen in on the reception speakers. I could use a good laugh. But if I even see a shadow twitch, I am out of here, and the machines are on their own."

She stomped around the desk and sat down hard in her chair. She tugged moodily at one of the larger piercings in her right eyebrow and glared at the phones set out before her, as though daring them to ring. And then she reached out, picked up all the receivers one at a time, and slammed them all down on the desk-top. She glared at Jonathan.

"Screw the regulations. I have my nerves to think of. Anyone wants to talk to the station, they can send us an e-mail. It's so much easier to officially ignore an e-mail."

She waited for Jonathan to argue with her and seemed a little surprised when he didn't. He nodded tiredly, in a resigned sort of way, and turned to the waiting Ghost Finders.

"Can we please go upstairs now? Felicity will be getting really impatient; and I hate it when she throws things."

"I'll stay down here with you, Sally," said Kim. "Keep you company. We can have a nice little chat and a gossip— all girls together."

Sally looked at her suspiciously, clearly trying to figure out why she hadn't noticed Kim before. "Who are you? And where did you come from?"

"I am Kim Sterling, and I am from London. I am a Ghost Finder! What I don't know about ghosts isn't worth knowing and would probably only upset you anyway."

"You're with them?" said Sally. "But you look so . . . normal!"

"It's a gift," said Kim.

"You're not really normal?"

"Not even close."

"Good!" said Sally. "Because neither am I!"

Kim and Sally grinned at each other.

"You two play nicely," said JC. "Hold the fort, don't speak to any strange spirits, we won't be gone long." He looked at Kim. "You're going to talk about me behind my back once I'm gone, aren't you?"

"Of course, sweetie!" said Kim. "Don't worry. I'm sure I'll find something nice to say about you. Eventually . . ."

Jonathan gestured at the rear door, imploringly, and JC gathered up Happy and Melody with his gaze. They all followed Jonathan to the back of the room, some more willingly than the others. Melody walked arm in arm with Happy in case he looked like bolting. As Jonathan held the rear door open for them, JC moved in close on Melody's other side, so he could murmur in her ear.

"Since when do your machines need looking after? I understood them to be heavily armed, and quite capable of defending themselves?"

"They are," said Melody. "I wanted Sally back inside so the machines could look after her. I don't think it's safe for anyone to be on their own in this place, inside or out."

"Kim's here," said JC.

"Kim can't touch anyone," said Melody. "Whereas my machines can. Suddenly and violently and with extreme prejudice."

"Fair enough," said JC.

::::::::::::::::::::::::

They all went up the back stairs to the next floor. Jonathan led the way, staring firmly straight ahead. He stamped his feet down hard on every wooden step, making a lot of noise, as though to ensure that everyone knew he was coming. When they reached the top of the stairs and stepped out onto the landing, Happy pulled his arm free from Melody and hung back, looking quickly around him. Melody stuck close, watching him carefully, knowing better than to try to touch him.

"Do you . . . See anything, Happy?"

"No," he said.

"Is this where you saw . . . the other me? The future me?"

"Yes. You were dead but still suffering. Monstrous, but still you. You said my name and I recognised you. Even in that awful state, I knew you." He looked at her, holding her gaze with his. "I need you to trust me, Mel. I swear I won't let that happen to you. I will do whatever it takes. I will put my life on the line for you. I will put my death on the line . . ."

"Hush," said Melody. "Hush. I know that; I've always known that. We're going to get through this, together; and neither of us is going to die. You need to trust me on that."

They managed a small smile for each other. It was hard to tell who was comforting whom.

A little further down the landing, JC cleared his throat, and Happy and Melody followed him and Jonathan along the landing to studio one, where Captain Sunshine was standing outside the closed door, talking quietly with Tom Foreman. They looked round sharply as they heard the others approaching, then relaxed a little as they saw who it was. The Captain looked more interested than nervous. Tom looked tired and jumpy and not at all happy to be there. He nodded quickly to Jonathan.

"I was saying how sorry I was, to the Captain. About

leaving him alone in the studio, to be ambushed by that voice on the phone."

"No problemo, kemo sabe," said Captain Sunshine. "That spooky shit doesn't bother me."

JC studied Tom openly. Of everyone he'd met at the radio station, Tom seemed the most honestly scared. JC wondered if perhaps Tom didn't want to be alone in the studio for the same reason that Sally didn't like to be alone in the reception area. Because they could both feel things they couldn't put into words . . . A thought struck JC, and he stepped forward to face Tom.

"Pardon me for asking, but I thought you were supposed to be doing your broadcast from the other studio? What were you doing in studio one, anyway?"

Tom looked down at his feet before looking up to meet JC's gaze.

"Normally we keep both studios going, so that if there's a problem, one can cover the air for the other," he said quietly. "But something's gone wrong with the equipment in studio two. Again. I've done everything I can with it, Jon. You know I have. It's like the bloody tech doesn't want to work."

"Easy, Tom, easy," said Captain Sunshine, cutting in before Jonathan could say anything, and giving the station manager a warning glance. "Everything's cool, we get it. We really do. Nothing that's happening here is your fault. Is anybody's fault."

Tom didn't say anything. He didn't have to. Jonathan sighed and shrugged briefly.

"You can all share the same studio, Tom. If that'll make things easier . . ."

"Always a warm seat," the Captain said calmly. "There

is strength in togetherness, people. Am I right, or am I right?"

Tom managed the beginnings of a smile. "Sometimes, you can be a bit too understanding, you know that?"

"Yes," said the Captain. "I know that."

He produced a thick spliff from somewhere, stuck it in the corner of his mouth, and lit the twisted end with a battered old Zippo. He took a good puff and filled the air with aromatic smoke. He put the Zippo away again and smiled serenely about him. Happy started to move towards the Captain. Melody pulled him back.

"I need you and the Captain to stick around for a while," Jonathan said to Tom. "We'll be shutting the station down early tonight, right after Felicity has finished her show. Apparently, Mr. Chance here feels the need for a group discussion, about . . . recent events."

"Sure," said the Captain. "Suits me."

Tom didn't look at all pleased but finally nodded briefly. "All right. But I won't stay long. Not here. Not after it starts getting dark."

"Come on, Tom," Jonathan said urgently. "Talking things through, making sense of things, is exactly what we need. Something to settle our nerves. Mr. Chance promised me he'll provide us with some answers, at last."

"You think answers are going to help?" Tom said angrily. "I don't need to know what's going on! I don't need to know what's behind all this weird shit! I've had enough . . . I won't spend one more night in this house. No, Jon! Don't say anything! I don't care any more. The moment this discussion is finished, I am leaving, getting in my car, and driving to the nearest hotel. It's been so long since I had a good night's sleep . . ."

"What about your things?" said Jonathan.

"I'll send for them," said Tom. He looked defiantly at Jonathan. "I stuck it out here because you asked me to. I supported you, for as long as I could . . . You know I have! But I can't do it any more. I have to get out of here, while I still can."

He broke off, abruptly. Everyone could see he was on the edge of tears; and he didn't want to let himself down in front of everyone. The Captain gave his shoulder a friendly squeeze.

"Let's go downstairs, brother. We can always go for a stroll round the gardens. I like gardens. Flowers are righteous, man . . ."

He gently steered Tom down the landing towards the stairs, keeping up a soothing level of casual conversation along the way. Tom didn't say anything. Jonathan watched them go; and he didn't say anything either. He opened the door to studio one and ushered the Ghost Finders in. They lined up in the outer room, before the separating window, to watch Felicity Legrand at work. She was swivelling impatiently back and forth in her chair, before her microphone, with one of the Captain's records playing to fill air time—the Judy Collins cover of "Both Sides Now." Jonathan knocked on the separating glass, and Felicity immediately sat up straight and looked round. She glared at the Ghost Finders and gestured urgently for them to come in and join her. Jonathan opened the door to the inner room and stepped back. JC strode past him with all his usual bravado, smiling easily at Felicity Legrand. Happy and Melody brought up the rear.

Felicity smiled at each Ghost Finder in turn; and it was a cold, professional thing. A predator's smile. She gestured for them to sit down facing her, on the other side of the table. A second microphone had been set up there, one for all three of them. JC sat down facing the mike, with Happy on one side and Melody on the other. Jonathan hovered in the doorway.

"Well, unless you need me for anything . . ."

"Go," said Felicity, without even looking at him. "I've got everything I need, right here."

"I could stay and . . ."

"Go!"

JC grinned easily at Jonathan. "You run along. Join the others, downstairs. Play count-the-piercings with Sally. We'll be fine."

"I can take a hint," said Jonathan.

He left, almost but not quite slamming the door behind him. JC watched him leave the studio, then gave his full attention to Felicity. She smiled at him, and he smiled at her. Big, meaningless, professional smiles. Like two gladiators sizing each other up in the arena. Melody sat slumped in her chair, her arms folded, scowling glumly at Felicity over the top of her glasses. Happy peered around him in a vague and unfocused sort of way. Felicity considered him, thoughtfully.

"Happy Jack Palmer . . . that is what they call you, isn't it? My, what big pupils you have . . ."

"You should see them from this side," said Happy. "All the better to see things no sane person would want to see . . . It's a man's life, being a telepath in the Ghost Finders. I don't recommend it."

"I can't believe you've had the nerve to turn up to a live radio interview, stoned out of your skull," said Felicity.

"Don't go there," said JC.

Felicity immediately stabbed him with her cold glare. "Why not? I never agreed to anything being off-limits in this interview."

"Play nicely," said JC. "Or I'll throw Melody at you."

"And I will kick your bony arse all around the studio," said Melody. "Live, on-air."

Felicity looked at her, then looked away. She knew a genuine threat when she heard one. She made a great show of checking through the big pile of notes set out on the table before her. JC sniffed loudly.

"Notes are rarely a good thing," he said. "They speak of preconceptions. And ambushes."

"Just doing my job," said Felicity. "I am, after all, a professional."

The Judy Collins song came to an end, and Felicity quickly worked the control panel before her with one hand while removing the needle from the old single with the other. She then leaned forward to address her audience; and her voice changed to its on-air persona. Warm and friendly and inviting.

"Hello, everyone, this is Felicity Legrand, welcoming you all to the *Felicity Legrand Hour*. Cheerful chat and casual conversation, about all the important and interesting aspects of the day. Stay tuned for a very special show! We are fortunate to have with us today, right here in the studio, three of those amazing and very mysterious people, the Ghost Finders. JC Chance, Melody Chambers, and Happy Jack Palmer. They have agreed to be interviewed about all

the strange things that have been occurring here, at Radio
Free Albion. Mr. Chance is a very handsome young fellow
who never removes his sunglasses. Ms. Chambers is the
self-confessed girl science geek of the team. And last, but
in no way least interesting, the supposed telepath, Happy
Jack. Why do they call you Happy, Jack?"

"Because I'm so cheerful," growled Happy. "Smell the
irony . . ."

"Moving on," Felicity said smoothly. "Let's start with
the team leader himself, JC Chance. You don't really expect my listeners to believe that you're all experts in the
supernatural, do you?"

"No," said JC.

Felicity blinked, caught off guard. She looked briefly at
her notes for confirmation and support, then pressed on.
"Then, why . . . ?"

"It doesn't matter what you or your listeners believe,"
said JC. "We are here to do a job. And part of that job is
to protect and reassure the innocent bystanders. If it helps
you to think we know what we're doing; all the better. But
we really don't care whether people believe we're sav-
iours or frauds or showmen as long as you stay out of our
way while we're working. Let us get on with what we
have to do. We're here to help; settle for that."

"I am interviewing you to inform my audience," said
Felicity. "I'm only interested in the truth."

"You couldn't handle the truth if we hit you over the
head with it," said Melody. "The truth is a slippery beggar,
when it comes to the hidden world. Science can help pin
down the corners, but there's still a lot we don't understand.
May never understand. The world is not only stranger than
we imagine, it's stranger than we can imagine. Yes, yes, I

know, JC, play nice. I will if she will. Look at her, hunched over before her mike like a praying mantis, looking for something to leap on. She's already made up her mind about what the truth is."

"There's a reason why we don't let you do public relations," JC murmured. He smiled easily at Felicity. "You must excuse Melody; she's just being herself. Do feel free to ask me anything you want."

"I will," said Felicity, matching his smile with her own.

"And I will feel free to tell the truth, or lie, or make shit up, as I please," said JC. "It comes with the job."

"Oh, this can only go well," said Happy.

He got up out of his chair and wandered around the cramped studio, peering closely at things and running his hands over them. As though he wasn't entirely sure where he was or whether any of it was really real. Melody got up and went after him. She took Happy firmly by the arm and led him back to his chair. She sat him down, with enough emphasis to make it clear she meant it, then took her own seat again. While all this was going on, Felicity kept her attention fixed only on JC, throwing one question after another at him. He answered them all easily enough, sitting calm and relaxed in his chair, apparently unmoved by any of it.

"Welcome to the Felicity Legrand interview," Felicity said to her audience again, after the two of them had duelled each other to a standstill. "Where we always get to the bottom of things, no matter how deep we have to dig. For those of you who came in late, we are talking with JC Chance, Ghost-Buster."

"Ghost Finder, Felicity," said JC. "There's a difference. We're real."

"And they're copyrighted," said Happy,

"You still haven't answered my most basic question, JC," said Felicity. "Are you and your people really experts in the supernatural?"

"Inasmuch as anyone is, I suppose so," said JC.

"That's an interesting qualification, JC," said Felicity.

"Simply trying to be accurate," said JC.

"Do you honestly believe in ghosts?" said Felicity, with the air of someone going in for the kill.

"Believe in them?" said JC. "Hell, I'm sleeping with one!"

"It's true," said Melody. "He is. And if that freaks you out, think how we feel. We have to work with them."

"It'll all end in tears," said Happy.

"And, how is she?" said Felicity. "This . . . ghostly girl-friend of yours?"

"Very spirited," said JC.

Felicity grimaced, suspecting, quite rightly, that she was being set up for any number of ghost jokes and para-normal puns. She pressed gamely on.

"Let's talk about the voices, JC."

"Of course, Felicity. How long have you been hearing them? Do they tell you to do things? Naughty things?"

"I mean the voices all the staff here have been hearing! And the listeners! The voices that have been breaking in on our programmes!"

"Fine," said JC. "Let's talk about those voices. They are why we're here, after all."

"I don't suppose there's anyone left in our audience who doesn't know that Radio Free Albion has been plagued with . . . disturbing interruptions," said Felicity. "Unidentified voices, supposedly trying to warn us about some forthcoming catastrophe. Some of our listeners claim to have recognised some of these voices . . . as deceased and departed members of their families. Voices of the dead, in fact. What would you say to that, JC?"

"It's nothing to worry about," JC said smoothly. "In cases like this, it usually turns out to be something we call Electronic Voice Phenomena. Nothing more than auditory illusions. It'll all be over soon."

"What will all be over soon?" said Felicity.

"Everything," said Happy.

There was something in his voice . . . Felicity looked at him sharply; but one look into his eyes was enough to convince her she wasn't going to get anything useful out of him. She turned her attention back to JC, shuffling quickly through the papers set out before her. Like a gambler checking her hand to make sure the aces were still there.

"Now, JC, I am given to understand that you and your fellow team members work for that renowned, powerful, and yet very secretive organisation, the Carnacki Institute. Is that correct?"

JC leaned forward, for the first time. "What makes you think that, Felicity?"

She smiled triumphantly. "I did my homework on you, and your people, the moment the station manager told me you were on your way. I like to be prepared . . ."

"Interesting," said JC. "Given that Jonathan didn't know who they'd be sending. We didn't even know we were coming here until early this morning."

Felicity's smile wavered, and she looked uncertain for the first time. "Let's not evade the question, JC. Do you work for the Carnacki Institute?"

"Yes," said JC. "It is an honour and a privilege to serve,

and we were not in any way blackmailed into joining up. Not at all."

"What can you tell our curious listeners about this very private and clandestine organisation?"

"Not a lot," said JC.

"We could tell you," said Happy. "But then we'd have to haunt you."

Melody rocked with silent laughter, and she and Happy shared a high five behind JC's back.

"Ghost Finder humour," said JC. "The Carnacki Institute is basically a clearing-house for gathering and investigating information on all things supernatural, paranormal, and downright disturbing. It's a Ghost Finder's job to investigate the situation, interview everyone concerned, and do our best to figure out what's going on. Most of these situations turn out to have perfectly ordinary and reasonable explanations and outcomes."

"And the ones that don't?" said Felicity.

"Then I hit them really hard with the science stick until they stop bothering people," said Melody.

"What about those people who say the Carnacki Institute is nothing but a front for a far more insidious organisation?" said Felicity. "One that is answerable to no-one and follows its own rules and its own agenda?"

"What about them?" said JC. "Who are these people, exactly? And why are they saying these things?"

Felicity started to press the question, then stopped as Happy suddenly leaned forward across the table to interrupt her, staring unblinkingly into her eyes. He suddenly looked very focused and very dangerous.

"She doesn't know, JC," he said. "She doesn't know

who these people are or where her information comes from."

"What . . . ?" said Felicity. She tried to carry on, but couldn't, her gaze held helplessly by his.

"She doesn't know who told her these things," said Happy. "And it's never occurred to her till now to question that. And the fact that she now realises she didn't is scaring the hell out of her. Look at her notes, JC. There's nothing on those pages about us. They're everyday stuff: running times and schedules. Everything she's saying . . . is coming out of her head."

"Stop it!" said Felicity. "How do you know . . . What are you doing? What are you talking about?"

"Someone is using her," said Happy. "To take shots at the Institute."

"Interesting," said JC. "What are you talking about, Felicity? Who wants you to ask these particular questions?"

"This is a trick!" said Felicity, spitting the words at him. "You're playing games with me!"

"Someone is," said JC.

"Has Something got to her?" said Melody, leaning forward across the table to look Felicity over carefully. "She seems normal enough . . . I wish you'd let me bring some of my equipment, JC, so I could run some proper tests on her. See if there's anyone else inside her head apart from her."

"Someone knew we were going to be here before we did," said JC. "Which suggests that Felicity's information came from inside the Institute. The Boss was right—someone high up is briefing against her. We did wonder whether this case might be some kind of trap, bait to lure us in . . . Now I'm wondering whether this is the trap. This interview. Designed to distract us and make us reveal things the public isn't supposed to know. Only the situation here turned out to be far stranger, and more dangerous, than anyone suspected."

"What are you talking about?" whispered Felicity.

"Forget the questions, Felicity," said JC, not unkindly. "They're not your questions anyway. You're being used."

"No I'm not! This is my show! No-one's in charge of me but me!"

Her voice rose sharply, almost hysterically.

"Then where did you get your ammunition from, Felicity?" said JC. "Why are your notes not what you thought they were? Who first mentioned the Carnacki Institute to you?"

Felicity swallowed hard, then her head came up as she recovered some of her cold self-control. She met JC's gaze defiantly. "A journalist never reveals her sources!"

"Especially when you have no idea who they are," said Happy. "The inside of your head is a mess. Looking at it is giving me a headache."

Felicity snarled at him, a raw, ugly animal sound. The sound of it, and the realisation that her audience had heard it shocked her, and she pulled her professionalism about her.

"Let's go to the phones!" she said brightly. "It's that time in the programme when you the listeners get your chance to ask the questions you want answered! So if any of you good people listening today have a subject you want to raise, or something specific you want to ask today's guests, now is the time to phone in. You all know the number; but please remember I don't have an engineer with me today to help field the calls, so if you find you're having trouble getting through, please be patient. I'm doing this on my own. And already, we have our first caller! Go ahead, you're on the air, on the *Felicity Legrand Hour*!"

She fumbled with the control panel before her, and the first phone call came in over the studio speakers, loud and clear.

"Hello, Felicity! I wanted to say, we all think you're great! We love what you're doing! Don't you let those spooky bastards get away with anything!"

"Thank you, sir," said Felicity. "Could you tell us your name, please?"

"Oh, yes! This is Gareth!"

"Do you have a question for the Ghost Finders, Gareth?"

"I wanted to say, I keep hearing noises in my house, at night!"

There was a pause, until they all realised he'd said everything he was going to say. Melody leaned forward to address the mike.

"Have you had your house's plumbing checked recently?"

"Oh!" said the caller. "I hadn't thought of that . . ."

"Moving on to the next caller," Felicity said quickly.

"This is Father Xavier, of Stoneground Church," said a calm voice. "I have been following the unusual events affecting Radio Free Albion almost from the beginning, and I am very interested in what you've been saying on your programme. I do not believe that what we've all been hearing are Electronic Voice Phenomena. I also do not believe that the dead rise up from their rest to play games with local radio hosts. No, it is my belief that Radio Free Albion has fallen under demonic influence. If you wish, I can perform an exorcism . . ."

"Thank you, Father," said JC. "But should we decide that's necessary, I think we'll go with a professional."

The next caller was an excitable young man with a high-pitched and very intense voice. He refused to give his name. "I want to know if, you are part of the same Carnacki Institute who were involved with cleaning up that nasty business at Chimera House in London, a few years back? And making all the evidence disappear? You know, when they were testing that new drug on human volunteers, and it all went horribly wrong? Was that you? I've been following some really fascinating discussions about the Institute, on some very well-informed conspiracy sites . . ."

"If you don't ring off right now," said Happy, "the Men In Black will come round and take away your computer and tell the whole world what kind of porn you like to watch."

The line went dead. The next voice to phone in was that of an old woman, quiet and wavering but very sincere.

"That voice . . . the one who called in, and talked to Captain Sunshine, earlier . . . I don't know who it was, but I do think it sounded very familiar. That's all I wanted to say."

"Thank you, caller," said Felicity. "Is there anything you wanted to ask . . ."

But the old woman was gone. And although Felicity sat crouched over her control panel, there was only the quiet hiss of an open, empty line. There were no more callers. Felicity couldn't believe it.

"That's it?" she said loudly to her audience. "I go to all the trouble of assembling three of the most important people you're ever likely to encounter, right here in my studio, and you don't want to talk to them? Come on! Don't let me down; ask them something! Don't you have anything to say?"

"Is there anybody out there?" said Melody. "Is anybody still listening?"

The quiet dragged on.

"Apparently not," said JC.

"Something's here," said Happy.

And again, there was something in his voice that brought all their attention back to him. He was sitting very still, looking at nothing, a terrible helpless despair stamped on his face. Melody leaned in close.

"Are you sure, Happy?"

"It's here . . ." said Happy. "Listening . . . Talk to me, you son of a bitch."

A voice came through the studio speakers, across the open phone line. Felicity looked sharply at her control panel because she hadn't touched it. The new voice was smooth and horribly sweet, like an angel who'd learned to take a delight in the slaughter of innocents.

"Hello," said the voice. "Is there anybody there? It's time to pay the piper even if you don't like the tune."

"Cut the crap," said JC. "You want to talk to us, this is your chance. Get on with it."

"Hello, JC. You're looking good. Love the shades. It is time we talked, isn't it? We have so much to say to each other."

"This voice," Felicity said quietly. "It isn't coming in over the phone. I've shut all the lines down, but it's still coming through."

"Told you," Melody said to JC. "I don't know what kind of carrier signal the voices are using, but it isn't radio or phone."

"Of course not," said the voice. "I would never stoop to anything so crude."

"That's your voice, Mel," said Happy. "That thing is speaking with your voice!"

"I have no voice of my own, so I must use what I can find," said the voice.

"And that sounded like you, Happy," said Melody.

"Shut up!" said Felicity. "All of you, shut up! This is my show, you don't get to barge in and take over! Doing . . . stupid impressions!"

"Oh my sweet Felicity," said the voice, sounding like Felicity Legrand. "I'm going to have such fun with you . . ."

"What do you sound like when you're being yourself?" said JC, careful to keep his voice calm and unmoved. "Let's hear what you really sound like."

And then they all flinched back as a terrible blast of sound filled the studio. Animal sounds, mixed together; raw and vicious, harsh and brutal. The sounds of huge beasts and awful creatures, killing and being killed, living and dying, rutting and feasting. The sheer fury and ferocity in the sounds filled the studio, overwhelming everything. All the old animal instincts and impulses that mankind was supposed to have left behind and overcome, let loose, without conscience or restraint. Felicity lifted her control panel and slammed it down on the table-top, again and again, smashing it to pieces . . . but the sounds went on.

Growing slowly, steadily louder, as though the things responsible were drawing nearer.

Felicity clapped her hands over her ears. "Stop it! Stop it!"

*Stop it stop it stop it,* said the voice, rising over the massed animal sounds. It sounded like Felicity's voice, driven quite mad. And then the animal sounds cut off abruptly, and a blessed peace and quiet fell across the studio.

"There's nothing you can do to stop me," said the voice. A completely neutral thing, lacking any trace of human personality. "I'm so close, now. So close you could almost reach out and touch me. Prepare yourselves; after all this Time, I shall have my revenge upon you."

"Finally," said JC, "we're getting to something I can understand. Revenge is familiar ground to me. But revenge for what, exactly?"

"You know . . ." said the voice.

"Oh dear God," said Melody. "Are you . . . the Flesh Undying?"

"What?" Felicity said feebly. "What's that?"

"Hush, Felicity," said JC, not unkindly. "Grown-ups talking."

"The Flesh Undying?" said the voice. "I don't know what that is. Must be part of your world. I am nothing you know or could hope to understand, with your limited human minds."

"Why are you here?" said JC. "Why come to this radio station?"

"Because I knew you would be here," said the voice. "Time looks very different, when seen from the other side. For me, the future is another direction to look in."

"Are you saying, all of this, everything that's happened at Radio Free Albion, was to get us here?" said JC.

"Cause and effect are of your world, not mine," said the voice.

"But, the warnings . . ." said Melody.

"That isn't me," said the voice. "That . . . is my victims."

"I don't understand any of this," said Felicity. "I feel bad. I think I'm going to be sick."

"Dear Felicity," said the voice. "You sound so pretty. I could eat you up. And I will!"

"Stick to the subject!" said JC. "Why us? Why is it so important to you that we're here?"

"You shouldn't have left the door open, JC," said the voice. "Be seeing you . . ."

They all waited, looking quickly around the cramped studio; but it seemed the voice had said all it had to say. Melody turned to Happy.

"Is it gone?"

"I'm not sure it was ever really here," Happy said thoughtfully. "Or at least, not as such . . . It was superimposing its presence on our world, from outside. But . . . I think it can still see and hear us, from wherever it is."

"Or maybe, whenever it is," said JC. "I don't think Time and Space mean the same things to it as they do to us. Given that we've already decided the warning voices are coming back in Time, from the future . . . Maybe that's where our enemy is, too. Or will be."

*"What are you all talking about?"* Felicity said hysterically. Her face was stark white and beaded with sweat, her eyes bulging half out of their sockets.

"Easy, Felicity," said JC. "Breathe deeply. Concentrate on what's right in front of you. Don't upset the listeners if anyone out there is still listening . . . Hello, audience! Don't worry! This is all . . . weird phenomena. It doesn't necessarily mean anything. Leave it all to us; and we'll clear everything up, so you can have your nice radio shows back again. Felicity Legrand is fine; she doesn't feel like saying anything for the moment. So now the show is going to close. This is JC Chance, Ghost Finder supreme, saying, *Good night! And may the spiritual provider of your choice go with you.*"

Melody found one of the Captain's old singles, and put it on. The Doors, "People Are Strange." Melody looked at JC.

"By the time that record's finished, Jonathan should have taken the hint and shut down the broadcast. He did say he wanted to close the station down early . . ."

Felicity stood up abruptly, staring defiantly at all of them. "I don't believe this!" she said flatly.

"Don't believe what?" JC said politely.

"Any of it!" said Felicity. "I don't believe in the supernatural, or ghosts, or voices out of nowhere, or . . . or whatever that voice was pretending to be! You . . . You fixed that! You set it all up in advance, somehow! To distract me from all the legitimate questions I was going to put to you!"

"Sorry," said JC. "But no, we didn't."

"I don't believe you!" Felicity said viciously. "I'll never believe you!"

"Whatever helps you through the night," said Happy.

Felicity turned her back on them all and went to storm out the studio. Only to stop suddenly, as she discovered the door was gone. The only entrance and exit to the main studio had silently disappeared, and where it should have been there was nothing but an unbroken stretch of bare, plastered wall. Felicity looked at it for a long moment, then slammed both hands flat against the wall, as though she thought she could push through it. She cried out, in a loud, harsh voice, and beat her fists against the wall; and her wordless cries sounded like someone driven past their mental limits. JC nodded to Melody, and she went over to Felicity, put a hand on her shoulder, and pulled her gently away from the wall. JC moved forward to take her place. He studied the featureless wall, then ran his hands slowly over the bare plaster. It felt very smooth and perfectly ordinary. As though it belonged there and always had. Happy came forward to stand beside JC.

"It's not an illusion, JC," he said quietly. "Not a vision, or any kind of telepathic broadcast. Someone has interfered with the physical reality of our world. It would seem our unknown enemy is still here, messing with us. Moving around behind the scenes of the world, rearranging things for its own amusement. Which would suggest . . . it's getting stronger as it draws nearer."

"From the future?" said JC.

Happy shrugged. "Or from some other place, some other dimension. The Outer Reaches? The Shoals? The voice said, you left a door open, JC. Does that suggest anything to you?"

JC scowled at the blank wall. "Nothing specific. Could be something left over from any number of old cases. You know as well as I do, this world is riddled with weak spots. Where the dimensional barriers have grown thin, from different worlds rubbing up against each other."

"Or because someone poked a hole right through

them," said Happy. "I first raised that point back during the Fenris Tenebrae case, down in the London Underground. You didn't want to believe me then."

"I didn't know about the Flesh Undying and its agents, then," said JC. "It all seems so long ago now . . ."

"Could that case have anything to do with this case?" said Melody. She'd settled Felicity quietly into a chair and now came forward to join the discussion.

"Who knows?" said JC. "That kind of serious shit is way above our pay grade. Usually. For all we know, the voice is messing with us. Trying to make us look in the wrong direction. It's not like we have any shortage of old enemies, after all."

"But most of our old enemies are dead," said Happy. "Or worse than dead. This is either something we didn't kill or something we couldn't kill."

"You're sounding very lucid, Happy," said JC.

"Make the most of it," said Happy. "It won't last."

"What are we dealing with here?" Melody said impatiently. "What could be this powerful?"

"Only one thing it could be," said Happy. "It's a Beast."

They all looked at each other for a long moment, then JC shook his head.

"Let's be practical. If we can't leave through the door, there's still the window separating us from the outer studio. Smash the glass, and we can . . ."

He broke off, as Felicity cried out suddenly from behind them. When they looked back at her, she was pointing a quivering finger at the separating window. And when the Ghost Finders turned back to look, the window was still there, it hadn't disappeared like the door had . . . but the view beyond the glass had changed. The outer studio was gone, replaced by something else entirely.

Where it should have been, a great open wasteland stretched away forever. An ugly, blasted place, with no life at all, the ground cracked and broken apart. The sky was the colour of dust, and there was no sun and no obvious horizon. The air was dark yellow, burned orange, rippling slowly and heavily like heat haze. The look of this new place was oppressive to the eye, as though the light had curdled in this spoiled world. It was raining an endless stream of maggots, tumbling slowly out of nowhere, falling down to writhe and twist on the dry, dead ground. There was no sound, anywhere.

"What is that?" JC said quietly to Happy.

"Still not an illusion," said Happy. "Another place, another world. What you get when two different realities slam up against each other. Not a good place, JC. Looking at it is giving me a headache."

"Why is our enemy showing us this?" said Melody.

"I'm not sure this comes from our enemy," said Happy. "It feels more like . . . another warning. From the future. I have a horrible feeling we're being given a glimpse of what our world could be like if we don't do something . . ."

Melody looked sharply at Happy. "What is it? What are you Seeing that we're not?"

"I think . . . it's my turn," said Happy. "You saw your future self out in the car park, JC. And I saw the future Melody, out on the landing. We know what the two of you are going to become. Dead and worse than dead. Now it's my turn. I can feel me, feel my presence, on the other side of that glass, in the other place. This is my message, my warning, from the future."

"Could whoever's responsible have taken away the door?" said Melody. "Trapped us in here?"

"Yes," said Happy. "To make sure we get the message and can't run away from it."

"Is it really going to be that bad?" said JC.

"Look at the world that's waiting for us!" said Happy. "You think anything good would ever come from that? We've already lost, in that future. Lost the game, lost our lives, maybe much more. All they can do is reach back through Time, to try to warn us . . . Come on, you bastard. I'm here. Talk to me."

And immediately, there he was. Standing facing them, on the other side of the glass. Happy Jack Palmer. He looked normal. No obvious wounds. No monstrous distortions. The same grubby clothes and battered leather jacket. He looked steadily at the three Ghost Finders, from another place and another time. He looked . . . terribly sad. He turned his head slowly, searching one Ghost Finder face after another. Melody made a low, wounded sound; and the future Happy smiled briefly at her.

"Sweet Mel," he said. "I never thought I'd see you again, looking like yourself. And JC, old friend. You tried so hard, fought so bravely; and died so horribly. And there I am . . . looking so angry, so determined. I remember this moment, from when I was here before, looking at me. When I was you. Maybe this time, you'll listen."

"How is it that you're still alive when everyone else is dead?" said the present Happy. "I swore I'd die before I let Melody become . . . what I saw!"

"You tried," said the future Happy. "And you died. What kind of Ghost Finder can't recognise his own ghost? I made myself into a bomb, a psychic explosive. Sacrificed my life and all my hopes of resting peacefully; and all for nothing. This is the world where we lost. Where everyone lost . . ."

"Then tell us!" said the present Happy. "Tell us what we have to do, or avoid doing, to stop this from happening!"

"I almost got it right," said the future Happy. "Sacrifice. That's the key. But . . ."

And then he stopped, and looked up abruptly, as something fell towards him from out of the dusty sky. It dropped down impossibly quickly, its dark and rotting presence sending ripples through the surface of the world. The future Happy looked like he wanted to run but knew there was nowhere to run to. He looked like he wanted to cry but knew there was no point. The thing fell on him. The awful, distorted thing, that used to be Melody. Twisted like a fun-fair-mirror reflection, its exposed flesh dark with decay, its hands all claws and its mouth stuffed with teeth. The future Melody fell upon the future Happy and tore him apart. He screamed then, a terrible, lost, despairing sound. Driven on by some outside power she could not resist, the future Melody tore her Happy to pieces and scattered them across the broken ground. Where the maggots were waiting.

The present Melody cried out, in horror and fury; and the future Melody paused and looked at her. As though it had only become aware of the window into the Past just then. It looked at its previous self, and didn't know her.

The dead world disappeared. Beyond the separating window there was only the outer room of the studio. Even the intervening door was back where it should be. Melody turned away from the window, threw her arms around Happy, and hugged him tightly to her. Holding him like she would never let him go. Happy patted her absently on the shoulder, his eyes far away.

"I would never do that to you!" said Melody, her voice choked with tears she was damned if she'd shed. "Never!"

"But he said you were a ghost, Happy," JC said slowly. "So how could you be hurt, torn apart, like that? How is that even possible?"

"What do we know about what the dead can do in the future?" said Happy. "What do we know about what can be done to the dead in the world that's coming?" He looked at JC over Melody's heaving shoulder, and his face and his gaze were completely empty of emotion. "You said . . . when you encountered your future self, you were wounded, dying. Blinded . . . What happened to your eyes, JC? To your very special eyes?"

"He said, *They took them back*," said JC, as steadily as he could. "I'm assuming that means the forces from Outside who gave me these new eyes decided they wanted them back. Because I didn't see something I should have?"

"I hate this!" said Melody. "I hate this . . . What good does it do to see the future if we can't change it?"

"You know what?" said JC. "I have had enough of cryptic warnings. There must be something we can do, or what would be the point of contacting us? So why not simply tell us what to do?"

"Because they don't know who might be listening," said Happy.

"We have to do something!" said JC.

"We will," said Happy. "I think that's the problem."

He pushed Melody gently away from him. She grabbed hold of his hand and wouldn't let go. Happy opened the door, and they left the studio. JC went back to get Felicity

Legrand. She flinched away from him, but he coaxed her up out of her chair and got her moving towards the door.

"Please," she said, pitifully. "Please, I don't want to . . . I don't believe . . ."

"I know," said JC. "You don't want to believe any of this is real. Neither do I. But I don't think that's an option, now."

"Fight the future," Happy said loudly from the outer room. "It's not only a T-shirt."

# SEVEN

## TIME IS NOT ON OUR SIDE

Happy and Melody went striding down the long landing, side by side, keeping a watchful eye on every door and opening they passed, both of them looking as though they would very much like something to jump out of the shadows, so they could punch its head in. Which was really nothing new where Melody was concerned, but JC considered it a vast improvement on Happy's part. Unless it was all down to the pills, of course. JC followed on behind Melody and Happy, leading Felicity by the hand, coaxing her along. Her face was worryingly blank, her wide eyes lost and far away. She seemed to take no notice at all of her surroundings, but now and again she would jump, skittishly, for no reason and hang back, shaking her head. And then JC would have to murmur soothingly to her to get her moving again.

The landing seemed very still and very quiet, with all its doors safely and securely closed; but JC didn't trust

any of it. It was normal behaviour hiding something else.
The mask on the face of the monster. JC couldn't shake off
the feeling that he was being watched. Or that, at any moment, the landing might disappear, like the door in the
studio. It was a disturbing feeling, to know you couldn't
rely on your surroundings to stay your surroundings. That
you couldn't rely on anything . . . A door might become a
window to some horrible other place. The floor might turn
into mists, leaving you to fall all the way down to the
reception area. Nothing could be trusted to be what it
seemed. JC managed a small smile at that last thought. He
should be used to that after so many years working for the
Carnacki Institute.

He gave Felicity's arm a reassuring squeeze and hurried her along. There was no response, nothing to indicate
she even knew he was there. He pulled her a little closer
and tried to get her to move a little faster. The sooner they
were all safely back on the ground floor, the better. He
couldn't throw off a terrible suspicion that when they got
to the end of the landing, the staircase wouldn't be there.
That they'd keep hurrying down the landing and getting
nowhere, forever. He clamped down hard on the feeling.

They reached the head of the stairs without any further
incident. Happy and Melody led the way down, glaring
fiercely about them, with JC and Felicity close behind.
Their feet clattered loudly on the bare wooden steps. Normally, JC wouldn't have given a damn; but now it felt like
a really bad idea to be doing anything that might attract
unwelcome attention. He moved his sunglasses down
his nose, so he could look about him with his glowing
golden eyes, but couldn't See anything out of the ordinary.
He pushed the sunglasses back into place, cutting off the

golden light; and only then remembered that Felicity was
so close she could have seen his eyes. But she was still
staring straight ahead, paying no attention at all to him, or
their surroundings. In fact, he was pretty sure that if he let
go of her arm, she would stop moving and stay where she
was. JC was starting to feel a bit guilty about her condition. He should have realised sooner that someone as set
in her beliefs as she was would react badly when suddenly
presented with hard evidence that the world wasn't even
remotely what she thought it was. And never had been. It's
always the more solid minds that crack first, the ones with
less yield in them.

He should have done more to protect her. That was
what he was here for, after all.

\\\\\\\\\\\\\\\\\\\\\\\\\\\\

When they all finally burst through the rear door and back
into the reception area, everything seemed perfectly fine.
Still, and calm, and at peace. Apart from the people waiting there, who jumped half out of their skins when the door
slammed open. Sally was back behind her desk, Jonathan
and Tom were sitting side by side in two chairs they'd
dragged together, and Captain Sunshine was standing by
the open front door, staring out at the world, finishing off
the last half-inch of his funky hand-rolled. They all quickly
calmed down again; but they all looked like they'd been
prepared to run like hell if the new arrivals had proved to
be anyone else.

Sally slumped back in her chair, scowling and pouting.
The Captain turned unhurriedly away, to stare out at the
world again. Jonathan rose quickly to his feet once he saw
the state Felicity was in. He hurried forward to grab both

of her hands, and JC stepped back and let him do it. Maybe she'd react better to Jonathan. Tom rose up out of his chair, studying Jonathan and Felicity with a distinctly odd look on his face. She didn't react at all to Jonathan, even when he put his face right in front of hers. He said her name a few times, increasingly loudly, and turned to glare at JC.

"What have you done to her?"

"She's in shock," said JC. "Weren't you listening to what happened, during her show? She saw a lot of things she really wasn't prepared for. She'll come out of it, eventually. She needs time, to . . . process what she saw. Come to terms with it. She'll be fine."

"Probably," said Happy.

"You were supposed to be looking after her!" said Jonathan. "You were supposed to be protecting her. I should never have trusted you."

JC looked at him. He'd never seen the station manager this moved by anything, including the otherworldly attacks on his station. But a threat to Felicity really got him going. Which was . . . interesting. Jonathan realised JC had nothing to say. He led Felicity away and sat her down on the nearest chair. She went with him, unaware and unresisting. As though she didn't care where she was or what was happening. As though she'd simply withdrawn from a world that had become too complicated and too scary, and gone inside herself, to a place where nothing could hurt her. She sat in the chair Jonathan found for her, staring straight ahead; and if she saw anything at all, it didn't seem to matter to her. Jonathan fussed around her, trying to make her comfortable.

Tom glared at Melody and Happy. Happy ignored him,

and Melody glared right back at him. Tom turned his angry gaze on JC.

"I thought you were here to protect us from the bad stuff?"

"We do what we can," said JC. "But in a dangerous situation, it's inevitable that people will sometimes get hurt."

Tom turned his anger on Jonathan. "I told you we should leave the station! It's not safe here, for any of us."

"She wouldn't go," said Jonathan, not looking away from Felicity. "And I couldn't leave her here . . ."

Tom suddenly looked very tired. "Oh God, Jonathan, not again . . . Tell me you haven't been sleeping with Felicity. You promised me! When I came here to support your new venture, you swore you'd put all that behind you. You promised me you wouldn't sleep with the staff! After all the trouble that's got you into before . . ."

"Hold on; wait a minute!" said Sally, sitting up straight behind her desk and looking searchingly at Jonathan and Felicity. "He's been banging her? Jonathan? I thought he was gay!"

Jonathan looked away from Felicity for the first time. "Why on earth would you think that?"

Sally slumped back down in her chair and looked away, sticking out her heavily pierced lower lip. JC cleared his throat loudly, to get everyone's attention. But Tom was the only one who looked at him. JC raised an eyebrow.

"Excuse me, Tom, but I was given to understand that Jonathan's previous rocky employment history was down to his fondness for the booze?"

"Yeah, well," said Tom. "It was his fondness for . . . other things, that kept getting him into trouble. He was always a gentleman, always ready to take no for answer; but . . . there was always someone ready to say yes. Some bright young thing, headed for the top, looking for help and support from an authority figure. Usually someone with unresolved Daddy issues . . . Jonathan! You promised me it would be different, this time!"

"Yeah, well," said Jonathan, looking briefly at Tom and smiling wanly, "I can resist everything except temptation. I usually tell people the booze story because that kind of bad behaviour is more acceptable these days. In fact, it's almost fashionable. You're nobody if you haven't done rehab . . . Some forms of addictive behaviour are always going to be more . . . forgivable than others. I can honestly say, I never meant to hurt anyone. And if I was using Felicity, you can be sure she was using me."

"Oh well, that makes it all right then, doesn't it?" said Tom. "Jesus, Jonathan! That's pretty cold-blooded . . ."

"No," said Jonathan, "I was never cold-blooded. That's always been my problem. I do care for her; in my way. Felicity? Felicity, can you hear me, love?"

If she could, she didn't react, or reply. Jonathan pulled up a chair and sat down beside her. He took one of her hands in both of his and talked quietly to her. Trying to reach her. Waiting patiently for her to come back to him.

"Anything been happening down here, while we were going through hell upstairs?" said JC.

Tom looked around him, realised no-one else was going to answer, and shrugged quickly. "It feels quiet enough in here, but I don't trust it. I still think we should leave. All of us. While we still can."

"You could do that," said JC. "But I think . . . the voices would probably follow you."

Everyone looked at him then, apart from Felicity.

"What?" said Jonathan.

"It's clear the voices aren't in any way linked to the radio station," said Melody. She was back behind her precious array of instruments again, her gaze moving quickly from one readout to the next. Happy stood beside her, looking at nothing in particular. Melody ran her hands quickly over the keyboards, checking that everything was still as it should be. She talked on, without looking up.

"The voices you've all been hearing haven't been coming in over the radio, or the phones. They're coming directly to you. All of you. So if you did go, I think the voices would go with you. You couldn't leave them behind or shake them off because it isn't the radio station that attracted them in the first place. It's you. The only hope you have to escape from what's happening is to put a stop to it here."

"Why should we believe anything you say?" Tom said challengingly. "After what you let happen to Felicity? Look at the poor cow . . . We all heard you! We heard what happened during the show! You threw Felicity to the wolves!"

"That's not how it was," said JC. "She was in no more danger than any of us; she couldn't cope with what she saw. What she experienced. Not everyone can. There's a reason why so few people become Ghost Finders."

"And it has nothing to do with the appalling pay and conditions," said Happy. "And rather more to do with the fact that most of us are half-crazy to begin with."

"Really not helping, Happy," murmured JC.

"I know," said Happy. "It's what I do best."

"To hell with all of this!" said Tom. "I can't believe

anything you people say any more. I'm going! Right now! Don't try to stop me . . ."

"If you run away now," said Jonathan, quite coldly, "you might not have a job to come back to."

Tom turned on the station manager, looked at him disbelievingly, then fixed him with a cold, withering stare. "You really think that is any kind of threat?"

Jonathan ignored him, giving all his attention to Felicity. She was sitting perfectly quietly, with her hands neatly folded in her lap, looking at nothing and ignoring everything. After what she'd been through, she wasn't ready to come out and interact with the world, just yet. It was entirely possible, JC thought quietly, that she might never be willing to do that.

Melody finally finished checking out her instruments and shot a quick glance at Sally.

"Everything seems all right . . . Are you sure nobody's touched anything?"

Sally sniffed loudly, and several of her facial piercings jangled. "Kim and I have been busy talking; but we took it in turns to keep an eye on your precious toys. No-one's even been near them."

"Kim?" said JC. "Where are you?"

"Right here, JC," the ghost girl said brightly; and there she was, striding across the reception area to join him. The radio staff looked at her vaguely, only now realising that they hadn't noticed her for a while. No-one noticed Kim unless she wanted them to. She moved in close beside JC, and they shared a quick smile.

"You all right, Kim?" said JC.

"Nothing can get to me, sweetie. You know that. How about you? It sounded pretty awful up there."

"It was pretty bad," said JC. "But we've known worse in our time. How much of it did you hear?"

"Enough," said Kim. "I have to ask, JC . . . If you and Happy and Melody have all seen your future selves, why haven't I?"

"Perhaps because you're the only one of us who started out dead," JC said quietly.

"Oh poo!" said Kim. "There's always an excuse. You know I hate being left out of things."

"Trust me," said JC. "This isn't anything you'd want to be a part of."

"Well, if we're not leaving, what are we going to do?" Tom said loudly. "The radio station's shut down completely. Jonathan and I saw to that. Nothing going out, or coming in. Radio Free Albion is off the air. So what do we do now, *Mr. Expert*? All grab hands and hold a séance?"

"Probably not a good idea," said Happy. "Not after what happened with the last one."

"I would have to agree with that," said Melody. "On the grounds that we clearly did as much harm as good . . ."

Sally sat up, suddenly interested. "Why? What happened? What did you do?"

"Things . . . got a bit mixed up," said JC. "But I'm sure they'll sort themselves out again. Eventually."

"Shit happens, in the Ghost Finding game," Happy said comfortably. "More important, weird shit happens."

Tom went back to glowering at Jonathan. "Well, don't just sit there! This is your station! You must have an opinion as to what we should do!"

"Yes," said Jonathan. "Keep the noise down."

"Jonathan . . ."

"What do you want me to say, Tom? I am tired out,

worn-down, and running on fumes! The Ghost Finders are the only ones who seem to have a handle on what's happening here, so I am more than content to be guided by them."

"Even after what they did to Felicity?" said Sally.

"Shows how desperate I am," said Jonathan. "I understand radio and radio stations; but I don't have a clue what to do about hauntings . . ."

Tom shook his head firmly. "You know I don't believe in all that bullshit, Jonathan. There has to be a sane, rational, scientific explanation for everything that's happened; and if we can't see it, that's because we're not looking hard enough."

"Really?" said Melody. "A rational explanation? Such as?"

"Sabotage!" said Tom. "By another radio station! A more powerful signal, breaking in on ours and occasionally overpowering it."

"A signal strong enough to do that, which can't be detected by any of my very powerful machines?" said Melody. "One that can't be tracked back to any source?"

Tom shrugged angrily. "I'm only a general engineer; I don't understand the heavy science stuff."

"Clearly," said Melody.

"Anyway, why would any other radio station want to sabotage Radio Free Albion?" said Jonathan. "We're not big enough to be worth sabotaging!"

"I don't believe in the supernatural!" said Tom.

"Felicity used to say that," said Jonathan. "And look what's happened to her . . . Denial can get you killed here, Tom. Or worse."

Happy lost what little interest he had in the conversation and wandered away to join Captain Sunshine at the open front door. They stood together, looking out on the clear, quiet evening and the empty car park. It all seemed so very safe, and ordinary. The last of the light was going out of the day as the afternoon passed through twilight into evening.

"You see anything out there?" said Happy, after a while.

"No," said the Captain. He took one last drag on what was left of his spliff and sent the butt flying out into the car park with a flick of his finger. "All quiet, man. Like you could walk out into the embrace of the world, and leave all this down-beat shit behind. Except we can't. Like your friend said, we have to stay and face our demons." He looked at Happy with experienced eyes. "You are seriously maxed out, man. Definitely lacking in the mellow department. You want me to roll you a little fix-me-up?"

"No thanks," said Happy, politely. "With what I've got coursing through my veins, I doubt it would even touch me."

The Captain shrugged. "Might help you take the edge off."

"Last thing I need," said Happy. "I need to stay sharp. Cutting edge. Bad things are on their way, Captain."

"Aren't they always," said Captain Sunshine.

He went back into the reception area, to join the others. Happy took one last wistful look outside, at the tempting peace and calm of the car park; and then he turned his back on it and followed the Captain back in. He left the front door open, though.

ıııııııııııııııııııııı

In the end, JC got them all organised. It was what he did. With his usual mix of confidence, charm, good-natured arrogance, and a general sense of authority, he soon had a circle of chairs arranged, with everyone sitting facing each other. The radio staff sat together on one side, and the Ghost Finders took the other. It just worked out that way. Kim made it clear that she preferred to stand. She had to. Because sometimes she got so caught up in what was happening that her concentration would slip, and she would find herself floating an inch or two above the seat of the chair she was pretending to sit on. And she wasn't ready for the others to know she was a ghost. People always looked at her differently after that. And these people didn't need to be distracted from the things they should be afraid of. So she stood behind JC's chair.

"I feel like I should be organising some snacks, or drinks," said Jonathan. "Does anyone want anything? I could always make a quick trip to the kitchen, see what's in the fridge, maybe make some tea . . ."

"Do you really think going off on your own is a good idea?" said Tom.

"Probably not," said Jonathan.

"We could always phone out for some pizza," said the Captain.

"I am not touching any of those phones!" Sally said loudly.

"I've got a mobile phone built into my array," said Melody.

"Reception around here is really lousy," said Jonathan. "And yes, I am aware of the irony."

"Look," said Tom, "if we are going to do this whole big

discussion thing, we have to be honest with each other. I need some proof, some real evidence . . . that these Ghost Finders really do know what they're doing. That they understand what's happening here and why. And that they're capable of doing something about it!"

"You want evidence?" said JC. "Well, why didn't you say? How about this . . ."

He took off his sunglasses. Everyone jumped, and made startled noises, as his eyes glowed a deep disturbing gold in the growing gloom of the reception area. No-one could meet his golden gaze directly, not even the other Ghost Finders. JC looked casually about him, his eyes shining fiercely bright, as though the sun itself were looking out through his eyes. And then he put his sunglasses back on, pushing them firmly all the way back up his nose, so that not a single golden gleam got past them. Everyone relaxed a bit. Jonathan and Tom stared at him, fascinated. Sally looked genuinely scared, staring open-mouthed at JC. Captain Sunshine looked at him with a child-like delight, his lips silently forming the word *Groovy* . . . And Felicity slowly turned her head to look at JC. The golden glow from his eyes had reached her where nothing else could. She looked reassured. Character and personality seeped slowly back into her face, and she sat up straight in her chair.

While everyone else was still a little stunned, and a lot more compliant, JC took charge of the moment. Speaking slowly and carefully, he brought everyone up to date on what had been happening, and spelled out the current theory . . . That what they'd all been hearing were in fact voices from the future. Messages, warnings, sent back through Time. And having said all that, he sat back in his

chair and waited to see what they would all make of it.
Sally seemed to have found a whole new reason to sulk.
Captain Sunshine nodded slowly, rocking slowly back and
forth in his chair, conspicuously mellow. Tom and Jonathan looked at each other and didn't seem to want to say
anything. And Felicity seemed to be thinking hard.

"If all of this is true," Jonathan said finally, "it looks
like you were right all along, Tom. We should get the hell
out of here. Because we are in way over our heads. We
need to call in the authorities. Get more people involved.
Have them occupy Murdock House . . . and either defuse
it or blow it to pieces."

"We are the authorities," JC said flatly. "In cases like
this, the Ghost Finders of the Carnacki Institute are always going to be *The Authorities*. Because we specialise
in dealing with situations like this."

"Then call in more of your people!" said Tom. "With . . .
better equipment!"

"We have all the people and all the technology we
need," said JC. "And besides . . . even if I did call for reinforcements, by the time they could get here, I'm pretty
sure it would all be over. We are a long way from anywhere,
people; and we are on our own. Time is not on our side."

"Tomorrow," Jonathan said to Happy. "You said, the
world will end tomorrow."

"What?" said Tom. "Really? He said that?" He glared
openly at Happy. "When were you going to tell the rest of
us? And anyway, how can you be sure about something
like that?"

"I'm not," said Happy. "It could be later this evening . . ."

Sally made a loud and very rude sound. "I don't believe

in any of this shit, and you can't make me. I haven't seen anything . . ."

Everyone nodded understandingly, and talked right over her. It was clear she'd felt something because of all the breaks she'd been taking; but it was also clear that she would bolt like a startled deer if it even seemed like she might see something. Sally tried to make herself heard, then gave up, sitting stiffly in her chair with her arms tightly folded, taking it in turns to glare defiantly at different people, with utterly impartial scorn. Captain Sunshine smiled kindly on her.

"If you're not part of the answer, you're part of the problem. As we used to say, back in the day."

"Oh . . . stick it up your karma, you boring old hippie."

But she didn't make any move to get up or head for the open front door. The discussion, upsetting though it might be, was still interesting enough to hold her where she was. And there was still comfort, if not safety, in numbers.

"Can we all agree," said JC, "that the voices have become increasingly clearer, and more understandable? That's because we're drawing closer to them, in Time. The nearer we get to the future they come from, the more they . . . come into focus."

"There was something familiar about some of the voices," Captain Sunshine said slowly. "I'm sure I've heard some of them before, from somewhere . . ."

Everyone waited until it became clear that was the extent of his insight. He smiled gently around the circle, seeming more infuriatingly at ease than ever.

"Maybe we should . . . shut everything down," said Tom. "I mean permanently. Take Radio Free Albion off the air. I still think the station is drawing these voices here.

Like moths to a bright light. If there was no light, they might go somewhere else . . . and we'd be free of them!"

"We can't shut down the station completely!" Jonathan said immediately. "The new owners would never stand for it."

"Are you still going on about that?" said Tom. "Don't you think we've moved beyond that?"

"They don't know what's been happening here," Jonathan said doggedly. "They could fire us, replace us . . ."

"How can they hope to make any money out of this station if most of our audience is too scared to listen?" said Sally.

"I can't be fired," said Jonathan. "Not again. I'm too old to start over again."

"Listen to yourself!" said Tom. "We have more important things to worry about than unemployment!"

"Spoken like a man who's never been fired in his life," said Jonathan, bitterly. "We can't turn our backs on the station."

"Even though staying here puts your lives in danger?" said Melody.

"We're all going to die," said Happy.

"Stop saying that!" said Jonathan. He scowled at JC. "If we're really in trouble, get us more help! If your Institute can't get reinforcements here in time . . . There has to be someone else! Someone local!"

"You keep coming back to that," said JC. "Wanting the authorities you know to come in and rescue you. But what would you say to them if I could bring them here? If you tried to explain what you've experienced, what you've been through, they wouldn't believe you. They'd either arrest you for wasting their time, or fit you for a strait jacket. They're not equipped to deal with situations like this. You're much better off with us."

"And what about Felicity?" said Jonathan. "Is she better off because of you?"

"If she were to see us put things right," JC said carefully, "that might help to put her right."

"Might?" said Tom.

"It's always the ones who think they're strong who break the hardest when they're hit," said Kim. "Trust JC! He knows what he's doing. Don't you, sweetie?"

"Thanks for the vote of confidence, dear," said JC. "Look, you all need to understand what it is that's coming. When Happy says the world is coming to an end, he is not exaggerating. Everything and everyone we know is in danger."

"From what?" said Tom. "Voices?"

"No," said JC. "From what the voices are scared of."

"We're all going to die!" said Sally. "I don't want to die!"

"If we're all in such imminent danger," said Felicity, "do something!"

Everyone jumped and turned round in their chairs to look at her. Felicity was sitting up straight, her eyes clear. She still looked pale and drawn and had her hands clasped tightly together in her lap, so people wouldn't see how badly they were shaking, but her gaze was steady, and her mouth was set in a firm line. Jonathan squeezed her arm.

"Welcome back, Felicity. I was worried . . ."

She pulled her arm free. "Not in front of the children, Jonathan."

He smiled at her, almost fondly. "No point in trying to hide our . . . relationship, Felicity. That ship has sailed."

She looked fiercely at him. "You told them? Are you insane?"

"A lot has happened while you were . . . away," said Jonathan. "How are you feeling? Do you remember what you saw upstairs?"

"Yes," said Felicity. "I remember. I'm fine." She fixed JC with a cold, hard stare. "You claim to understand what's going on. So do something!"

"Don't think I'm not tempted," murmured JC. "Welcome back, Felicity. You seem . . . every inch yourself, again. But as I've already said, we don't have much time to work out what needs doing. Get it wrong, and we won't be the only ones to pay for our mistakes."

"I want to go home!" said Sally.

"I often say that," said Happy. "Never seems to happen, though."

"I'm not sure we'd be allowed to leave," said Melody.

"What?" Sally said immediately. "I'd like to see anybody try to stop me!"

"Up in the studio, the door that linked the inner and outer rooms, the only way in or out . . . disappeared," said Melody. "We were trapped in there. If whatever is behind this is prepared to change the material reality of our world, to make us watch a vision . . ."

"What might they be prepared to do to stop us leaving Murdock House?" said Happy.

Everyone thought about that; and it was clear from all their faces that none of them liked the implications. Sally looked fiercely at the open front door, clearly deliberating on whether she should make a dash for it while it was still there.

"You can't keep me here against my will!" she said

loudly; but she didn't sound as convinced of that as she had before.

"We can't," said Happy. "And we wouldn't. But we're not the ones making the decisions. We're not even sure whether it's the good guys or the bad guys who are trying to talk to us; though the voices do seem concerned that the end of the world is coming. And they do seem to believe we can do something about it. So it's up to us to do something. Or not do something. As the case may be. I hate it when Time gets involved in a case. It's always so complicated . . . trying to think in four dimensions. My head hurts."

"You're not alone," said Jonathan. "I'm not sure I'm understanding any of this."

"Situation entirely normal," said Felicity. "Stick to what you know and leave the important decisions to the better qualified."

"You really are back," said Jonathan. "How nice."

"I needed some time out," said Felicity.

"I know the feeling," murmured Jonathan.

"You've really been banging her?" said Sally. "You're old enough to be her father! And then some . . . No wonder she got her own show so quickly. Does she make you do nasty, demeaning things in bed?"

"You have no idea," said Jonathan. "And I loved every bit of it . . ."

"You should have talked to me first," said Tom. "I could have told you things . . . You have no idea how much she's been around. Or how much rough ground she's covered . . ."

"If we could please concentrate on the matter at hand," Felicity said coldly. She fixed her attention on JC. "Who are you people? Really? What can you do?"

"We're professionals," JC said calmly. "No-one knows more about weird shit than us."

"Then you have encountered situations like this before?" said Felicity.

"Well, no," said JC. "Not exactly like this."

"But you do know what to do, to stop it?"

Melody made a noise that suggested she strongly doubted it.

"Do you at least know how to protect us?" said Felicity.

"I wouldn't go that far," said Happy.

"Then what gives you the right to call yourselves professionals!" said Felicity.

"Who else have you got?" JC said flatly. "Who else can you turn to? The interview is over, Felicity. Accept . . . that we know enough about this sort of thing to know how much trouble we're in. That's something."

"I feel so much safer," said Captain Sunshine.

Sally stood up abruptly. "I don't care. I don't care what anyone says! I don't feel safe here, and I can't stand being in this room any longer. I am leaving! And there's nothing any of you can say that will change my mind."

That was when all the alarms built into Melody's array went off at once. Bells and sirens and flashing lights. Melody was up and out of her chair immediately, heading for her equipment, with Happy right behind her. She quickly had her fingers flying over her keyboards, her eyes darting from screen to screen. Sally stood where she was, frozen in place. Not sure whether to sprint for the open door or find something to hide behind.

"Did I do that?" she said. "I didn't do anything!"

"What is it?" said JC, raising his voice to be heard over the din of the alarms. "What's going on, Mel?"

"You remember the things called tachyons that aren't actually tachyons?" said Melody.

"Sort of," said JC.

"They're everywhere!" said Melody. "Massive energy spikes, coruscating temporal discharges and more kinds of strange radiations than I've ever seen in one place before!"

"But what does it all mean?" said Jonathan.

Happy's head jerked back suddenly, as he stared up at the ceiling. "Incoming!"

Objects appeared out of nowhere and fell from the ceiling. Hundreds of them, falling slowly at first, but quickly gathering speed. To begin with, they were hard to look at directly, only coming into focus completely as they fell through the air. By the time they reached the floor, they were all of them hard and solid and moving at speed. Some hit the polished wooden floor-boards hard enough to crack them, while others pierced the wood and stood upright, quivering with the violence of the impact.

Everyone in the reception area scattered the moment Happy yelled his warning. They ran to the edges of the large room and hugged the walls, pressing their backs flat as they watched the objects fall. Even Melody was forced away from her precious instruments because she knew they could protect themselves and she couldn't. Only Kim stayed where she was, staring about her with child-like wonder, because she knew she couldn't be touched or harmed by any of the falling objects. Finally, JC had to yell at her, to get her to move. Because he didn't want any of the others to see solid objects passing through her insubstantial form. On the grounds that might tend to give the game away. So she went to join him at the nearest wall, and they huddled together. Not quite touching.

More and more things appeared silently, blinking into existence under the ceiling, then falling down into the reception room. All kinds of things, all shapes and sizes; some immediately recognisable, most not. Falling and tumbling, like a hailstorm from a junk-shop. Like all the things you'd ever lost or misplaced, turning up again all at once. Nothing too big, nothing too small, falling down to form a great pile of assorted bits and pieces that covered the centre of the reception area.

Until finally objects stopped appearing. The last few pieces fell into place on the pile, and were still. A sudden silence fell across the room, as all of Melody's alarms snapped off. Even the flashing lights shut down. And one by one, everyone moved away from the walls, shooting quick glances up at the ceiling. They advanced, carefully and cautiously, on the huge pile of assorted objects.

"No more incoming," said Happy. "Knew I should have brought my umbrella."

Melody hurried back to her instruments. None of the objects had even come close to touching her array. She muttered soothingly to her machines in case they were worried.

Jonathan only moved a few reluctant inches away from his wall. He looked at JC. "Is it safe to come out now? Is it over?"

"Yes," said JC. "Unless it isn't; in which case, no."

"Experts," said Felicity, disgustedly.

She was already leaning over the great pile of objects, studying them closely. Jonathan moved slowly forward to join her. Tom and Captain Sunshine circled slowly round the pile, looking it over from what they hoped was a safe distance. Kim stuck close to JC as he considered the situation thoughtfully.

"Melody?" said JC. "Do you have anything useful to tell me?"

"It's all quiet now," said Melody, her eyes darting from one readout to another. "All the energy spikes have collapsed, no exotic radiations . . . it's clear all across the boards. Whatever that was, it's over. For now."

"But what was it?" said Sally. She seemed torn between a need to edge closer to the still-open front door and a fascination with all the things that had arrived out of nowhere.

"That was an apport," said Melody. "An old technical term from the occult for things that appear or fall out of nowhere. A typical example of naming a thing without in any way describing or explaining it."

"Like tachyons?" JC said innocently.

"I will hit you," said Melody.

Jonathan glowered at Captain Sunshine. "If you even look like you're about so say *Groovy* . . . I will slap you."

"Understood," said the Captain. "But it is . . ."

They all moved gradually closer to the piled-up objects, taking their time. Still glancing up at the ceiling now and again. They studied the accumulated objects with cautious interest, careful to look but not touch. Leaning well forward, bent over at the waist, with hands stuffed into pockets or held behind their backs, to be on the safe side. But as they drew closer, curiosity soon trumped caution, and one by one they reached out to touch various objects in the pile, then remove them and study them close-up. Turning things this way and that in their hands, growing

more confident as nothing bad happened, trying to get a
sense of what these sudden arrivals were and where they'd
come from. And why they'd ended up in the reception
area.

JC prodded a few things with a cautious fingertip, to
make sure they were really real, then shrugged and joined
in picking things up to examine them. Kim peered over his
shoulder. Melody came out from behind her machines
once it became clear even her best short-range scanners
couldn't tell her anything useful. She knelt by the pile and
thrust both her hands in, digging through the objects for
something of worth or interest. Happy stood beside her
and let her do it. He didn't pick up anything himself, but
he did take a polite interest in everything Melody selected.
Felicity pulled a face every time she touched something,
but she couldn't resist getting involved. Tom and Jonathan
picked things up and passed them back and forth between
them. And so it went, until people started finding things
no-one would want to touch.

"JC," said Jonathan, "do these look like . . . human
bones, to you?"

"Yes," said JC. "Quite definitely human. All kinds.
Charred, broken, and splintered. Gnawed on . . . And
fairly recently, too."

"So these are . . . tooth marks?" said Tom.

"I'd say so, yes," said JC. "Really big teeth, too. In fact,
I'd be hard-pressed to name any living creature in this
world that could make those marks and do so much
damage . . ."

"Maybe they're not from around here," said Happy.
"Maybe they're from the future . . ."

Everyone stopped what they were doing to look at him.

And then they looked at the pile of things that had appeared. And the ones they were holding.

"Apports from the time to come," said Happy. "It does make a sort of sense. If voices can come back through Time, why not objects? And who knows what kind of creatures they've got running around in the world that will replace ours? Remember those nasty animal sounds we heard, JC, when you asked the voice what it really sounded like? They didn't sound like any creature we might know or would want to meet."

"I've found a few things I recognise," said Tom. "Bits and pieces of this station's equipment. Smashed and torn apart but still recognisable."

"Are you sure, Tom?" said Jonathan.

"I should be," said Tom. "I've taken everything in this entire station apart and put it back together again more than once. Trying to keep things going, on a budget no self-respecting proper engineer would accept. Some of these things are compromise arrangements I cobbled together, to keep Radio Free Albion operating and on the air . . . Because putting in a request for a replacement would take too long. Where the hell did all this come from?"

Sally hugged herself tightly, holding herself together. She stayed apart, unable to bring herself to touch anything. "Don't you mean *when* did it come from? I don't like this. I don't like any of this!"

Kim looked at her approvingly. "Well done, dear! You're getting the hang of things nicely!"

"I don't want to get the hang of things!" Sally said miserably. "I want to get away from here. I want my life back."

"I feel like that a lot of the time," said Happy.

JC knelt, to sort through some fire-damaged materials. Pieces of clothing, torn and soaked with blood, some of it still wet to the touch. Most of the materials were too far gone to identify. He sat back on his haunches and looked over the pile.

"The only thing it all seems to have in common," he said slowly, "is that everything here could have originated in Murdock House."

"This definitely did," said Felicity. She held up the burned and charred remains of a poster. Enough of it remained, that they could all recognise it as the poster on the far wall, behind the reception desk. Saying WELCOME TO RADIO FREE ALBION. The poster on the wall was still there, completely undamaged. Everyone looked back and forth, from the poster on the wall to the one Felicity was holding. The same poster, in two different places. The one in Felicity's hands was already crumbling and falling apart. Too fragile to last long now. She pulled a face and dropped the remains back onto the pile.

"But why is it here?" asked Captain Sunshine. "Why is any of this stuff here? It makes no sense."

"These are clues from the future," said Melody. "Warnings about what's going to happen. Presumably they'll start to make more sense as we draw closer to the conditions that will produce them."

JC picked up a pair of cracked and broken sunglasses. He knew them, immediately. They were exactly like the ones he was wearing; only these very dark lenses were covered with a web of cracks and splashed with blood.

*What happened to your eyes?* he'd said. *They took them back,* his future self had said.

He closed the shattered sunglasses carefully and

slipped them into an inside pocket of his jacket. Right next to the bloody handprint.

"I've got it!" said Melody.

She scrambled back onto her feet and hurried over to her equipment array. Everyone watched interestedly as she worked her keyboards, glancing from one monitor screen to another. She spoke to the others without glancing up from what she was doing. "The tachyons are the clue! It's all about Time . . . My computers have been running tests on the various voice recordings, all this time, using the best filters and sophisticated comparisons . . . All the good stuff." She stopped suddenly to look at Captain Sunshine. "It occurred to me: if you could have two different versions of the same object, why not two different versions of the same voice? No wonder you thought you recognised the voice that phoned you, on the air. It was your own voice, Captain."

She fiddled with her controls and played the recording through her array's speakers. And without the distortion built into the incoming voice, everyone recognised both voices immediately. Now they knew what to listen for. Captain Sunshine stood very still. For the first time, he looked genuinely shocked, and shaken, as he listened to two versions of his voice talking to each other.

Take it easy, man, said the Captain. Be cool. The Captain is right here. And then his own voice answered him. Get out of there! Oh God, please listen to me . . .

"It is you," said Felicity, fascinated almost in spite of herself. "That was your voice, both times. Remember that old woman, who phoned into my show, earlier? She said she recognised the voice . . ."

"This is seriously weirding me out," said the Captain,

barely hanging on to his cool. "What do you think it means?"

"Something really bad is going to happen," said Melody. "Something so bad, it's sending ripples back through Time. From the future to the Present. Like a haunting in reverse."

"Can this future be stopped?" said Sally. "Or at least avoided?"

"If we did stop it," said Felicity, "there wouldn't be any really bad thing happening, to impress itself upon Time and send its ripples back into the Past. Our Present. The very fact that we're experiencing these warnings means the future is inevitable."

"We're all going to die!" said Sally. "I'm not ready to die!"

"Time doesn't work like that," said Melody. "Tell her, JC."

"There are an infinite number of time-streams," JC said confidently, "and, therefore, an infinite number of potential futures."

"Are you sure about that?" said Jonathan.

"Not as sure as I'd like to be," said JC, looking at the pile of future apports. "We could run, I suppose. But if the future that's coming is as bad as it seems, there might not be anywhere to run to . . ."

"The world will end tomorrow," said Happy.

"Stop saying that!" said Felicity. "You can't be sure of that!"

"Yes I can," said Happy. "I've seen the world that's coming. And I think it's fair to say that if I weren't already heavily medicated, I would be very upset. I don't think I want to be around when it happens . . ."

"We can still stop this," JC said firmly. "We can work together, to understand the warnings and figure out what we need to do."

"Are you sure about that?" said Jonathan.

"Of course," said JC. "I have to be. Because all the other alternatives are unacceptable."

# EIGHT

## SEE WHAT'S COMING

In the end, JC had to shout everyone else down to get them to pay attention to what he was saying. When they finally settled into a rebellious silence, he glared round at them all impartially.

"Do you understand what I've been saying?" he said, loudly. "Because it is really important that you do! All those voices you've been hearing are your own voices. Your voices, from your future selves. You are the ghosts who've been haunting Radio Free Albion."

Felicity glared right back at him, openly challenging everything he said and his authority to say it. "So you keep saying, Mr. Expert! In the face of all reason and sanity. But even if that is the case . . . what do you propose to do about it?"

JC sighed, quietly and inwardly. He'd known someone was going to say that. Like somehow this was all his fault and therefore his responsibility to fix it. He took a deep breath and considered his words carefully.

"Think about it: all these voices from the future, reaching back through Time, trying desperately to warn us. But it still isn't clear about what. Or what they want us to do. So I say, why not ask them? Let's make contact with these people in the future, these older versions of ourselves, and get them to spell it out. Tell us exactly what it is that's coming, and what we need to do to prevent it."

"How do we do that?" said Jonathan, sounding like someone trying very hard to be reasonable in the face of extreme provocation.

"Some of us have already encountered future versions of ourselves," JC said carefully. "Happy, Melody, and I have all seen what's in store for us."

"Here?" said Tom. "At Murdock House? Why didn't you say something?"

"Because all of these encounters were . . . disturbing," said Melody. "Not the kind of thing you want to talk about."

"You've actually spoken to your future selves?" said Sally. "Did they tell you anything?"

"Wasn't that kind of encounter," said Happy. "Everything we saw was horrible. We don't die well, any of us. I always suspected that came as standard, once you signed up with the Carnacki Institute. But it still comes as a shock, and a kick to the heart, to see yourself dead and know for a fact you're not going to rest in peace."

"We still have a chance to change that," said JC as firmly as he could manage.

"But how can we make contact with the future?" said

Sally. Her voice was wavering, but she was still hanging on to her self-control, if only by her fingertips. "How is that even possible? I mean, unless you've got some kind of time machine tucked away in that array of yours, Melody . . ."

"Not as such, no," said Melody. "I have enough problems dealing with the Present and all its troubles without dragging in other options. I think we need to keep this simple. They've been talking to us, so maybe they're listening. Waiting for a response, a reply. We need someone capable of shouting loudly enough to attract their attention."

She looked at Happy; and after a moment or two, so did everyone else. Happy straightened up and scowled back at them.

"I'm really not going to like this, am I?"

"Do you ever?" said JC. "What do you have in mind, Melody?"

"We need what's in his mind," said Melody. "Sufficiently refocused and boosted . . . My scanners have been picking up tachyon emissions for some time. Yes, I know, they're not really, but let's all pretend they are . . . They're still here, along with the unnatural energies that produced them. I am pretty sure I can get my machines to lock on to these energies and reproduce the conditions that made contact with the future possible. Establish a sort of bridge, or tunnel, between Here and Now and whatever lies ahead. And then you, Happy, will blast a tightly focused telepathic bellow along this bridge to whoever's listening in the future."

"I can see a problem already," said Happy. "Even if I could shout that loudly, without all my little grey cells leaking out my ears, I won't only be attracting the attention of our future selves. That kind of telepathic volume would be heard by all kinds of nasty things from Outside. The kinds of things we really don't want to notice us."

"That's why I said *tightly focused*," said Melody.

"You really believe I can generate a telepathic voice loud enough to reach the future?" said Happy. "I'd be hard-pressed to reach London from here. On a good day! And good days seem to be in increasingly short supply as I get older."

"We can boost your signal," Melody said carefully. "With the right chemical support and inducements."

"The drugs do work," said Happy. "It's the after-effects . . ."

The radio staff looked at each other. It was clear they weren't following any of this. The Ghost Finders ignored them, intent on their own business.

"I don't want to do this," said Happy. "I really don't, JC. I'm already so full of pills that different parts of my brain are beating each other up. There's a limit to what even my system will put up with. I haven't found it yet, but logic says there has to be one."

JC frowned thoughtfully. "Do you think this is a good idea, Melody?"

"I think it's necessary," said Melody. "It's dangerous, yes. We have no idea what kind of dosage Happy will need. I'll help work it out, but . . ."

"But the world is going to end," said JC. "Tomorrow."

"All right!" said Happy. "I get it . . ."

"No you don't," said Melody. "You can't properly appreciate all the risks involved because you've never tried anything like this before. JC . . . I need time to work this through. To calculate the proper dosages and the best combinations . . . Put in some safeguards! To give him the best possible chance of surviving this."

"We don't have time," said JC.

"I won't let you force him into this!" said Melody.

"It was your idea," said JC.

Melody glared at him. "We can't . . . mess with his head without taking proper precautions!"

"Yes we can," said Happy. "Remember; I saw what the future did to you. I swore I would put my life on the line, put my death on the line, to make sure that future you would never happen. And I meant it. I will do anything, risk anything, to save you from that. So, no more talk, Mel. Let's do it."

Melody came forward and stood before him, staring into his eyes. And then she took him in her arms and held him. Happy let her do it. He patted her back comfortingly. Melody hadn't realised how much he was shaking until she held him. After a while, she let him go and stepped back. They shared a small smile, then she took him by the hand and led him over to the reception desk. Once again, they sat down together, and Happy took out all his pill boxes and bottles. He set them out before him, and Melody began sorting through them.

"What the hell is going on there?" Felicity said loudly. "Are those drugs?"

"Far too small a word, for what these little beauties can do," said Happy, not looking up from what he was doing. "Call them medicines, if that helps you feel more comfortable."

"I get it," said Captain Sunshine. "I have been here before . . . Feed your head, expand you consciousness, right? Like injecting rocket fuel into the motor of your mind. What my generation used to call the mind's true liberation."

He wandered over to the reception desk and watched, fascinated, as a massive collection of pills slowly assembled in front of Happy. The Captain leaned right over the table for a better look at the discarded empty boxes and bottles, his lips moving slowly as he worked out the handwritten labels. And then he straightened up again and looked doubtfully at Happy.

"Damn, man, I thought I'd seen pretty much everything in my time; but I don't recognise half this shit. Mandrake Root? St. John the Conqueror's Elixir? Red Death, Green Wyrm, Blue Meanies. In my day, it was all brown acid and purple hearts . . ."

"I could provide you with the chemical formulae," said Melody, not looking up.

"It would all be wasted on me," the Captain said cheerfully. "You don't need to know how a television set works to turn it on. I have to ask, though . . . some of those pills are seriously dangerous, right?"

"Right," said Melody.

The Captain nodded ruefully and moved away from the desk. "If the medicine didn't taste bad, you wouldn't know it was doing you good . . ."

Melody pushed a few last pills forward, her lips moving quickly as she added up dosages in her head. She considered adding a few more, decided against it, then she and Happy quietly considered the huge assortment of multi-coloured pills. Happy smiled, briefly.

"I am seriously impressed! Even a few years ago, I would never have dared attempt some of these dosages, never mind all of them together. A rainbow collection, a chemical cornucopia. Boys and girls, just say, *Fuck no!*"

"You don't have to do this," said Melody.

"Yes I do," said Happy.

"You don't have to do it for me, Happy!"

"Yes I do, Mel. For you; and the world. Perhaps because I wouldn't want to live in a world that didn't have you in it. You as you. The future will make you into a monstrous thing, Mel. A thing, made to kill other things. I was dead in that future world; and the Beast made you kill me again and again. Can you think of a better definition of Hell, for you and for me?"

Melody shook her head slowly. "How did we come to this?"

"Comes with the job," said Happy. "I've always known that."

They both looked at the piled-up pills. Happy reached out and pushed a few pills around with a fingertip. As though he still couldn't quite believe what he was contemplating doing.

"Think this is enough?" said Melody, trying to smile. "Think this will do it?"

"I think there's enough chemical dynamite here to blow the Doors of Perception right off their hinges and into next door's garden," said Happy. "Enough medical mayhem to let me see God and make me brave enough to spit in her eye. With all this blasting through my head, I could make anyone hear me. But there's no way I can drop this much shit into my system, and not suffer the consequences. The pills will send my mind up and out; but there's a more than reasonable chance that I won't be coming back, afterwards.

So I need you to promise me, Mel. Don't let me linger. In some hospital back room, with only machines to keep me going. Promise me. If you have to, you'll do what's necessary."

"Don't talk like that," said Melody.

"I have to. Who else can I trust?"

"I promise," said Melody. "Now take your damned pills."

"I am going to need a really big glass of water for this," said Happy.

"I'll get you one."

..............................

While all that was going on, Jonathan and Felicity joined forces to interrogate JC. Not an easy task, given that they didn't properly understand what was happening or what the proper questions were to ask. JC nodded and smiled politely, gave them as much truth as he thought they could handle, and remained properly evasive over everything else. On the grounds that even if he could make them understand all the consequences and implications of what they were about try, they almost certainly wouldn't thank him for it.

"So this is your big idea?" Felicity said finally, after JC had walked them through it for the third time. "You're going to feed your pet junkie mind-reader a massive overdose, so he can shout at the future?"

"Got it in one!" JC said happily. "I knew we'd get there eventually."

"And you really think this is going to work?" said Jonathan.

"The theory seems sound," JC said carefully. "If you

have any other ideas, I am definitely willing to listen . . .
No? Well, colour me surprised. Look, people, we're going
to do this because we don't have anything else. And a
really awful future is heading straight for us like a racing
train with really big horns on the front. Let us hope that
when we finally do place our call to the future, someone
will be there at the other end of the line. Someone who can
tell us whatever the hell it is we need to do."

He broke off. They all looked round, at the sound of
someone sobbing. Captain Sunshine was holding Sally in
his arms and doing his best to comfort her, as she cried
like a hurt child. The young receptionist had her face buried in the Captain's chest, tears streaming down her face,
cutting tracks in her make-up. She clung to Captain Sunshine like a small child hanging on to a parent because
something had come out of the dark to frighten her.

"I want to go home," she said miserably, forcing the
words past her ragged sobbing. "I don't want to be here . . .
It's horrid here."

"Hush, hush," said the Captain. "Hang in there, girl.
It'll all be over soon."

He shot a look at JC, who nodded. All be over soon.
Yes. One way or another.

Captain Sunshine got Sally settled onto a nearby chair
and stood protectively over her. He was still holding one
of her hands because she wouldn't let go of it. She was
still crying.

Jonathan and Tom moved off together, talking quietly.
Felicity glared around at everyone but had run out of
things to say. JC watched silently as Melody fed Happy
his pills, one at a time, with a lot of water. The telepath's
throat worked convulsively, as he struggled to get some

of them down. Melody held on to his free hand, doing her best to be quietly supportive. Her mouth was firm, her eyes bright with tears she refused to shed in front of Happy. She didn't say anything. There was nothing left to say.

She was feeding him poison, death in small doses, and they both knew it.

All the colour dropped out of Happy's face as he forced down the pills. Sweat broke out in heavy beads all across his forehead, then coursed down his face, to drip off his nose and his chin. His hand shook inside Melody's. But he got them all down; and then sat back in his chair, breathing hard. Like a runner before a race; like a warrior before a battle; like a man scared out of his mind by what he was doing but doing it anyway.

Not for the world, or even for the future. For the woman he loved.

"How are you feeling, Happy?" said Melody.

"I don't know . . . Hot. Sick. Exhilarated and enlightened. Everything seems so far away from me. Including me. Better do this soon, Mel. While I still remember what it is I'm supposed to be doing."

"I have to talk to JC for a moment," said Melody. "I won't be far."

"That's what you think," said Happy.

*"Man,"* Captain Sunshine said respectfully. "That was what the blessed Timothy Leary would have called a properly Heroic Dose. Are you sure you can find your way back from the trip you're going on?"

Happy didn't answer him. He didn't look as though he'd even heard the Captain. His face was flushed and twitching and running with sweat. His gaze was fixed on something far away, something he didn't like looking at. JC moved in beside the Captain.

"Happy will have a life-line," said JC. "Melody's building it right now."

Melody worked hard behind her machines, ripping bits out from here and there, improvising wildly as she cobbled together something she hoped would do the job. The others wanted to watch, but JC knew Melody didn't take kindly to being observed, so he chivvied everyone into taking seats around the reception desk, setting them in a rough semicircle facing Happy. One look at his strained face, and his wide staring eyes, was enough to make them all distinctly uneasy. Sally didn't want to be there at all, but the Captain persuaded her, and made a point of sitting next to her. Jonathan and Tom kept looking at JC, hoping for some sign of reassurance. Felicity scowled at him, making it clear that as far as she was concerned, whatever happened next was all his fault.

"The machines are working," Melody said finally. "Renewing the necessary conditions for a controlled temporal break, a direct link between the Present and the future, cutting out the middleman and slamming the edges together."

"How?" said Tom, desperately trying to understand. "How is any of that even possible?"

"It wouldn't mean anything to you if I did explain, which I probably couldn't anyway, so what's the point?" Melody said reasonably. "I'm making this shit up as I go along. What amazes me is how often that works . . . Hello; we're getting something."

They all looked at her. Her array of instruments shook and juddered, rattling on their supports and bouncing up and down. Strange lights blasted out of the monitor screens, and dark, crackling energies danced on the air above the array, like fuzzy ink-blots staining the air. Melody carefully withdrew her hands from the keyboards.

"Okay, that's interesting. The computers seem to be doing the rest of the work on their own, programming themselves. Crafty little beggars; they've been holding out on me. Ah well, time for phase two. Work your worry beads if you've got them."

She grabbed her cobbled-together piece of tech and carried it out from behind the array, holding it out before her as though it was both very fragile and very dangerous. She knelt and placed it carefully on the motorised trolley, which hummed loudly and importantly to itself. Melody then unrolled a length of heavy cable, plugged one end into her shaking array and the other into the back of the machine on the trolley. She went back to her array, slapped at one of the jumpier computers until it settled down, then studied her readouts for a long moment. She nodded to herself in a satisfied but still-uneasy way, and tapped a series of cautious commands into her main keyboard. The trolley chugged steadily away, out into the open centre of the reception area, the heavy cable unravelling behind it. The trolley reached its destination, a carefully judged distance away from everything else, and stopped.

"Right," said Melody. "That particular piece of tech should act as a homing signal, or beacon, for Happy's mind to hang on to. So he can find his way home. Not a particularly pretty piece of tech but not bad for something I knocked together in a hurry. In fact, I'm not at all sure I understand how it works . . . I get the feeling I may have picked up the necessary information from this room. Happy said the aether here was saturated with information. I think . . . our future selves sent back the necessary information, along with their voices, and we're only picking it up now we need it. Clever future selves . . . Anyway, once we're ready, I'll goose the array, and it should establish our bridging tunnel. Then it's up to Happy to shout his head off. Happy . . . Happy! Are you listening to me?"

"Yes, I can hear you," said Happy. His voice seemed as distant as his eyes. He didn't look at her.

"The tech is your anchor, Happy! Don't lose hold of it, no matter how far you send your thoughts. It's your way home."

"How are you feeling, Happy?" said JC.

"I wish people would stop asking me that," said Happy. "Isn't it obvious?"

"Not really, no," said Melody.

He looked like shit. They could all see that. But none of them wanted to say it.

"I am large," said the telepath. "I contain multitudes. And they're all running round and round in my head, fighting to get out." He turned his head slowly back and forth, seeming to finally take in the people seated before him. His eyes were large and dark and unblinking. "I can See you all . . . shining, so very brightly. If you could only see how wonderfully you all shine, in the dark of the world . . . Let's do it."

Melody's hands moved quickly across her keyboards. The motorised trolley trundled forward a few yards, went round and round for a bit, then stopped as it found exactly the right place. It beeped self-importantly, and the mechanism it carried glowed suddenly, in a series of brisk pulses.

Everyone sitting around the reception desk sat up straight in their chairs and looked quickly about them.

They could all feel something forming in the room, gathering strength and purpose. A growing presence, as though another person had appeared in the room. Happy's chemically augmented mind reached out in some new direction that they could all sense but not name. *Happy,* they all thought. *It's Happy. He's doing it. He's really doing it.*

Melody's machines roared and chattered as they blasted all kinds of light around the room. She had to turn her head and look away from some of them, they were so bright. Deep, impenetrable shadows gathered, at the furthest edges of the reception area, as though something were closing in. The trolley jumped up and down in place, but the piece of tech it was carrying didn't seem to be doing anything at all. The conditions weren't right yet. Happy sat very still in his chair, his face empty, but they could all feel the power gathering around him. Nothing they could see or hope to understand; but they knew it was there. There was a sense . . . of a gulf forming. Like staring down into a deep, deep well, with something at the bottom, staring back.

"This is it, people," Happy said suddenly. In a perfectly normal voice. "Here we go. Fasten your seat belts. It's going to be a very bumpy ride, and you don't want to be thrown off."

The room shuddered violently, as though the whole building had taken a direct hit. Murdock House seemed to lurch from one side to the other, then back again. The floor rose and dropped back. Everyone cried out, holding on to their chairs and each other, like passengers on a ship that had struck something unexpected. JC dropped into a chair by the reception desk and hung on grimly.

"What was *that*?" yelled Felicity.

*"Timequake!"* yelled Melody.

"What does that even mean?" said Jonathan.

"Beats the hell out of me," said JC. "Brace yourself and hang on."

And then their voices were drowned out as a cacophony of horrible sounds broke out all around them. JC recognised them immediately. It was the same awful animal sounds he'd heard before, up in the studio. Grunts and howls, screams and the sound of things dying. Sounds of hunting, and killing, and feasting. A terrible appetite pulsed on the air, heavy and overpowering, so physical they all felt they could reach out and touch it. Or it could touch them.

And oh, it's so hungry.

The animal sounds raced round and round them, closing in and falling back, like nocturnal creatures emerging from the jungle shadows to study their prey around a camp-fire. A great force was building, establishing itself in unnatural ways. Everyone sitting around the desk was crying out now, despite themselves—raw sounds of horror and fear. Even JC and Melody, experienced as they were. But not Happy. He sat very still in his chair, his hands resting loosely in his lap. His eyes were squeezed tightly shut: either because he didn't want to see what was happening or because he didn't need to. He was smiling. A wild, exultant, death's-head grin.

Flashing visions filled all their heads, brief glimpses of other worlds, come and gone in a moment, as a new reality fought to impose its own conditions on theirs. The future, elbowing the Present aside. Raging fires broke out all over the reception area: fierce but without heat. As yet. The flames weren't clear enough, weren't real enough yet. The walls of the room silently exploded, rushing away in all directions, receding into the distance. As though they could no longer contain all the space inside them. The floor and the ceiling vanished, dismissed by a new reality that didn't need them any longer. Because they would only have got in the way of letting everyone see the new world.

The world that was coming. The future.

Everywhere they looked, the world was on fire. Great flames leaping up, into a sky raining blood, and shit, and streams of maggots. Great jagged cracks split the sky apart, opening it up, so that Something could peer through from the other side. Cities exploded, buildings blown away on a terrible bright wind. Whole city blocks dropped into the earth, swallowed up by crevices appearing suddenly beneath them. Roads collapsed or tied themselves in knots. And all around, things and people fell into bottomless pits or were snatched up and carried away or burned for no reason.

It was the end of everything, the end of the world that was. A terrible future being born.

A new set of operating conditions replaced the old. The light curdled and spoiled, becoming feverish and foul. Almost unendurable to merely human eyes. Massive trees burst up out of the cracked ground, forcing the earth apart as they exploded into the rotten air. Driving up, like nails driven down. The ground acquired a covering of flesh, of skin. Stretched taut, flushed and sweating, heaving in slow, sluggish waves. The trees were big as buildings, bigger, and made entirely of meat. Their branches thrashed violently, clutching at the air like grasping tentacles. Living things ran through the meat forest, horrible creatures, hunting and being hunted. They jumped and ran and slithered through the living jungle. Huge and small and everything in between, they fell upon each other with boundless hate and hunger. Everything feasting on everything else. Killing and being killed, eating and being eaten, over and over again.

Because death was not an end, here.

People, recognisably human people, were running and hiding and screaming helplessly as awful things pulled them down. Men and women were torn apart, eaten up . . . dying horribly everywhere. Because that was all that was left for them to do, in this newborn future world. They never stood a chance. They were prey, there to be played with.

"Oh God," said Melody. "I know this . . ."

Her quiet voice cut clearly through the bedlam. Perhaps because she was so much closer, or realer, than anything else.

*"You know this?"* said Felicity.

"JC, we've seen this place before!" said Melody.

"Of course we have," said JC. "From the students, and their séance. This is the world of the Beast."

"You mean you've been here before?" said Jonathan, his voice rising hysterically. "How the hell . . ."

"We get around," said JC. "On another case, we had to break into a world like this, to rescue some kidnapped souls. We brought them safely home again; and we shut the door behind us. I know we did. But I'm starting to wonder . . . whether we should have locked it, too."

"Talk to us properly!" Tom said angrily, using his anger to hold his fear at bay. "Tell us what's going on! We need to understand what's happening!"

"The world we entered wasn't this world, exactly," said JC. "It wasn't the future, then. It was another world, another place. We defeated the Beast; and I thought that was it."

"It's our future now," said Melody. "Unless we do something. Happy? Happy! Have you made contact yet?"

"We closed the door after us; but the door was still there," said Happy. Not looking at her, not looking at anything. "We left a trail of bread-crumbs, and the Beast followed us home. And brought its home with it. Time means nothing to the kind of things that see it from the other side. The Beast has come, will come, through the door . . . and it brings the rules of its own reality with it. It wants revenge on us, JC; and oh, it's so hungry . . ."

"Concentrate, Happy!" JC said harshly. "Remember what you're doing, and why! The bridging tunnel is in place. Yell out to our future selves! Make them hear you! Make them talk to us!"

"I have made contact," said Happy. "They're here."

The front door slammed shut behind them. They all turned around in their chairs, surprised to find the front door still there. Standing alone, in its frame. The wall around it was gone. The door opened and slammed shut, then swung open again as the future JC came through. Standing tall and composed, in his immaculate white suit. No trace of his death wounds, not yet. Only the dark and empty eye-sockets where his glorious golden eyes should have been. Bloody tears had run down his face, leaving dark crimson trails on his cheeks. JC could feel the broken sunglasses he'd picked up, in his inside jacket pocket, pressing against his heart, under the bloody handprint. The future JC strode forward, heading straight for the group sitting around the reception desk. He stopped abruptly and turned his blind face to JC.

"Took you long enough to make contact," said the future JC. His voice was rough and strained, as though simply standing there before them was an almost unendurable strain. "Pay attention, people. We don't have much time. We have to get this done before the Beast realises what's happening, and shuts this down."

JC got up from his seat and moved cautiously forward to face his future self. He could feel his heart hammering painfully fast.

"How far?" he said. "How far into the future is this? How far have we come to meet you? Do you know?"

"Of course I know," said the future JC. "I remember this meeting as though it was yesterday. I remember this conversation from the first time around, when I was you. This is tomorrow. The day after this meeting. Yes . . . It really did all go to hell so very quickly . . . Let me walk you through it, for all the good it will do you. The Beast found the door again, from the other side. You closed it . . . but the door, or the possibility of a door, was still there. The Beast had all the time it needed, to work out how to open it again because the years pass so differently in this place. The Beast is very old, and very powerful, and not used to being defied. It's so hungry . . . because you made it hungry for revenge . . ."

Melody looked at the future JC but stayed put behind her machines. "What about the Flesh Undying? How did the Beast overcome that?"

"The Beast ate the Flesh Undying," said the future JC. "That's what the Beast does: it eats flesh. Over and over again."

"What happened to you, JC?" said Happy. His voice was quite calm and composed.

"Happy . . ." said the future JC, turning his blind face unerringly in the telepath's direction. "Yes, I remember your being here. When you were still alive. You made all this possible. How can I ever thank you?"

"Stop that!" said Melody. "This is the Beast's fault!"

"No," said the future JC. "We should never have meddled, never have got involved with the Beast. But what the hell, let's be generous. There's more than enough blame to go around."

"What happened to our eyes?" said JC. He had to know.

"They took them back," said the future JC. "Because I should have seen this coming, and I didn't. Too full of myself, you see, and too easily distracted. The forces from Outside have withdrawn their support for this world. Given it up, as lost. Too many disappointments in their chosen agents . . . They have decided Humanity isn't worth saving."

"How can the Beast be this powerful?" said Melody.

"Because it's the Beast," said the future JC.

"What happened?" said Happy. For the first time, his voice sounded angry. "Show us what happened. Show us how we got to where you are, from where we are."

"Visions?" said the future JC. "You ask for visions, from a blind man? Well, why not? We'll start with Melody, shall we? Poor Mel, so convinced her precious machines would save her."

A vision of Melody appeared, standing amidst the ruins of Murdock House. In a clearing in the meat jungle. Melody stood alone, behind her array of instruments, surrounded by a great pack of vicious creatures. She worked fiercely at her keyboards, while a shimmering force shield surrounded and protected her. The crackling energies barely held the horrid creatures back; but still they pressed forward, driven by rage and hunger and other, worse, appetites. They threw themselves against the killing energies of the force shield; and even as it destroyed them, more pressed forward to take their place. They slammed against the shield, again and again, pushing it back and edging that little bit closer. Until finally, inevitably, the shield collapsed, overwhelmed by the sheer weight of numbers.

Melody opened fire with her machine-pistol. Heads shattered and chests exploded, blood flying on the air; and still the awful things pressed forward, driven on by a will outside their own. The never-ending enmity of the Beast. She held them off for a while, dead things piling up before her. She stood her ground, didn't run. Wouldn't run. Until the creatures came scrambling up and over her array of instruments, even as the machine-pistol shot them down. And then, quite suddenly, they fell back, as Something appallingly, impossibly, huge came walking forward through the meat jungle. Too big to be seen clearly, too foul for the human mind to accept. The Beast came walking, and the ground cracked open under its terrible weight.

Melody fired her gun at the Beast; and it didn't even notice. It towered over her and its army of creatures. It looked down on Melody, and she withered and twisted under the weight and force of its regard. Her physical presence was reworked and reshaped; and when it was done, the distorted monstrous thing that used to be Melody Chambers knelt at the feet of the Beast and worshipped it.

And somehow, everyone watching knew there was just enough consciousness left inside the creature to know what it was doing and to hate it and despair.

"Where's Happy?" said Melody. "Why didn't he protect me? He would have, I know he would . . . unless something happened to him. Talk to me, damn you; what happened to my Happy?"

The vision changed. Happy was standing alone in an empty clearing in the meat jungle. Looking up past the thrashing trees, at the Beast standing over him. He glared up at it, refusing to look away. Even though it must have hurt him more than anyone because he could See it more clearly. They could all feel the effort his defiance was costing him. He raised his voice, to the Beast.

"You destroyed my Mel, you bastard! I warned you! I warned you what would happen if you took away the only thing I cared about. There's an old trick, the first thing the Institute teaches all E.S.P.ers, before they're allowed out in the field. One last dirty trick to throw at our enemies, when all is lost. The psychic bomb. The real suicide bomb. Where you take everything you have, everything you are, and throw it at your enemy. So to hell with you, Beast."

He concentrated, focusing his thoughts in a single, implacable way; and then he exploded, in a great blast of released psychic energies. A light that burned so brightly even the Beast had to turn its head away. Meat trees were ripped up out of the ground and thrown away. More burst into flames, cooking in the heat, blackened and charred. Every living creature watching from the shadows was blown apart or consumed by flames, all in a moment. As Happy did his best to wipe the rotten world clean with one last dying effort.

It didn't work.

When his light finally died away, the clearing was much larger, but the meat jungle still remained. There was death and devastation all around, but the Beast was still standing. Untouched and unharmed. Because it was the master of its own world—the world it made for itself. The Beast looked slowly around, and wherever its gaze passed, the meat jungle was restored. All the trees, and all the creatures, and Happy, too. The ghost of Happy returned, made solid and held in the world against his will, held in place by the power of the Beast.

Happy's ghost turned his head suddenly, to stare back into the Past, and speak to all the people there watching him. He could see them though it was clear the Beast couldn't.

"The power provided by my psychic suicide allowed us to open a door in Time, so we could send our warnings back to you. To make the bridging tunnel possible. To make this meeting, this conversation, possible. I died, to give you this chance. Don't waste it."

"What happened to me?" whispered Felicity. "Where are the rest of us, in this future? What is the Beast going to do to us?"

"Nothing you'd want to know," said the future JC. "And certainly nothing you'd want to see."

"Show us!" said Tom. "We have a right to know!"

"Some people never learn," said the future JC.

The vision changed again, to show the fate of the staff of Radio Free Albion in the burning wreckage of the reception area. Jonathan Hardy had been impaled, on a single twisting tree branch. The long, writhing thing had threaded itself through him, in one end and out the other, finally bursting out of one bloody eye-socket. Jonathan was still alive, still aware, still suffering. Tom had been nailed to a wall with a broken-off beam. He was on fire, burning and screaming forever. Felicity had been stretched out, her body spread across a whole wall. Her taut-stretched skin was constantly splitting and cracking, and repairing itself. Only her face remained recognisably the same as she sobbed endlessly.

"I know that sound," said Sally. "I've heard that crying before. A woman sobbing, right here in this room. Oh my God; it was you I heard. I heard you crying, Felicity."

The vision pulled back to show a huge insect creature, with a bulging head and compound eyes, standing over the reception desk. It held Sally's severed head out before it, so the head could see all the horrors in the room. Now and again, the creature would drag a single clawed finger down Sally's face, leaving a long, bloody gouge behind. The severed head screamed and screamed. The sound carried on and on even though there were no longer any lungs to support it.

Melody had seen the severed head before, hanging in mid air above the reception desk. Screaming endlessly. And now she knew why.

"What about me?" said Captain Sunshine. His voice was surprisingly strong and steady. "What happened to me?"

The vision changed again, to show a red-and-purple-veined thing, lurching slowly across the floor, slick and shapeless, with all its organs on the outside. The Captain had been turned inside out and left that way.

And then the voice of the Beast was back, beating on the corrupt air, lazy and amused. You all helped to make my triumph possible! You and your precious radio station! See how I reward you all. Forever!

''''''''''''''''''''''''''

Everything stopped. A moment, frozen in Time. And then the visions disappeared and the reception area went back to how it was. Everyone was struck dumb, shocked silent. Except for JC, who fixed his future self with a cold stare.

"All right," he said. "How do we stop this?"

"You can't," said the future JC.

"What?" said JC. "Then . . . why are we here? Why all the warnings?"

"They didn't come from us," said the future JC. "The Beast owns us all; we do what it wants. And it does so love to play with us, now and then. It's having such fun . . . Except, I don't think it ever really believed you'd be able to do this. So learn from what you've seen. Go back, get the hell out of here. Run, while you still can."

He broke off as the Beast's voice was heard again, crashing upon them in heavy, overwhelming waves.

*Little creature, this is not what I instructed you to say. All of you exist by my will, now; you speak only because I allow it.*

"You know what?" said the future JC. "Screw you." He looked straight at JC, with his empty, bloody eye-sockets. "Get back to your own time. To yesterday. I'll hold it off, for as long as I can. And once you're back, shut down the tunnel." He grinned, briefly. "I'd say good luck; but we both know that's not on the cards. But maybe you'll think of something I didn't and save the day at the last moment. That's always been what we do best, after all."

The Beast roared its displeasure—a vast, foul sound that hammered on the air. It leaned in over the roofless room. The future JC moved forward, to put himself between the Beast and the Past. And the distorted monstrous thing that had been Melody Chambers fell on him from out of the broken sky. She hit him hard and tore at him with her clawed hands. And he stood there and took it, holding the Beast's attention, so his Past self could get away. He would not retreat, would not fall back even a single step, even as he died again and again.

JC turned to Happy, still sitting motionless in his chair. "Break contact! Shut down the bridge!"

"I can't," said Happy. "I'm lost . . . I can't find the Past. I can't find my anchor, anywhere . . ."

Melody came running out from behind her array. And the piece of tech sitting on the trolley exploded, scattering sharp pieces like shrapnel. The Beast laughed, mockingly. Melody turned away and threw her arms around Happy, in his chair. She held him tight, her face pressed against his, her mouth at his ear.

"I'm your anchor, Happy. I'm right here. Come home, to me!"

"I never left you," said Happy.

Suddenly, the future was gone. And everything was as it had been, again.

।।।।।।।।।।।।।।।।।।।।।।।।।

Happy collapsed in his chair, almost sliding out of it. Only Melody's grip held him in place. His eyes were closed, and he was breathing harshly. Everyone else scrambled up out of their chairs and backed away from the desk, needing to distance themselves from what they'd seen. The whole reception area was back, everything as it had been. No fires, no destruction; no sign anywhere of the awful things to come. The radio staff stumbled about, not even looking at each other. Trying to come to terms with what they'd seen and learned.

"How is he, Melody?" said JC. "How is Happy?"

"Out cold," said Melody. She checked Happy's pulse, then sat him up in his chair as best she could. "His breathing is uneven, his pulse is thready; he's got a really bad colour, and he's cold to the touch. God alone knows what that experience did to him, never mind all those pills we made him take. He said he might not come back from this, JC . . . So we'll have to wait and see." She looked grimly at JC. "Well? Was it worth it?"

"Too soon to say," said JC. "But it was . . . interesting. We learned some useful things."

"He's a tough little fellow," Melody said fondly, brushing the hair back out of Happy's face with a gentle hand. "A dosage like that would have killed anyone else outright."

"Let him rest," said JC. "He's earned it."

Felicity lurched forward to face him, her expression almost feral. "Do something! Think of something! We can't let that nightmare happen!"

Jonathan came and took her by the arm and led her away, making soothing noises. She had no strength left to resist him.

"There has to be a way to prevent this," said JC, as much to himself as anyone else. "Or the Beast wouldn't have been so determined to stop us, there at the end."

"We closed the door on the Beast, back in the students' flat," said Melody. "I know we did. All my instruments confirmed it."

"Maybe it found another door," said JC. "Or made one. It had all the time in its world . . . to work out how . . ."

He stood there—frowning, concentrating, thinking hard. While all around him people stared numbly at each other, horrified and traumatised. JC knew he should be doing something to help them, comfort them. That was his job. But all he could really do for them now was think. Jonathan and Felicity clung together, like survivors of some terrible shipwreck. Tom stumbled round and round in circles, muttering to himself. Captain Sunshine led a trembling Sally to a chair and sat her down. She grabbed his hand in both of hers and wouldn't let go.

"Don't leave me alone. Please, don't leave me alone . . ."

"It's all right, girl," the Captain said gently. "I'm right here."

Melody went back to her instrument array but couldn't seem to concentrate on it. She looked at JC.

"Still think the Boss just happened to send us here?"

"There was no briefing, no case file," said JC. "If she'd known, she would have told us . . . something. Prepared us, so we could fight better. No, she was preoccupied with the Flesh Undying and all its agents. I think the Beast slipped this one past her. Past all of us . . ."

Jonathan left Felicity, for the moment. He approached JC in a determined way. "What just happened? What did it all mean?"

All the radio staff looked to JC; and he did his best to talk them through it; but he could tell from their faces that they were no wiser and no happier when he'd finished. Perhaps fortunately, he was interrupted then by Kim, who came walking urgently through the left-hand wall to join them. All the radio staff jumped, and Felicity actually produced a small scream. Kim looked down her nose at them all.

"Yes! I'm a ghost! I'm the only ghost in the Ghost Finders. Get over it. We have more important things to talk about."

"Where have you been, Kim?" said JC. "And why didn't I notice that you weren't with us, in the future?"

"How many times, JC?" said Kim. "No-one notices me unless I want them to. I could feel the Beast approaching, so I hid myself away and watched it all, unobserved. Do you remember how the two of us stopped it the first time, together?"

JC nodded and looked at the radio staff to explain what they were talking about. And then he decided not to. They didn't look in any condition to cope with more explanations.

"She's a ghost, but she's on our side!" he said loudly. "And she's come up with a really good idea. Something we can do . . ."

Felicity lunged forward and thrust her hand through Kim's unsubstantial back. She waggled her hand about, then snatched it away again.

Kim turned and fixed her with a hard stare. "If you ever do that again, I will haunt your mirror for the rest of your life."

Felicity retreated so quickly, she almost fell over her own feet. Jonathan put an arm around her, and she let him. Kim drifted over to the reception desk, to stand beside Melody and look sadly at Happy. He wasn't moving, barely breathing.

"He's dying, isn't he?" said Melody.

"He was so very brave," said the ghost girl. "But even his system couldn't handle that kind of overdose. Nothing human could."

"I know," said Melody. "And I helped him do it. Encouraged him to do it. Because I thought it was necessary. Maybe he'll get some rest, now. He's earned it."

"Not if he doesn't help us stop the Beast, he won't," said Kim. "You saw what will happen to him, in the future."

Melody's head snapped round suddenly, to meet her gaze. "Wait a minute. Is that it? Is that the paradox we need, to break the chain of events between here and there? If Happy dies now, the Beast can't make him die later. Without his psychic suicide, none of this could happen! His death, here and now, could save us all. He'd like that."

"No he wouldn't," said Kim. "He'd much rather go on living, with you. Trust me on that. All Happy's death would do is rob us of a weapon we could use against the Beast! JC, come here. We're needed."

JC hurried over to join her, and at the last moment she stepped forward to meet him and move inside him. The two of them joined together on so many levels; and a gentle golden glow surrounded JC. The radio staff cried out again, this time in quiet awe and wonder. Something wonderful had come into the room, and they could all feel it. JC, with Kim contained within him, removed his sunglasses and looked on Happy with his fierce golden glare. And Happy took a deep breath and sat bolt upright, his eyes wide with surprise.

"I feel good!" he said loudly. "Really good! Wow, what a rush . . . What the hell was *that*? It was like I was finally getting a good night's sleep and going down for the third time; and then someone called my name! Like God, spotting me in the middle of a crowd. So I came back. Oh, hello, Mel. How are you? Why are you crying?"

Melody whooped with joy, grabbed both his hands, pulled him up out of his chair, and danced him round the room, stamping her feet and grinning wildly. Happy went along, laughing breathlessly.

"I'm back! I'm fine!" he said. "I can feel it. What happened?"

"We happened," said Kim, stepping out of JC. The glow disappeared from around him. JC winked a glowing eye at Happy and put his sunglasses back on.

Happy stopped dancing and looked steadily at Melody. "I remembered something . . . Something the Beast said, about how the radio station made his triumph possible." He looked across at Jonathan. "Have there been any changes made here, recently? Any new equipment installed?"

"Well, yes," said Jonathan. "There's a whole bunch of new equipment down in the cellar. The new owners insisted on it when they took over. It's supposed to increase the strength of our broadcast signal, so we can cover a larger area, reach more people."

"Talk about hiding in plain sight," said Melody. "And you didn't think to mention this to us before, because . . .?"

Jonathan shrugged uncomfortably. "Didn't seem relevant, with all the weird shit going on."

"I need to take a close look at this new equipment," Melody said firmly. "See what it's really doing. Would I be right in saying, Jonathan, that all your problems here started after this new equipment was installed?"

"Well, yes. But . . ." said Jonathan.

"I think your new owners are almost certainly a front for Something Else," said JC. "That's if they even exist as such. The Beast has had a lot of time to move things around behind the scenes."

"The radio signal must have been altered, to broadcast on unnatural frequencies," said Melody. "That's what brought the Beast here. Like a beacon; something it could home in on. I think that's what the warnings were really all about. When the signal reaches a certain strength, or perhaps even a certain frequency, it will open a door for the Beast, make it possible for it to come through. We did lock the door, JC, so it had to make another! Everything that has been happening here, the voices, the visions, have all been distractions. To keep us away from what really mattered—the equipment in the cellar! JC, I think we should go down there and do something seriously annoying."

"It's about time," said JC.

# NINE

..............................

## SOMETHING BEASTLY IN THE CELLAR

"A cellar?" said Captain Sunshine. "There's a cellar, here under Murdock House?"

"All these years, and you never noticed we have a cellar," said Jonathan. "Why am I not surprised?"

"You can talk," said Tom. "How many times have you ever been down there since we moved in?"

"I'm the general manager," Jonathan said loftily. "I leave such menial things to the members of my staff."

"I notice we're not getting any closer to going down there," said JC. "Is there a problem?"

Jonathan shot a quick glance at the far end of the reception area. "I don't know why, but thinking about going down into the cellar is giving me the creeps, big time. Anybody else feel that?"

"No," said Felicity immediately.

"I don't even like it up here," said Sally. "Look, you don't need me down in the cellar. Someone should stay up here to keep an eye on things."

"Good idea," said Happy. "I'll keep you company. We can hide behind each other."

"Everyone goes down," JC said firmly. "I don't think it would be safe for anyone to be left on their own here once we start making trouble down below."

"What kind of trouble did you have in mind?" said Melody.

JC grinned at her. "Oh, the usual. Violent and destructive and seriously upsetting to the Bad Guys."

"Ah," said Melody. "The usual."

"I'll lead the way, then," said Jonathan. But he didn't seem at all happy about it.

They all followed him to the door at the back of the reception area. JC and Happy and Melody stuck close behind Jonathan, to make sure he couldn't change his mind, while the others brought up the rear. With varying levels of confidence. Felicity looked fascinated, Tom looked resigned. Sally and Captain Sunshine stuck close together for mutual support. Kim was in there, too, somewhere; but no-one noticed exactly where. There was at least a general sense of purpose in the group now they'd committed themselves to a course of action.

Jonathan pushed the door open, took a sharp turn to the left, and led everyone down a narrow, dimly lit stairway. Dull metal steps sounded loudly under their descending tread, as though to warn whatever lay in wait that company was coming.

The first thing that struck JC was the smell. It hit him hard the moment he started down the steps, a thick, nasty, and corrupt smell . . . that reminded him irresistibly of dead things piled up and left to go off. He wrinkled his nose and pulled a face despite himself. Other people began to make loud noises of disgust and distress as the stench got to them.

"I told you we needed to get someone in, to see about the plumbing," Tom said to Jonathan. "It smells like something is seriously backed up down there."

"Easy for you to say," said Jonathan. He peered ahead into the dim light, being very careful about where he put his feet. "Do you have any idea how much a plumber charges by the hour? All right, I should have listened to you; I didn't realise things had got this bad. But as long as the smell stayed down here and didn't come upstairs to bother the rest of us, I had more important things to worry about."

"This isn't plumbing," said JC. "It smells like . . . game meat, like carrion left to hang and decay."

Happy took a deep breath. "I'm getting . . . organic materials, I'm getting phosphates and nitrates, noble rot and weird shit," he declaimed, in his best wine-taster's delivery. "What I'm not getting . . . is anything remotely like radio-station equipment."

"I have to admit, I'll be interested to see what this new machinery looks like," said Jonathan.

"You've never seen it?" said Melody.

"None of us have," said Tom. "The new owners sent in their own installation team, and they did all the work. Wouldn't even let me help unload the stuff from their trucks. Or go down and watch them work—in case we got in the way. Delicate instruments, they said. Very temperamental. Hell, I can take a hint."

"And that didn't seem in any way suspicious?" said JC. "That they wouldn't even let you supervise the connections? In your own radio station?"

"They seemed to know what they were doing," said Tom, defensively.

"As long as the cost of the installation wasn't coming out of my budget, I didn't want to know," said Jonathan.

"Did you notice any difference, afterwards?" said Melody. "Any improvement in the range or quality of your transmissions?"

"No . . ." said Tom. "But it really wasn't my business to say anything . . ."

"I kept meaning to ask," said Jonathan. "But . . ."

"You didn't want to say anything that might attract the new owners' attention," said Felicity. "Or do anything that might get them mad at you."

"Exactly," said Jonathan. "And as long as you were left alone to run your show, you didn't care about anything else. Did you?"

"No," said Felicity. "Nothing else mattered."

They'd almost reached the bottom of the stairs when they all slammed to a halt, stopped right where they were, as though they'd hit an invisible wall. None of them cried out, or protested, or asked questions. They were afraid; and they didn't know why.

A nameless fear had them all by the throat, a sudden conviction that to descend any further was to put their lives in danger. That something was waiting for them down below, something with bad intent. They didn't know what or why; but they knew, beyond any shadow of doubt. Some of the radio staff started to turn around in the narrow space, to go back upstairs; but JC stopped them and held them in place with his loud, implacable voice.

"It's all right! Don't panic! I know what this is. The threat isn't real, there is no immediate danger; it's all in your head. This is what's called an aversion field. The psychic equivalent of a barbed-wire fence and a KEEP OUT! sign. It can't affect you if you don't let it!"

One by one, they all calmed down. Once they thought about it, and realised there was nothing actually threatening anywhere near them, the feeling didn't seem nearly as bad. But it was still there. A lot of looking back and forth took place as everyone waited for someone else to take the plunge.

"Do you want me to go back upstairs and fetch some of my equipment?" Melody said to JC. "I'm sure I could whip up something to disrupt whatever's generating the aversion field."

"I don't feel anything," said Kim. And most people jumped as they realised she was with them.

"Of course you don't," JC said kindly. "This kind of thing only affects the living. And you stay right where you are, Melody. I don't want the group splitting up. Happy, I think this is more in your line. Can you do something about this field?"

"From the feel of it, it's not being generated by any machine," said Happy. "This has the flavour of something produced by a living mind. A telepathic broadcast. Definitely my line of work. And from somewhere really close, too."

"From the cellar?" said JC.

"Wouldn't surprise me at all," said Happy. He frowned, concentrating. "It's so . . . diffuse, it's hard to pinpoint. But since this all comes from a living mind, I can hit it with my mind."

He lashed out with a blunt and brutal psychic attack. The aversion field shuddered enough for everyone to feel the difference. And then it surged forward again, recovering its strength, falling upon them like an angry attack dog. They all cried out as the weight of the field closed in on them, clinging to them and holding them in place, like falling layers of invisible cobwebs. Everyone cried out in shock and disgust, struggled against the unseen force that held them. Happy closed his eyes and struck again, putting all his strength into it, pushing the field back and back. Until it stretched, and snapped, and disappeared, blown apart by the force of his mind.

Everyone on the stairs breathed more easily and patted at themselves numbly, to make sure nothing still held them. Once the aversion had been banished, they couldn't even remember what it had felt like or why it had such power over them. But they all felt the relief.

Happy put his shoulder against the cold, stone inner wall and leaned on it heavily, his eyes still closed. Melody moved in close beside him.

"It's all right, Mel," he said, without opening his eyes to look at her. "I'm tired. I've been through a lot today; and I don't know how much more I've got left in me. I'm running on fumes."

"Do you want some of your pills?" said Melody, carefully.

"Always," said Happy. "But not right now."

"Lead on, Jonathan," said JC. "We're almost there. Let's go see what's in the cellar that Something doesn't want us to see."

............................

They finally reached the bottom of the stairs and clustered together in the cramped little space before the closed metal door. Not much light, lots of shadows. The air was close and hot and sweaty. The smell was stronger than ever. Thick and pungent; filling their heads. It reminded JC of a zoo at feeding time.

"Smells like you've got an animal caged up in there," said Melody. "And a big one, too."

"I think we'd have noticed that," said Jonathan.

They all looked at the door before them. A great slab of solid steel, blocking the way. Their distorted reflections stared impassively back at them. There was no handle, only a computer keypad on the wall next to the door. Jonathan gave the door a good push, just in case, but it didn't budge. He made a surprised sound and snatched his hand away. The metal was uncomfortably warm to the touch.

"Let me try," said Tom.

He leaned over the keypad, a little self-importantly, and tapped in his security code. The door still didn't want to move. Tom scowled and tried again, hitting each key very firmly to make sure he'd got it right; and still nothing. He turned to Jonathan.

"They swore to me that code would open the door."

"They lied," said Jonathan. "Who would have thought?"

"All right," said Tom. "Try your managerial override."

Jonathan punched in his code; but the door didn't want to know. Jonathan gave the door a good kick, then fell back, wincing and favouring his throbbing foot. The dull sound from the kick made the door seem even more solid and immovable.

"That code should have worked!" Jonathan protested. "I'm supposed to have full access to everything at this station!"

"Obviously no-one was supposed to have access, once

the special new machinery was installed," said JC. "If you could see what was in there, and what it was really doing, you might not approve."

"How are we going to get in?" said Felicity. "That door looks like it could laugh off dynamite."

"Doors," sniffed Kim, dismissively. She strode forward and ghosted right through the solid steel. The radio staff tried not to jump this time. Kim disappeared beyond the door; and there was a long pause. JC scowled. He didn't like Kim's going places he couldn't follow, to back her up. Because she was dead she thought bad things couldn't happen to her. And then Kim came running back through the steel door, and came to a halt before JC. Her face was shocked, her eyes wide. She tried to say something, then shook her head helplessly.

"What is it?" said JC. "What did you see in there?"

"It's bad. Really bad," said Kim. "We have been places, JC, and we have seen things; but what's in there . . . It's alive. Nasty. And ugly. I mean really, horribly ugly."

"Is it dangerous?" Happy said immediately. "Yes, I know, goes without saying."

"We still need to get in there!" said Felicity.

"Do we?" said Sally. "I've heard nothing so far to convince me that we do."

"The world is going to end tomorrow," said Happy. "Unless we get in there and do something."

"Well," said JC, "we could always try being polite, I suppose. If there is something alive on the other side of that door, there's always the chance it will respond to a reasonable approach."

"Bets?" said Melody.

JC stepped up to the metal door and knocked smartly.

Something immediately struck the other side of the door, in response—violent, vicious, thunderous blows. So hard the steel door jumped and shuddered in its frame. JC stepped carefully back from the door.

"Okay . . ." said Happy. "Not good. Not in any way, shape, or form good, or even helpful. Something is at home, and it really doesn't want to be disturbed."

"You're the telepath," said JC. "You tell us what's in there."

Happy smiled, briefly. "I knew you were going to say that." He glowered at the door, in a considering sort of way. His brow furrowed, and his eyes narrowed. "It's . . . definitely alive. Don't ask me what it is, though. It's hard to get my head round its true nature. Like . . . nothing I've ever encountered before. It's definitely not human, JC. Not in any way human."

"So what is it?" said Melody. "Alien? Mutant? Something from Another Place?"

"Could be," said Happy. "I've never sensed anything even remotely like this; and I've been around. Making contact with it is creeping me out on an industrial scale. I'll tell you this; it knows we're out here, and it isn't afraid of us. Not even a little bit."

"Could it be one of the creatures from the Other Place?" asked JC. "Something from the Beast's world?"

"Yes . . . and no," said Happy, reluctantly. "It's not the Beast. I'd recognise that in a heart-beat. But it does have something of that flavour about it."

Melody produced her machine-pistol, so suddenly none of the others could be sure exactly where it came from. She aimed the gun at the keypad, and everyone edged back as far as the cramped space would permit. The sound of gun-fire was painfully loud in the confined space; and bits of broken keypad flew through the air, showering over everyone. The door swung back a few inches.

"What is a Ghost Finder doing with a gun?" said Felicity, pointedly.

"Is that a trick question?" said Melody. She turned up her nose at the shattered keypad. "Think of this as a pick-lock with attitude."

She made the machine-pistol disappear about her person, stepped forward, and placed one hand flat against the steel door. She braced herself and pushed. The door gave way before her. The stench was suddenly that much worse, rich and foul and acrid, rolling out past the door in heavy waves. Everyone coughed hard and turned their heads away. Melody stood her ground and pushed the door back some more. Heavy sucking sounds came from inside the cellar and a slow, steady susurrus, like something large breathing. Melody glanced back at JC. He nodded, and she threw all her strength against the door.

Tom moved in beside JC. "Where, exactly, does she keep that gun?"

"Trust me," said JC. "You don't want to know."

"You don't know, do you?" said Tom.

"Ask Happy," said JC. "He's sleeping with her."

Tom looked to Happy, who shot him a disturbing smile. Tom shuddered, briefly.

"Brave fellow . . ."

"I've always thought so," said JC.

"I can hear you!" said Melody, not looking round.

JC moved in beside her, and together they pushed the door all the way open. A bruised red and purple light fell out into the corridor. The stench was almost overpowering.

Happy moved up alongside Melody, and the three Ghost Finders moved cautiously forward, into the cellar. Followed, slowly and very reluctantly, by the radio staff.

᠎᠎᠎᠎᠎᠎᠎᠎᠎᠎᠎᠎᠎᠎᠎᠎᠎᠎᠎᠎᠎᠎᠎

The cellar was packed full, from wall to wall and from floor to ceiling, with awful things. The humans stood bunched together, inside the doorway, feeling small and insignificant, overwhelmed by the sheer scale of what lay before them. The cellar spread out in all directions, easily the same size as the huge reception area above it; and there was barely an inch of open space left anywhere. Strange organic shapes pressed up against each other, alive and even blossoming, in an utterly unnatural way. *Unearthly,* thought JC. *Not of this world.* Rounded surfaces oozed dark, tarry liquids as they heaved and swelled and subsided. Protuberances thrust out here and there but not in any way that made the shapes make sense. It was like looking at alien organs, torn from some inconceivable body, which had somehow learned to thrive on their own. Strange sounds beat heavily on the still air. Something that might have been a slow, sullen heart-beat, and something else that might have been breathing. A thick, viscous mulch, like bloody vomit, covered what could be seen of the floor.

The radio staff were the most affected. They clung together, making quiet noises of distress. The Ghost Finders took it more in their stride.

"I've seen worse," said JC.

"Really?" said Melody. "When? Not on any case we worked together."

"This is so above our pay-scale," said Happy. "We're

supposed to deal with ghosts. Does this look in any way spiritual to you? I say we all back out, very carefully, and send for the SAS. Or anybody else with really big guns and a careless attitude to high explosives."

"What is this?" said Jonathan. He had both hands pressed tightly over his mouth and nose, trying to keep out the smell.

"This is disgusting," said Tom. "I saw the machines, as they were unloaded from the trucks; and they didn't look anything like this! I mean, I would have said something . . . Where did all this come from?"

"Looks to me like it grew here," said JC. "From a pre-programmed seed, probably. Biotech. Organic machines. Once it was established here, it kept growing until it filled all the space available."

"You've encountered things like this before?" said Felicity.

"No," said JC. "But I have read some files . . ."

He broke off as several of the nearer shapes expanded suddenly, the glistening surfaces stretching disturbingly taut. Dark shapes burst through, popping out onto the dank air. Disturbingly human eyeballs on the end of long, wavering tentacles, dripping thick, glutinous liquids. The eyes stared balefully at the newcomers.

"Told you," said Happy. "It knows we're here."

"You had to knock," Melody said to JC.

All across the cellar, strange living shapes bulged and heaved and pressed against each other. Protuberances thrust out, lengthening and thickening. Everything was some shade of red or purple, an angry, violent colour under the bruised, sullen light that seemed to seep from everywhere at once. It made everything seem that much more . . .

fleshy. JC thought of rotten fruit, and mushrooms, and fruiting mushrooms. The bulging shapes pushed up against each other, and sometimes a large shape would engulf a smaller, swallowing it up.

Everything was connected to everything else by long, warty tubes that pulsed and twitched, like connecting nerve fibres. More tendrils hung down from the ceiling, like jungle liana, stirring and curling as though moved by some unfelt breeze. Or dreaming thoughts. More eyes popped out on wavering stalks, bobbing on the air as they swept this way and that, concentrating on first one human face, then another. One eye lunged forward, straight at Felicity, studying her with malignant interest. She slapped at it with her hand. The eyeball dodged her blow easily and withdrew a few feet.

Another eye advanced on Captain Sunshine. He stood where he was, frozen in place by its unwavering gaze. Sally stepped quickly forward, putting herself between the Captain and the eye. She punched it, hard. Her fist sank deep into the eyeball, but the surface didn't rupture. The eye retreated quickly until it was well out of range. Sally looked at her dripping hand, slimed from contact with the eyeball, grimaced, and wiped her hand clean on the back of the Captain's jacket. He didn't react.

"Bad trips are bad enough," he said slowly. "But when they want to reach out and touch you . . ."

"Feel how hot it is in here," said Melody. "I'm sweating like a pig. It's like a greenhouse; or a forcing-house for something delicate, that needs supporting and protecting . . ."

"Organic machines," said JC. "Living computers. Put here to do . . . something. What?" He glared at Jonathan.

"How could you not know this was going on down here? Right under your feet?"

"I didn't know! All right?" Jonathan said angrily. "I didn't have a clue. None of us did!"

"Remember the aversion field, JC," said Melody. "It's quite probable these things were generating a *Don't think about it* message, as well. That's why it never occurred to them to do anything about the smell."

Long, undulating tentacles arched across the walls and stretched between and around the curving shapes, criss-crossing in mid air in insanely complicated ways. Like diagrams of roads in Hell. Every square inch of wall was covered with thick mats of the stuff, like a fleshy, creeping ivy. Tendrils writhed and twisted around each other, dripping dark, oily fluids. The thick mulch on the floor squelched loudly as JC led the group slowly forward. They had to pull their feet free after every step, with an effort, being careful not to lose their shoes. The floating eyeballs retreated steadily before them. JC peered past the heavy layers of bulging organic shapes and thought he could make out, in the exact centre of the cellar, a single shape bigger than all the others. A dark purple barrel, rising all the way up to the ceiling, covered in shapes and protrusions that rose and fell in intricate patterns. The sound that wasn't a heart-beat, and the sound that wasn't quite breathing, all seemed to emanate from this large central mass.

"What are we looking at?" said Jonathan. "What's it for?"

"I love the way you keep asking me questions, like I've got any answers to give you," said JC.

"You're supposed to be the expert," said Felicity.

"No-one is an expert on this shit," said Happy. "We're all tourists on this ride."

"But why did the new owners want this installed?" said Tom. He looked down at something he'd trodden in and grimaced. "I mean, it must serve some purpose even if it's not what they said it was for . . ."

"It's horrid," Sally said flatly. "I hate it. Looking at this stuff is putting my teeth on edge. It doesn't belong here, not in our world. It makes me want to . . . step on it all! Crush it, grind it, under my heel! Set fire to everything and watch it burn . . . You only have to look at this to know it's not on our side."

"Machines made out of flesh . . ." said JC. "I think I detect the hand of the Flesh Undying in this . . ."

"Not the Beast?" said Melody.

"Maybe the Beast saw what was happening here, from its place outside of Time, and took advantage," said JC. "It does love to manipulate things to its advantage. Remember when we thought this whole set-up might be a trap, for us? Maybe this . . . is a trap within a trap. The Flesh Undying sets this up to draw us in, and the Beast makes use of it, reworks it . . . to create a doorway from its world to ours. And an opportunity to take its revenge on us at the same time."

"You really are making this shit up as you go along, aren't you?" said Jonathan. "You don't understand this any more than we do!"

"I may be guessing," said JC. "But it is at least an educated guess. If you've got a better interpretation of what's happening here, I'll listen."

"Assume you're right, JC," said Melody. "For the sake of not arguing. Assume that central mass is working to create a door, or perhaps more properly a tunnel, between our reality and that of the Beast's. What do we do?"

"Drive a stake through its heart," said Happy. "Or fire. Fire's always good."

"That was my idea!" said Sally.

"Excuse me," said Felicity. "But you mentioned something called the Flesh Undying. You've talked about it before. What the hell is the Flesh Undying?"

"Classified," said JC. He shot her a smile, then turned to Jonathan. "These new bosses of yours. Have you ever met them?"

"Well, not in person, no," said Jonathan. "The sale and transfer of the radio station was a done deal by the time I got to hear about it. I was given the choice of going along or finding employment somewhere else. All I've ever seen are e-mails from the parent company: Strictly Substitute Sausages. They are a real company; I looked them up. But we've never had a visit from any of their representatives. I've never even spoken to anyone on the phone. Which is a bit odd, now I come to think about it. I always assumed they were maintaining a professional distance, in case they decided to shut us down. I figured as long as they were leaving us alone, it was better not to do anything that might rock the boat . . ."

"Could be a front for the Crowley Project," said Melody. "They often use existing companies as masks or fronts for their nasty little schemes."

"Who are the Crowley Project?" demanded Felicity.

"Even more classified," said JC. "You don't want to know."

"Yes I do!" said Felicity. "That's why I asked!"

"Look, if we're the Good Guys, they're the Bad Guys,

all right?" said Happy. "We mend things, they break them. Except . . ." He looked at JC. "I have to wonder if this could be connected to the forces working inside the Carnacki Institute. If the Flesh Undying's agents are involved . . ."

Felicity's ears pricked up immediately. "This thing has agents? Inside the incredibly secretive Carnacki Institute? Oh this gets better and better! Are you saying all the conspiracy sites I've been boning up on are actually onto something? The Institute really is up to things? Disturbing, secret . . . illegal and immoral things?"

"You might say that," said JC. "I wouldn't dare."

Surprisingly, Felicity grinned briefly. "Tease . . ."

JC looked around him. "We have to shut this down. Every last bit of it, with extreme prejudice and balls-to-the-walls violence. If we destroy the doorway, then the Beast can't get into our world. And the terrible future we saw will never happen."

"Sounds like a plan to me," said Melody. "I should be able to whip up some incendiary devices . . ."

"Fire!" said Sally. "I said fire!"

"And a timer?" said Happy. "So we could get away to a safe distance, first?"

"Perfectionist," said Melody.

"You do realise," said Felicity, "that if we do actually survive this, and save the whole world in the process, I am going to grill you all unmercifully on the Beast and the Flesh Undying and the Carnacki Institute. And then tell the whole damned world what happened here. There's a story in this, and I want every last bit of it!"

"Even if we did tell you," said JC, "you wouldn't be allowed to tell anyone. And even if you did, no-one would be allowed to publish it."

Felicity sniffed. "There's this thing they have these days, called the Internet . . ."

"You'd be nothing more than another voice," said JC, "ranting in the wilderness."

"Maybe," said Felicity. "It doesn't matter. Sometimes . . . I need to know the truth. For its own sake. Though I have to say it does my heart good to know for a fact that the Powers That Be really are conspiring to keep secrets from the rest of us! God, I feel so vindicated . . ."

"Welcome to my world," said Happy. "We have T-shirts and everything."

"And you don't even want to know what the *and everything* involves," said Melody.

"You said something very encouraging about incendiary devices," said Sally. "And I do wish you'd get on with it. I won't feel safe until we've blown everything here to shit and roasted the remains. I will personally volunteer to stamp on anything that survives that's bigger than a very small thing."

"I could make some Molotov cocktails," said Captain Sunshine. "It's been a while, but you never really forget . . ." He realised everyone was looking at him and smiled vaguely. "One of the things you picked up, back in my day. Everyone did . . . Don't need to be a Weatherman to know which way the wind's blowing, and all that . . ."

"These organic machines are almost certainly a lot tougher, and better protected, than they look," JC said carefully. "The Beast wouldn't put its faith in anything that could be easily destroyed. Or couldn't take care of itself . . . But you are right, Sally. Everything must go."

"Everything must go up!" said Happy.

"All of this stuff functions as machines," Melody said slowly. "And I suppose . . . in its own appalling way, under all the fleshy trappings, this is still some kind of technology. So possibly, I might be able to reprogramme these computers and shut down their defences. This might be organic, but it's still machinery; and I know all about getting machines to do what I want. Except . . ."

"And you were doing so well there," said JC. "Except what?"

"Except . . . I don't even know where to start!" said Melody, glaring about her. "There's nothing here I can recognise as any kind of tech. No obvious operating systems, or computer access points, nothing to get at . . . For all I know, this whole system works through chemical relays . . ."

JC turned to Happy. "Does anything here have a mind, as such? Some kind of Artificial Intelligence, or organic consciousness? Anything you can read or influence, with your E.S.P.?"

"I've been picking up something, ever since I came in here," Happy said reluctantly. "But it doesn't make any sense! It's like listening to the buzzing of bees, or termites in a hill . . . Not just inhuman, actually alien. Wherever the original designs for these living machines came from, it definitely wasn't anywhere around here. Maybe this all came from the Beast's original world. I always got the sense the Beast created that Other Place, where we found it, to have somewhere it could play. That's how it was able to control everything in it so utterly."

"Hold it," said Melody. "Could it be . . . that this isn't the work of the Beast or the Flesh Undying, but . . . Something Bigger, from Outside?"

"I don't know!" said Happy. "Stop trying to complicate things!"

"I say, let's deal with what's in front of us," JC said carefully.

"Fair enough," Melody said briskly. "Let's make a start with the death and destruction."

She had her machine-pistol in her hand again. Everyone edged away. Melody took careful aim at the bulging central mass and opened fire. But not a single bullet got anywhere near it. The moment she started firing, all the fleshy shapes surrounding the central mass slammed together to provide cover for it. The thick, pulpy masses soaked up the bullets, suffering no obvious harm. And every other organic shape in the cellar began to stir and shake angrily, rising and swelling up, throwing out new tentacles and protuberances. Everything in the cellar seemed to lurch forward, heading for the human intruders. Melody swept her machine-pistol back and forth, raking the organic shapes with a steady rate of gunfire, hitting everything she aimed at; but it didn't even slow them down. Tentacles hanging down from the ceiling lashed out at her, stretching in her direction.

Melody lowered her gun and looked at JC. "Time to escalate to things that go bang."

"Sounds like a plan to me," said JC.

The radio staff were already hurrying back through the open doorway, wedging themselves together in the narrow gap. The Ghost Finders had to stand their ground, to protect the others. Melody kept up a steady stream of fire, cutting through lashing tendrils and stretching protuberances as they reached for her. Black blood spattered everywhere as severed ends flailed wildly. Happy turned his E.S.P. on the nearest organic shapes, hitting them with furious telepathic blasts. The living machinery shook and shuddered under the impact. Some fell apart, unable to maintain their focus. A few exploded, blown apart by internal pressures run amok. JC took off his sunglasses, and the nearest advancing shapes halted immediately wherever he turned his glaring golden eyes on them. They didn't seem hurt, or damaged, but they couldn't press forward as long as he was looking directly at them. But everywhere else, everywhere he wasn't looking, the bulging shapes came on.

Interestingly enough, none of the organic things wanted to go anywhere near Kim. She stood where she was, looking around, and all the organic shapes went out of their way to go around her. Even though she was entirely insubstantial. Or perhaps because of that.

Felicity was stuck at the back of the crowd by the door; partly because she hadn't reacted quickly enough when the shapes started advancing, partly because she was still fascinated by everything that was happening and reluctant to leave until she absolutely had to. She turned away from the struggling crowd for another look, and a dozen thick tentacles snapped down from the ceiling and wrapped themselves around her. She struggled fiercely, but her arms were pinned to her sides, and she was quickly lifted off the floor and dragged away, towards the central mass.

Melody looked around as Felicity cried out, and opened fire on the tentacles above Felicity's head. But for every one she shot through, more spilled down from the ceiling to take its place. Jonathan came running back from the door. He jumped up and grabbed Felicity's legs, and his weight was enough to pull her back down to the floor again. He tore at the clinging tentacles with his bare hands, and they broke apart under his impassioned strength. They let go of Felicity, and she fell to the floor, gasping for breath. The tentacles whipped around Jonathan instead, and dragged him away. Kicking and struggling, he disappeared between the shielding organic shapes, towards the waiting central mass.

JC and Happy went after him, forcing the organic shapes out of their way through sheer willpower, but so many things threw themselves in the way that they couldn't keep up. Melody fired at the ceiling's tentacles until she ran out of bullets and had to stop to reload. The great central mass split from top to bottom, and opened up, the two sides curling back like great fleshy petals to form a gaping mouth, or wound. Jonathan saw the dark maw waiting for him and fought even more fiercely. To no avail. The tentacles threw him into the waiting opening, and the central mass swallowed Jonathan up. Felicity cried out in shock and scrambled to her feet, dripping thick mulch from the floor.

She started towards the central mass. JC grabbed her by the arm and held her back. She fought him, crying out Jonathan's name.

"You can't help him!" said JC. "We have to get out of here and find something we can use to reach him . . ."

Felicity stopped struggling and looked at JC. "I don't understand! Why would he sacrifice himself, for me?"

"Because he loved you, you silly bitch," said Tom. He'd come back from the door to help Jonathan but stopped when he saw there was nothing he could do.

"I never loved him," said Felicity.

"He knew that," said Tom.

JC started to urge them all back towards the cellar door, then everyone stopped as the great central mass opened up again, and Jonathan came out. Or what remained of Jonathan. He'd been reworked, remade, inside the central mass, altered to suit its purposes. Things had been done to him, layers of strange flesh added to him, until he was half as large again as he used to be. He didn't move like anything human any more, lurching and sliding along, half-buried under new alien organs, his face hidden behind a thick scarlet mass. Tentacles burst out of his sides, lashing at the air. A single unblinking eye stared from his forehead; and when his mouth opened, the sound that came out was utterly alien. Happy winced and clapped both hands over his ears. JC could feel a new presence, beating on the air. Something new had been born in the cellar; and it was trying to get inside his head. Melody shook her head sickly, trying to shake off the influence. Tom and Felicity stood where they were, all traces of personality seeping out of their faces.

Sally and Captain Sunshine turned away from the doorway and came back into the cellar. Something in the sound Jonathan was making had got inside his friends and colleagues and taken over. He was broadcasting a signal, like a living radio, and the signal controlled the radio staff.

JC and Happy and Melody fought the signal, refusing to give in to it. Kim looked anxiously at them, not feeling it, not understanding. Because the signal only affected the living. The radio staff pressed forward, trudging through the thick mulch on the floor, coming to kill the enemies of the living machines.

But all Ghost Finders from the Carnacki Institute are thoroughly trained in how to defend themselves against psychic attacks. One by one, JC and Happy and Melody threw off the living signal, and turned to face the advancing radio staff. Their movements were off, their faces empty, but they all moved with a single will and purpose. There was nothing human left in them to stop them doing terrible things to the enemies of the living machines.

"What do we do, JC?" said Melody. "I can't just shoot them! Or at least, I don't want to. Think of something!"

"I'm thinking, I'm thinking!" said JC. He looked desperately around him.

"No other way out of here," Happy said immediately. "I already checked. Come on, boss; they really are getting very close now."

JC turned his golden glare on the advancing radio staff, and that slowed them down a little, but only as long as he was looking at a specific person. The others kept coming. He looked quickly from one person to another, but it soon became clear that wasn't going to be enough. Melody raised her machine-pistol, then lowered it again. Happy stepped forward to meet them; and a tentacle snapped down from the ceiling to wrap itself around him. He barely had time to cry out . . . before the tentacle snapped away from him, releasing him. It writhed and convulsed in mid air, then fell deathly still. The Ghost Finders looked at it; and then JC and Melody looked at Happy.

"All right," said JC. "What did you do to it, Happy?"

"I didn't do anything!" said Happy. "It touched me and died!"

"It's your sweat!" said Melody. "We're all sweating like pigs in this heat; but your sweat is still full of the residue of all those pills you took! You poisoned it!"

"Oh come on," said Happy.

"No!" said JC. "That's the answer! Now, take it to the next level. The living machines may be alien in nature, but they still work by chemical processes. Which we can disrupt, with your appalling medications. Force-feed the head of the central mass, and it should shut itself down in mass confusion."

"Usually works for me," said Happy. "Except for all those times when it doesn't . . ."

Kim stepped forward to block the way of the advancing radio staff, buying her colleagues some time.

"Give me every pill you've got, Happy," said JC. "I'll take them inside the central mass."

"No," said Happy. "It has to be me. Because the only way you can get the central mass to take in the pills is if you take them yourself, then let the central mass take you. Like it took Jonathan. And you couldn't hold as heavy a dosage as me. Come on, JC; you know whoever goes inside that thing probably isn't coming out again."

"I know," said JC. "That's why it has to be me. I'm team leader. That makes this my responsibility."

"No," said Happy. "It has to be me. Because I'm dying already."

"No!" said Melody.

Happy turned and smiled at her. "You know it's true, Mel. And if I'm going to die, I'd rather it was to some good purpose."

"I'm not ready to lose you yet," said Melody.

"You never would be," said Happy.

"No-one has to die!" Kim said loudly. "There's a better way."

They all turned to look at her. She smiled dazzlingly, and hurried back to step inside JC, fitting her form to his. The two of them joined together, and a golden glow formed around JC's body. The radio staff fell back, unable even to look at him, and the transformed Jonathan and all the organic shapes fell back, too.

"Don't worry," said Kim, through JC's mouth. "I'll bring him back safely."

"Give me the pills," JC said to Happy.

Happy emptied out his pockets, opened up all the bottles and boxes, and poured the contents into JC's waiting hands. JC closed his glowing hands over them and turned to face the central mass. He strode steadily forward, and the living machines had no choice but to retreat back out of his way. The transformed Jonathan tried to block his way and couldn't. JC put a hand on Jonathan's arm, and his glowing fingers sank deep into the fleshy layer as he gently pushed Jonathan to one side. He walked up to the central mass, and it opened slowly, reluctantly, before him unable to defy his glowing presence. JC and Kim walked forward, together, into the central mass. It closed behind them, taking them within itself.

................................

Inside, the joined JC and Kim found a whole new reality waiting for them. Behind them—a door back into the world they knew. Ahead of them—an entrance into the Beast's world. They were standing in a blank, featureless place, an artificial construct, a single, colourless cube. Utterly without distinguishing details, it was an abstract shape, designed only to have form and purpose. JC threw the pills at the walls around him with inhuman force, and they sank into the colourless walls like bullets. The cube soaked up the new chemicals like the machine it was.

Something changed, ahead of them. JC and Kim looked round to see the entrance ahead of them open, and the Beast walk through. Determined to protect the tunnel it had made, connecting its reality to the human world.

The Beast looked huge to begin with. But as it approached the entrance, it shrank, in sudden fits and starts, till it was barely more than human in size and scale. It had to do that to enter the tunnel. It had to change itself, to exist in the bridging place, which still embraced the rules and realities of the human world, for the moment. The Beast was still a terrible thing, but now it was hardly bigger than JC. And like the machines it had made, it shrank away from his golden glow. It didn't look nearly as impressive, now. Its flesh slipped and slid across its bones as though it couldn't make up its mind what it wanted to be. It still had teeth and claws, and its eyes were the same as it glared fiercely at JC.

"What have you done, little creature?" it said, in a human-sized voice.

"Sowed a few seeds," said JC. "Sowed madness, and confusion."

The cube was trembling all around them now as the central mass absorbed the powerful psychoactive drugs that Happy took every day and took for granted. The sides of the cube lurched this way and that, stretching and ballooning out, losing definition, as its working principles became confused. The Beast took another step forward.

"It will take more than a few poisons to destroy my wonderful bridge-head! It will last long enough to allow me entrance to your world; and I will bring the rules of my world with me. And then; oh, the fun I'll have! Playing with you and all your kind until you break . . ."

"I know that was the plan," said JC. "But now it's time for a change in plans."

"You can't stop me!" said the Beast. "I control my world, I rule my world and everything in it!"

"But you're not in your world any more," said Kim, with JC's voice. "And we've poisoned the tunnel you made, so you have no strength here. Come and say hello to our world."

And, together, they grabbed hold of the Beast. It cried out as their glowing hands clamped down on its slipping flesh as they dragged the Beast across the cube and out the door, into the human world. It fought them; but together, in that place, their strength was greater by far. It should never have left the world it ruled, the world it made. They hauled the Beast through the door and threw it out into the cellar.

ıııııııııııııııııııııııı

Exposed to the scientific laws of human reality, the Beast shrank in upon itself. Like a creature brought up from the depths of the ocean, it was destroyed by its own internal processes. Its power fell away from it, and what was left of the Beast crashed to the floor, struggling to hold itself together. It tried to crawl back to the central mass; but the joined JC and Kim blocked its way. All the strength went out of the Beast, crushed by the remorseless logic of the human world. It stopped moving, and the light went out of its eyes. Its flesh fell off its bones, already rotting and decaying. Because it was a thing that couldn't exist in our sane and healthy world.

And as the Beast died, so did all the organic machines it made. Unable to continue without the driving will that fashioned them, and sustained them, and gave them form and purpose. Bulging organic shapes collapsed all across the cellar, falling in upon themselves; great dark patches of decay spreading everywhere. It all fell apart, slumping down, collapsing into the thickening mulch on the floor. Including all the layers of flesh that had been wrapped around Jonathan. They fell away, leaving him standing alone. Human, and confused. And without his overpowering signal, the rest of the radio staff woke up and were themselves again.

Kim stepped out of JC; and they grinned at each other. Happy and Melody came forward to join them; and then they all looked down at what remained of the Beast.

"Such a small thing, in the end," said Melody.

"It was only big in the world it made for itself," said JC. "It should never have tried to come here, after us, to such an uncompromising world."

"So! We're not all going to die, after all," said Happy. "Good, good . . ." He glowered at JC. "Did you have to take all of my pills?"

"I'm sure you've got more stashed in the car," said JC.

Happy smiled. "How well you know me."

JC looked around at the shaken radio staff. Felicity was holding Jonathan tightly in her arms.

"I'll never understand," she said, "why you did that for me."

"I know," said Jonathan.

Tom clapped him on the shoulder. The Captain and Sally were holding hands.

"Just this once!" said JC. "Everybody lives!"

"What should we do, with all of . . . this?" said Jonathan.

"Bury it," said Happy.

"Burn it!" said Sally.

"Burn it, then bury it," said JC. "And then salt the ground afterwards; to be sure."

"Traditionalist," said Melody.

# TEN

## WHAT DO WE DO NOW?

Sometime later, everyone sat around in the reception area. Slumped in their chairs, getting their strength back, and their mental second wind. The room was quiet and peaceful, mostly because no-one felt like talking. The radio staff looked liked they'd been through a war, which was fair enough. The Ghost Finders were still coming to terms with having seen themselves die in a future they had just made sure would never happen. Outside the open front door, night was falling over a very ordinary world.

"Is this what your cases are like, most of the time?" said Felicity, eventually.

"Pretty much," said JC.

"Whatever the Carnacki Institute is paying you, it's not nearly enough," said Tom.

"I have been known to say that," said Happy.

"Though there are fringe benefits," said Melody.

Happy smiled at her. "Nicest thing you've ever said about me."

Jonathan stirred in his chair. "If the new owners of this station really aren't who and what they're supposed to be, where does that leave Radio Free Albion?"

"Dead in the water," Tom said immediately. "Come on, Jonathan; I think I can speak for everyone here in saying that the moment we all get our breath back, we are out of here. At speed, heading for the nearest horizon, not even glancing back over our shoulder."

"Damn right," said Sally. "I want to put all this behind me and move on."

"All right," said Jonathan. "One last gift for you, Sally. In return for sticking it out at your post, for so long. You are fired. I'll even put it in writing. That should help you with the social-services people, right?"

"Thank you, Jonathan," said Sally. "You're too kind."

"I shall be hitting the road, too," said Captain Sunshine. "Too much bad karma in this place. Time to go somewhere else, be someone else."

"It's all right for you," said Jonathan. "What am I going to do? No-one's going to want to take over Radio Free Albion. Even if we could clear all the weird shit out of the cellar with no-one's noticing, the station's reputation is hopelessly tarnished . . . And our audience is traumatised. The name of this place alone will be enough to give people nightmares, for years to come. No-one's ever going to employ me in radio again; and I am too old to learn new tricks. What am I going to do?"

"Easy," said JC. "You sell your story to the media."

"What?" said Felicity, sitting upright in her chair. "I

thought you said we wouldn't be allowed to tell anyone the truth about what happened here?"

"Not the truth, no," said JC. "The Carnacki Institute does tend to frown on the truth getting out. But a story— that's different. If you want to tell some tall tales about how Radio Free Albion was haunted, with dead people phoning in to your shows . . . That would be a whole different matter. The Institute has always been quite happy with people telling stories and muddying the waters . . ."

"And," said Melody, "if you all tell different versions of the story, so much the better. You could make a very successful living, touring the chat shows and loudly disagreeing with each other."

"You've done this before, haven't you?" said Tom.

"You have no idea," said Happy.

"Book deals," Felicity said dreamily. "Film deals . . . *Based on a true story . . .*"

"Sounds like a plan to me," said Jonathan. "Of course, I'd need someone who understands these things, to talk me through it."

"I think I might know where you could find someone like that," said Felicity.

They smiled at each other.

One of the phones on the reception desk started ringing. Everyone sat very still and looked at it.

"I am not answering that," said Sally. "I don't work here any more."

Jonathan prised himself up out of his chair and went over to the desk. He picked up the phone, listened for a moment, then turned to JC.

"It's for you."

"Of course," JC said resignedly. "It would have to be."

He got up out of his chair and went over to take the phone from Jonathan.

"Yes?" he said. "What do you want? And why can't it wait?"

"I take it you have finished dealing with such a minor case by now?" said Catherine Latimer. "Good. Now come back to London. We're finally ready to go after the Flesh Undying."

"Well," said JC. "It's about time."

# SPIRITS FROM BEYOND

### A Ghost Finders Novel

The Carnacki Institute's newest assignment takes JC and the team to a famously haunted inn where, according to legend, a traveller trapped by an unusual thunderstorm simply vanished. An unusual thunderstorm—like the one that begins raging outside shortly after they arrive...

The team is forced to face some hard truths—truths that may push one of them over the edge into the madness.

simonrgreen.co.uk
facebook.com/AceRocBooks
penguin.com

From *New York Times* Bestselling Author
### SIMON R. GREEN

# THE BRIDE
# WORE BLACK LEATHER

### A Novel of the Nightside

Meet John Taylor: Nightside resident, Walker—the new representative of the Authorities—and soon-to-be husband of one of the Nightside's most feared bounty hunters. But before he can say, "I do," he has one more case to solve as a private eye . . . which would be a lot easier to accomplish if he weren't on the run, from friends and enemies alike.

And if his bride-to-be weren't out to collect the bounty on his head . . .